Heidi

At last, little Heidi is going back to her mountain village. She can hardly wait to breathe the fresh air once again and to listen to the murmuring wind in the pines. She misses Peter and the goats, her dear Grandfather, and the simple life in the country— for Heidi herself is as delightful and unspoiled as the Swiss mountains she loves!

Heidi is the heart-warming story of a young girl who brings sunshine and joy wherever she goes. Her adventures will take you up into the beautiful Swiss countryside and into the big city where Heidi is educated. And, along with Heidi, you will be surprised by all the wonderful things that happen when she finally returns to her beloved mountains.

Heidi

Johanna Spyri

A WATERMILL CLASSIC

Contents

Chapter 1
Up to the Alm Uncle

From the pleasant village of Mayenfeld a path leads through green fields, richly covered with trees, to the foot of the mountain, which from this side overhangs the valley with grave and solemn aspect. Where the path begins to grow steeper, begins also the heath with its short grass; and the perfume of sweet mountain plants seems to advance as if welcoming the traveller. From this spot the footpath rises almost perpendicularly to the summit.

Along this steep mountain path a stout, healthy girl was climbing, one clear, sunny morning in June, leading by the hand a child, whose cheeks were so glowing red that she looked as if an inward flame were shining through her sunburned skin. And little wonder, for the child was as much wrapped up on this sunny June morning as if to protect her from bitter frost. The little girl could be scarcely more than five years old; but her natural size could not even be guessed at, for she had on two, if not three, dresses, one over the other, and over all, wound round and round, was a great red woolen shawl; so that the little shapeless figure, with its heavy hobnailed mountain shoes, toiled hot and weary up the steep hillside.

They had gone on in this way perhaps an hour from the valley, when they reached the hamlet lying halfway up the Alm, which is called Dörfli. Here the wanderers were hailed and greeted from almost every doorway, now from a window, and once from the road; for the girl had reached her native village. She did not, however, pause at all, but answered all questions and greetings as she went along, till they reached the end of the hamlet, where only a few scattered cottages stood. Here some one called from a doorway, "Wait a minute, Dete! I will go with you if you are going farther."

As Dete stood still, the child freed herself from her grasp, and seated herself upon the ground.

"Are you tired, Heidi?" asked her companion.

"No, but hot," replied the child.

"We are almost at the top. You must exert yourself a little more, and take very long steps, and in an hour we shall be there," said Dete encouragingly.

A broad, good-natured-looking woman came from a doorway, and joined the pair; and the little one followed the two old acquaintances, who were deep in conversation about the inhabitants of

Dörfli and the surrounding cottages.

"But where are you really taking the child, Dete?" asked the newcomer. "It is of course your sister's child, the one she left when she died."

"It is," said Dete. "I am taking her up to the uncle's; she must stay with him."

"What, leave this child with the Alm uncle! You have lost your senses, Dete. How can you think of such a thing? He will soon send you to the right about with your plans."

"No, that he cannot do; he is her grandfather, and must do his share. I have cared for the child up to this time; and now, Barbel, I have the offer of a situation which I cannot afford to lose because of this child. Let her grandfather now take his turn."

"Yes, if he were like other people, Dete," rejoined Barbel anxiously. "But there, you know all about that. What can he do with the child? Such a small one, too! It will never succeed. But where are you going?"

"To Frankfort," explained Dete, "where I am promised an unusually good place. The family were at the baths last summer. I had the care of their rooms in the hotel, and looked after their comfort so well that they wanted to take me back with them then. Now they have come again, and repeat their offer; and you may believe that I mean to accept this time."

"I should not like to be in this child's place," said Barbel, with a gesture of aversion. "No one knows how he lives up there. He will have nothing to do with other people, year in year out. He never sets foot in a church; and when he comes down here once a year, with his thick stick, every one avoids him, and is afraid. With his thick gray eyebrows, and his frightful beard, he looks so like a heathen and a barbarian, that every one is thankful not to meet him in a solitary place alone."

"But for all that," said Dete defiantly, "he is the grandfather, and must take care of the child. He will probably do her no harm, or will have to answer for it if he does. It is not my affair."

"I should really like to know," said Barbel inquiringly, "what that old man has on his conscience, that he casts such glances about him, and lives all alone up there on the Alp and never lets himself be seen. They say all sorts of queer things about him. But you must know the truth from your sister, do you not, Dete?"

"Certainly, but I will not tell, for if he should ever know that I had said anything, what a scolding I should get!"

But Barbel had long wanted to know why the Alm uncle had such a look of dislike to other people, and why he lived alone up on the mountain; and why people spoke so cautiously about him, as if they could not say anything favorable, and would not speak against him. Neither did Barbel know why the old man was always called in Dörfli the Alm uncle. He could not be the real uncle of all the inhabitants; but as they always called him so, she did the same.

Barbel had been married only a short time, and came to live in the village after her wedding. She formerly lived in Prättigau, and therefore did not know all the ins and outs of the life there, nor the peculiarities of the people in Dörfli and the neighborhood. Her good friend Dete, however, was born in Dörfli, and had always lived there with her mother until her death; then she went to Ragatzbad, and served in the big hotel as chambermaid with very good wages.

That very morning Dete had come with the child from Ragatz; a friend had given them a ride in a hay-cart as far as Mayenfeld. Barbel, having learned this much, hastened to improve the opportunity to find out still more. So she laid her hand confidentially on her friend's arm, saying, "From you, Dete, one can know the real truth about the Alm uncle, and not be dependent on what the people here say. Do tell me. What is amiss with the old man? Has he always been feared, and always seemed to hate his fellow beings as he does now?"

"Whether he has always been like this I cannot be expected to know exactly, as I am just twenty-six years old, and he is at least seventy; so you will not require me to tell you how he was when young. If I could only be sure that what I tell you will not be directly known in all Prättigau, I might give you some information, for my mother and he both came from Domleschg."

"O Dete!" replied Barbel, somewhat offended, "what do you mean? They are not such terrible gossips in Prättigau, after all, and I can keep a secret, if necessary. So tell me, do, and you shall never have reason to be sorry for it."

"Well, I will, but mind you, keep your word," said Dete warningly.

She turned to look behind, to see if the child were near enough to hear what they said, but Heidi was nowhere to be seen. She must have ceased following for a long time, but they were too busy talking to notice her absence. Dete stopped, and looked about in every direction. The path made one or two curves, but yet the eye could follow it almost down to Dörfli. There was no one visible for its whole length.

"I see her now!" exclaimed Barbel. "Down there—don't you see her?" And she pointed to a spot quite distant from the mountain path. "She is climbing up the cliff with Peter the goatherd and his flock. I wonder why he is so late today. It is lucky for us, for you can go on with your story while he looks after the child."

"It will not be necessary for Peter to exert himself much in looking after her," said Dete. "She uses her own eyes, and sees all that goes on. I have found that out, and it will be of use to her now, for the old man has only his two goats and the Alm hut."

"Did he once have more?" asked Barbel.

"He? Yes, indeed. He had much more, formerly," replied Dete eagerly. "He had once the very best peasant's farm in Domleschg. He was the elder son, and had only one brother, who was quiet and steady. But the elder would do nothing but play the gentleman, and travel through the country with bad company, about whom no one knew anything. He lost his whole property at play and in extravagance, and when it became known, his father and mother died one after the other from mortification, and his brother was reduced to beggary, and obliged to go no one knows where, for vexation. Then the uncle, who no longer had anything but a bad name, also disappeared. At first, no one knew where he had gone, but after a while they learned that he had joined the army, and gone to Naples.

"Nothing more was known for twelve years or more. Then he all at once appeared in Domleschg, with a half-grown boy, and sought to introduce him to his relations there; but every door was closed against him. This made him very bitter. He said he would never set foot in Domleschg again, and so he came to Dörfli. He lived here with his boy, and must have had property, for he gave Tobias, his son, a trade. He was a nice fellow, a carpenter, and well liked by every one in Dörfli.

But the old man trusted no one. It was said that he had deserted from Naples. He had a bad time of it, having killed some one, not in battle, you understand, but in a brawl. But we recognized the relationship, because my great-grandmother and his mother were sisters; so we called him uncle, and as we are related to every one in Dörfli, on our father's side, gradually everybody called him uncle. Since he has moved up there on the Alm, he is known to every one as the Alm uncle."

"But what happened to Tobias?" said Barbel, who had listened eagerly.

"Only wait. I am coming to that. I can't tell everything at once.

"Tobias was sent to learn his trade in Mels, and when he had learned it he returned to Dörfli and married my sister, my sister Adelheid, whom he had always liked. They were married and they got along well enough together, but that did not last long. Two years after his marriage, as he was helping to build a house, a beam fell on him, and killed him, and he was brought all crushed to his home. Adelheid fell ill from the shock and from sorrow and had a fever from which she never recovered. She, who was formerly so strong and hearty, fell often into swoons, so that one could not tell if she were waking or asleep. Only two months after Tobias's death we buried Adelheid.

"Everybody was talking far and wide of the sad fate of these two, and they said softly, and then aloud, that it was the punishment that the uncle deserved for his godless life; and the pastor, appealing to his conscience, told him that he must now do penance. But he became more and more gloomy and morose, spoke to no one, and at last every one avoided him. Then we heard that he had gone up on to the Alm, never coming down, but living a solitary life, at war with God and man.

"We took Adelheid's little child to live with us, my mother and I. Heidi was a year old. Then, after my mother's death, I decided to go to the baths to earn something, and taking the child with me, I gave her in charge of old Ursel in Pfäfferserdorf. I could remain at the baths during the winter, for there was plenty of work for me, and I can sew and mend very nicely. The same family returned early this spring from Frankfort whom I served last year, and they again wish to take me back with them. So I am going the day after tomorrow, and it is a good place, I assure you."

"And you will leave the child up there with that old man? I cannot understand what you are thinking of, Dete," said Barbel reproachfully.

"What do you mean by that?" answered Dete. "I have done my share for the child, and what more can I do? It is not to be expected that I can carry a child five years old to Frankfort with me. But where are you going, Barbel? Here we are already halfway up the Alm."

"I am almost come to the place," said Barbel. "I

have something to say to the mother of Peter the goatherd. She spins for me in the winter. So goodbye, Dete! Good luck to you!"

Dete held out her hand to her companion, and stood still while the latter went toward the small dark-brown cottage which stood a little way from the path, in a hollow where it was somewhat protected from the mountain winds. Standing halfway up the Alm, it was fortunately situated in the sheltered hollow, and yet looked so crazy and weatherworn that it must have been a dangerous dwelling when the Föhnwind blew strongly over the Alm, making everything shake and tremble, and setting all the rotten beams a-creaking.

It could not have stood long in its present condition on the summit, but would speedily have been swept down into the valley. This was the dwelling of goat-Peter, the eleven-year-old boy whose business it was to drive the goats from Dörfli every morning up on to the Alm, to let them pasture on the short, succulent bushes that grow there. In the evening he led his nimble-footed herd down into Dörfli again and gave a shrill whistle on his fingers, at the sound of which the owners came to the little square to fetch the animals that belonged to them. Generally little boys and girls came for the animals—such gentle creatures could do no harm—and thus Peter was for a short time every day with companions of his own age. Otherwise he lived during the entire summer only with his goats.

To be sure, he had his mother and his blind grandmother; but he left the hut early in the morning, and returned late from Dörfli, because he liked to amuse himself with the children there as long as possible, spending only enough time at home to swallow his bread and milk as fast as he could, to get off early with the goats in the morning, and to his pillow at night.

His father, who followed the same business, and was also called goat-Peter, had been killed while felling wood the year before. His mother, whose name was Brigette, was always spoken of as goat-Peterin, or goat-Peter's mother, from the connection; and for everybody far and near his blind grandmother had the same name.

Dete stood waiting for certainly ten minutes, looking in every direction for the children and the goats, who were nowhere to be seen; then she climbed still higher to get a view of the valley, searching in every direction, with signs of increasing impatience on her face and in her movements. In the meantime, the children had gone round in quite another direction, for Peter knew of many spots where all sorts of bushes and herbs grew that were good for his goats to nibble at, and to reach which he twisted and turned about from one place to another with his flock. At first Heidi climbed after him, but with the greatest difficulty. Enveloped as she was in her heavy

11

wraps, and suffering from their weight and moreover from heat, she was obliged to exert all her little strength.

She said nothing, however, but looked fixedly at Peter, who, with his bare feet and light trousers, sprang here and there without the least trouble. Then she observed the goats, which, with their thin, slender legs, climbed still more easily over the stocks and stones, and even up the precipices. Suddenly the child sat down, pulled off shoes and stockings as quickly as possible, stood up again, threw off the thick red shawl, unfastened her dress, cast that away, and had still another to strip off; for Dete had put on all the child's Sunday clothes over her everyday garments, for convenience' sake, so that no one else need carry them. In a twinkling the child tore off her everyday dress too, and stood in her light petticoat, stretching her bare arms with delight out of the short sleeves of her little shirt in the cooling wind.

Then she folded all her clothes together into a neat little heap, and leaving them, climbed up after the goats to Peter; going with them as lightly and easily as the very best.

Peter had not noticed what the child was about while she stayed behind, but when she sprang up beside him in her new dress, he grinned in the most comical way. Then, looking back, he perceived the little heap of clothes, and his grin became wider, until his mouth seemed to extend from ear to ear, but he said never a word.

Now that the child felt herself so free and comfortable, she began to talk to her companion, and he had to answer all sorts of questions. She wanted to know how many goats he had, where he was taking them, and what he did when he reached his destination. At last, however, the children and the goats reached the hut, when Aunt Dete caught sight of them. As soon as the latter saw the little company of climbers, she shouted out, "What are you about, Heidi? How you look! What have you done with your two dresses and the shawl, and the new shoes that I bought you for the mountain, and the new stockings I knit you myself? Are they all gone, all? Heidi, what have you done with them?"

The child pointed quietly down the mountain side, saying only, "There."

Dete looked; and following the direction of the child's finger, she saw something lying, on the top of which was a red spot. Could that be the shawl?

"You mischievous child!" she cried, in great excitement. "What are you thinking of? Why have you taken everything off? What does it mean?"

"I do not need them," replied the child, and did not look sorry for what she had done.

"Oh, you unlucky, thoughtless Heidi! Have you no idea about things?" said Dete, scolding and complaining at the same time. "Who is to go down for them? It will be at least a half-hour's work. Come, Peter, run down and fetch them for me! Don't stand there staring as if you were nailed to the ground."

"I am too late already," said he slowly, and stood without stirring from the spot, with his hands in his pockets, just as he stood when Dete's cry of alarm first reached his ears.

"You stand there, and open your eyes as wide as you can, but do not stir," cried Aunt Dete to him again. "Come now, you shall have something nice. Do you see this?" showing him a new, shining threepenny piece.

In an instant he ran down the mountain, taking the shortest way, and reaching the clothes by great strides, seized them in his arms, and he was back again so quickly that Dete was forced to praise him, while she gave him the promised threepenny piece without delay. Peter stuck it quickly deep into his pocket, while his face beamed and shone with pleasure; for a like treasure rarely fell to his lot.

"You can carry the bundle for us up to the uncle's. You are going that way, I believe," said Dete, while she applied herself to climbing the steep path that made an abrupt ascent from behind the goat-herd's hut. He was quite ready, and followed her, carrying the bundle under his left arm, while he swung his rod with his right.

Heidi and the goats sprang joyfully about in every direction.

In this manner the little procession reached at last the summit of the Alm, after about three-quarters of an hour's climbing. There stood the old uncle's hut, exposed, it is true, to all the winds of heaven, but getting the advantage of every ray of sunlight, and commanding too a most beautiful view of the valley.

Behind the hut stood three big, very old pine trees, with long, thick, untrimmed branches; and then the mountain background rose up, up to the old gray rocks, first over beautiful slopes covered with succulent herbs, then through thickly strewn boulders, and at last came the bald, steep pinnacles.

On the side of his hut overlooking the valley, and fastened there securely, the uncle had placed a bench. Here he was now seated, his pipe in his mouth, his hands resting on his knees, looking quietly down at the children, the goats, and Aunt Dete, as they came clambering up.

Heidi reached the summit first, and going directly toward the old man, stretched out her hand to him, saying, "Good morning, Grandfather."

"Well, well, what does this mean?" answered the Alm uncle harshly. He gave his hand, however, to the child, looking at her with a long piercing gaze from under his bushy eyebrows.

Heidi returned his look with equal steadiness, not once letting her eyes swerve from his face.

Such a strange-looking man as her grandfather, with his long beard, his gray eyebrows growing together in the middle like a bush, seemed to her worthy of study.

In the meantime Dete and the goatherd stood beside Heidi, Peter looking on to see what was to happen.

"I wish you good day, Uncle," said Dete, stepping up. "I bring you Tobias and Adelheid's child. You will scarcely recognize her, for you have not seen her since she was a year old."

"And what has the child to do with me?" asked the old man. "You there!" he called out to Peter, "go on with your goats. You are none too early. Take mine along with you."

Peter heard, and obeyed; for the uncle had looked at him, and that was enough.

"The child must stay here with you," asserted Dete. "I have done my share for her these four years past. Now it is your turn."

"Indeed!" said the old man, casting a withering glance at Dete. "And if the child begins to cry for you, and whimper, as these senseless little creatures do, what is to be done then?"

"That is your affair," said Dete. "I mean, no one told me how I was to manage with her, when she was thrown on my hands a year-old child, and I had already as much as I could do for my mother and myself. Now I must go with my employers, and you are the next-of-kin to the child. If you won't keep her, do with her as you like. If anything happens to her, you know, there will be no further trouble."

Dete's conscience was not easy about this proceeding, and therefore she was working herself into a passion, and said more than she really meant. As she uttered these last words, the uncle stood up, and looked at her so strangely that she involuntarily drew back several steps. He stretched forth his arm, and said in a commanding voice, "Go back to the place from whence you came, and do not show yourself here again in a hurry."

"Then farewell, and you also, Heidi," said Dete, not meaning to wait for a repetition of these words; and she ran down the mountainside, without stopping, till she reached Dörfli, for her inward excitement drove her onward as if she were impelled by steam.

In Dörfli, everybody called to her, even more clamorously than before, for all were curious to know what had become of the child. They knew Dete very well, and to whom the child belonged, and all her former history. So they called from door and window, "Where's the child?" "What have you done with the little one, Dete?"

She shouted back impatiently, without stopping, "Up there with the Alm uncle, I say. Don't you understand?"

But she was very uncomfortable, for the women

all exclaimed, "How could you do such a thing?" "That poor child!" "The idea of leaving such a helpless child up there!" and again and again, "The poor little tot!" and so on, and so on.

Dete ran on as quickly as possible and was soon beyond the reach of their voices, for she was not happy about her conduct, as her mother had given the child into her charge on her deathbed. But she tried to quiet her conscience by saying to herself that she could do more for the child when she had earned something. It was a relief to get away as quickly as possible from her old friends, who questioned her too closely, and to go into service with a good family.

Chapter 2
At the Grandfather's

After Dete had left, the old man sat down on his bench again, blowing great clouds of smoke from his pipe, while he looked fixedly on the ground, and was silent.

Heidi looked about in the greatest delight, discovered the goatshed and peeped in, but finding nothing, pursued her investigations. At last she went behind the hut to look at the old pines.

The wind was sighing and moaning in the branches, and the topmost bough swayed to and fro. Heidi stood listening, but the wind lulled, and she went on again until she came to where her grandfather sat as she had left him. Planting herself directly in front of the old man, she put her little hands behind her, and looked fixedly at him. After a few moments he raised his head, and asked, as the child continued to stand motionless before him, "What will you do now?"

"I want to see what you have in there, in the hut," said Heidi.

"Well, take up your bundle, and follow me." Her grandfather rose to enter the dwelling.

"I don't want it any more," said the child.

He turned, at these words, to examine the little girl, whose black eyes were dancing with eagerness to know what the hut contained.

"At least she is not wanting in intelligence," he said half aloud, then louder, "Why shall you not need them, my child?"

"I want to go about like the goats," said Heidi, "they have such light legs."

"You shall do that," replied her grandfather, "but bring in the bundle, and we will put it into the press." She raised the bundle as he bade her; he opened the door, and they entered the large room which made up the entire hut.

In one corner was the bed; in another a big kettle hung over the hearth. There was also a table and a chair. In the wall was a big door, which the grandfather opened. It was the press. There hung his clothes; on the shelves were shirts, stockings, handerkerchiefs, cups, plates, saucers, and glasses; above was the smoked meat, cheese, a round loaf of bread—in short, all that was needed for daily use. While he held the door open, Heidi stepped up with her bundle, which she stuffed in behind her grandfather's things, as far out of sight as possible. After this she looked carefully about the room, saying, "But where shall I sleep, Grandfather?"

"Wherever you like," was his answer.

This pleased the little girl. She ran about the room, searching every corner, to find the place that would best suit her. Opposite her grandfather's bed was a ladder, that led into the hayloft. Up this ran Heidi, and found it strewn with fresh, sweet-smelling hay, while from a round hole in the rafters one could look far, far away into the valley.

"Oh, I must sleep here! It really is beautiful," cried the child. "Come up!" she called to the old man. "Come up, and see how beautiful it is here."

"I know all about it," he answered from below.

"I am making my bed here," said Heidi again, while she worked busily away, "but you must come up, and bring me a sheet. There must be a sheet on the bed to lie on."

"Well, well," replied her grandfather. He went to the press, searched about, and at last pulled out from under his shirts a long, coarse linen cloth, that was certainly something like a sheet.

He then mounted the ladder with it; and behold! There was a dear little bed all piled up with hay, and where the head was to lie was raised quite high, and so arranged that the occupant could look directly through the open hole.

"That is well done," said the old man. "Now we must put on the sheet; but stop a bit." He took more hay, piling the bed up till it was twice as thick as Heidi had made it, that she might not feel the floor through the hay. "Now bring me the sheet."

Heidi seized the sheet, but could hardly lift it, the linen was so heavy—and that was good, for the hay could not penetrate such thick stuff—and now they both spread this sheet over the hay. As it was much too long for such a little bed, Heidi busily tucked it well under. Now it was a charming resting-place to look at, and the child stood in admiration of it for a long time, thoughtfully. "We have forgotten one thing, Grandfather," said she at last.

"What is that?"

"A coverlid, to be sure, for when one goes to bed, one must creep in between the sheet and the coverlid."

"Do you think so?" said he. "I fear I have none."

"Oh, then, no matter!" said Heidi. "I can get more hay instead." She ran to fetch some, but her grandfather stopped her.

"Wait a moment," he said. He descended the ladder, and went over to his bed; then, climbing up again, placed a heavy linen sack on the floor, saying, "Is not this better than hay?"

Heidi strove with might and main to spread out the sack, but her little hands could not manage the heavy stuff. With her grandfather's help, however, it was soon arranged; and then the bed looked so nice and firm, that Heidi stood entranced in admiration, and exclaimed, "This is a beautiful coverlid, and a perfect bed! I wish it were night, Grandfather, that I might lie down."

"I think, however, that we could eat something first. What is your opinion about that?" asked the old man.

Heidi had been so much interested about her bed that she had forgotten everything else. Now she remembered, and felt suddenly very hungry. She had eaten nothing since breakfast, when she had a piece of bread and a little weak coffee, and had since made a long journey. Heidi replied heartily to her grandfather's question, "Yes, I think so, indeed."

"Well, go down then, since we agree," said the old man, and followed his grandchild down the ladder. He went over to the fireplace, removed the big kettle, hung a smaller one in its place on the chain, seated himself on the three-legged stool with a round seat before him, and blew the fire till there was a blaze, and the kettle began to boil. Next, he held a long iron fork over the fire, with a big piece of cheese on it, which he turned slowly round and round till it was of a golden yellow.

Heidi watched him with keen interest; but suddenly an idea came into her head, and she sprang away to the press, then back to the table, and again many times. When her grandfather came with the pot, and the roasted cheese on the fork, there lay already the round loaf, two plates, two knives, all neatly arranged; for Heidi had noticed everything in the press, and she knew what was needed for the table.

"Now, this is nice that you can think of things yourself," said the old man, and put the cheese upon the bread. "But there is something more needed still."

Heidi saw how invitingly the pot was steaming, and dashed to the press again. Only one mug could she find, but did not remain long in perplexity. Two glasses stood at the back of the press; in an instant the child was back again, with a glass and the mug.

"That is right. You are very helpful. But where will you sit?" said he; for he sat on the only high stool himself. Like an arrow the child was at the fireplace, brought the little three-legged stool back again, and sat down.

"Well, you have a seat, at any rate," said the grandfather, "but rather low down. You would be rather too short, even on mine, to reach the table. But you must have something to eat at once, so begin."

He stood up, filled the mug with milk, set it upon the high stool, drew the latter up to Heidi so that she had a table to herself, and sitting on the corner of the table began his dinner, bidding her also to eat.

Heidi seized her little mug, and drank and drank without once stopping, for all the thirst of her journey seemed to rise up at once. Then she drew a long breath—for in her eagerness to drink, she had not been able to stop to breathe—and set down her mug.

"Does the milk taste good?" asked her grandfather.

"I never drank such good milk," said the child.

"Then you must have more," said he, and filled the mug again quite to the top, and placed it before the child, who was eating her bread, spread thickly with the hot cheese, which was like butter from the heat, and tasted delicious. She now and then drank her milk and looked meanwhile perfectly happy.

When they had finished eating, the old man went out to the goats' house, and put things to rights there, while Heidi observed him carefully, how he first swept everything up with the broom, then strewed fresh straw about for the animals to sleep upon. He then went to the wood pile near by, cut round sticks of the right size, cut a board to the right shape, bored holes in it, stuck the sticks in, and had soon a stool like his own, only higher. Heidi watched him at his work, speechless with wonder.

"What do you call this, Heidi?" said he.

"That is my stool, because it is so high. How quickly you have made it!" said the little one, in the greatest wonder and admiration.

"She knows what she sees. She has her eyes in the right place." remarked the old man to himself, as he moved round the hut, and drove a nail here, or made something fast there, going with his hammer and nails and pieces of wood from one place to another, finding constantly something to do, or to mend. Heidi followed him step by step, watching everything that he did with unflagging attention, for all that happened interested her very much.

At last it was evening. The wind began to sigh through the old trees. As it blew harder, all the branches swayed back and forth. Heidi felt the sounds not only in her ears, but in her heart; and she was so happy, so happy, she ran out under the pines, and sprang and leaped for joy, as if she had found the greatest pleasure imaginable.

Her grandfather meanwhile stood in the doorway, and watched the child.

Suddenly a shrill whistle was heard. Heidi stopped her jumping, and the old man went out. Down from the mountain streamed the goats, one after the other, and Peter was in their midst.

With a joyous shout Heidi vanished into the midst of the flock, to greet her old friends of the morning, one and all.

When they reached the hut, they all stopped; and from out of the herd came two beautiful slender goats, one white and one brown. They went to the old man, and licked his hands, for he held a little salt for them every evening when they came home. Peter vanished with the rest. Heidi stroked the goats gently, one after the other, then ran to the other side, and did the same. She was as joyful as possible over the charming creatures.

"Are they both ours, Grandfather? Will they go into our stall? Will they always stay here with us?" Heidi poured out her questions in her excitement, her grandfather having hardly a chance to repeat a continual, "Yes, yes, child," now and then.

When the goats had licked up all the salt, her grandfather said, "Go fetch your little mug and some bread."

Heidi obeyed, and he milked the goats into the mug, into which he cut bits of bread, and said, "Now eat your supper and then go to bed. Dete left another bundle for you. There are your night-gowns, and so on, in it. You will find them in the press. I must put up the goats now. Go, and sleep soundly."

"Good night, Grandfather, good night," shouted Heidi after him, as he disappeared with the goats. "What are their names?"

"The white one is called Schwänli, the other Bärli."

"Good night, Schwänli; good night, Bärli," shouted the child at the top of her voice to the goats, who were already going into their stall.

The little girl sat down on the bench to eat her bread and milk, but the wind was so strong that it almost blew her off her seat; so she ate as fast as she could, went into the cottage, climbed up to her bed, and was soon fast asleep. Indeed, she slept all night as comfortably as a princess.

Not long after, but before it was quite dark, the old man also went to bed, for he was always up by sunrise, and that was very early in summer on the mountain. During the night the wind arose. It blew so hard that the hut shook, and the beams all creaked. The wind roared and moaned through the big chimney as if in anguish. In the old pine tree, too, it blew a blast that broke old branches off as if in anger. In the midst of it all the old man rose, saying to himself. "The child will be afraid."

He mounted the ladder and went softly into Heidi's chamber. The moon was shining brightly in the clear sky, but in a moment the driving clouds flew across, and everything was dark. In another moment she shone clearly forth, through the round hole in the roof, and her beams fell on Heidi's bed. The little one slept with rosy red cheeks under her heavy covering, quiet and peaceful, with one round arm under her head, and certainly dreaming of something that made her happy, for her little face beamed with contentment. Her grandfather stood long, looking at the lovely, sleeping child, until the clouds again obscured the moon. Then he turned and went down the ladder.

Chapter 3
In the Pasture

Heidi was awakened on the following morning by a loud whistle. As she opened her eyes a yellow sunbeam, shining through the opening, fell on her bed, and turned it, and all the hay that was spread about the loft to glistening gold. She looked about her with astonishment, and could not make out where she was.

Soon she heard her granfather's deep voice, and it all came back to her: how she came there, and that now she lived with her grandfather upon the Alm, and no longer with the old Ursel, who was quite deaf, and so chilly that she was always sitting by the kitchen fire or by the stove, where the child must sit also, or quite near, in order that the old woman might see what she was doing, as she could not hear. Poor Heidi always had felt it stifling and close in the room, and longed to get out. How glad she was to awake in her new home; to remember how much she had seen the day before that was new; and to think of all the coming day had in store for her—above all, Schwänli and Bärli!

She sprang up and soon had on all her clothes of the day before, and they were few enough. Down the ladder she ran, and away out of doors. There stood Peter with his goats; and her grandfather brought his out from the stall, that they might join the flock. Heidi bade both him and the goats a good morning.

"Would you like to go with them to the pasture?" asked the old man.

The child could only jump for joy, she was so delighted.

"First, however, you must wash and make yourself clean; or the sun will laugh at you, while he is shining so brightly up there, and sees you all dirty and black. Look there—everything is ready for you." He pointed to a big tub of water that stood in the sun before the door. Heidi splashed and rubbed herself till she shone again. Her grandfather in the meanwhile went into the hut, and soon called out to Peter, "Come here, goat-general, and bring your knapsack."

Peter obeyed in surprise, and opened his bag in which was his poor little dinner.

"Wider, wider," said the old man, and put in a big piece of bread and another piece of cheese. Peter opened his eyes as wide as ever he could, for the pieces were each twice as large as his own.

"Now the mug goes in, too, for the little one can't drink as you do from the goats themselves. No, indeed. And you must milk this twice full at noon, for the child will go with you, and stay till you come back in the evening. Now, take care that she does not fall off the cliffs."

Heidi was soon ready, and came running to say, "Now can the sun make fun of me, Grandfather?"

In her fear of the laughter of the sun, she had rubbed her face, neck, and arms so roughly with the coarse towel she found by the tub, that she was as red as a lobster, as she stood there before him.

He laughed a little, but said soothingly, "No, he will find nothing to make fun of now. But do you know something? In the evening, when you come home, you must go into the tub all over, like a fish; for when you go about like the goats, you will get very black feet. Now go on your way."

And on they went, climbing joyfully up the Alm. The wind had swept the last trace of cloud from the sky, which was of a wonderful dark blue. The green Alp was covered with blue and yellow flowers, and their wide-open petals seemed laughing back at the sun, while everything shimmered and shone.

Heidi scampered hither and thither, shouting for joy. Now it was a whole group of red primroses; one place was perfectly blue with lovely gentians; and here and everywhere the tender blossoms of the yellow buttercups nodded and laughed in the sunlight. Carried away with delight by all the beckoning, glistening flowers, the child forgot the goats, and Peter also. She was running now forwards, now back again; first on this side, then on that side; for here they were like red, and there like yellow sparkles, and she was tempted in every direction. She gathered great handfuls of flowers and stuffed them all into her apron; for she must carry them home with her, and place them in the hay in her bedroom to make it look there as it did on the Alp.

Poor Peter was obliged to keep his eyes about him today; and those round eyes, that were not in the habit of moving very quickly, had enough to do. For the goats were like Heidi: they ran about everywhere, while Peter must whistle and shout and swing his rod to bring together all the wanderers.

"Where have you got to now Heidi?" he called out, somewhat angrily.

"Here," came back the reply from—somewhere. Peter could see no one, for Heidi sat on the ground behind a little mound that was covered with the sweetest-smelling prune flowers, and the whole air was perfumed. Heidi had never breathed anything so perfectly delicious. She seated herself among the bushes, and drew in the scent in long, full-drawn breaths.

"Come here now," shouted Peter. "You must not fall over the precipices. Your grandfather has forbidden it."

"Where are the precipices?" asked the child, but did not stir from her seat, for with every breeze the sweet perfume was wafted to her nostrils.

"Up there, aloft. We have still a good bit to climb, so come along. Up there, at the very top sits the old eagle, and screams!"

This stirred the little girl. She jumped up and ran toward her companion with her apron full of flowers.

"Now you have picked enough of these," said he, "else you will be always stopping. Besides, if today you pick them all, tomorrow you will find no more."

This last reason convinced Heidi; moreover, she had stuffed her apron so full that there was not room for another flower, and tomorrow she must see them again.

She now kept along with Peter. The goats, too, went in better order, for they scented the sweet herbs from their pasture on the heights afar, and pushed forward without pausing.

The pasture where Peter usually stopped and made his resting place for the day lay at the foot of the peak, which rose steep and naked toward the sky, clothed from its base with scrub trees and bushes. On one side of the Alp the great rocks were divided by steep clefts and chasms, and the old man was quite right to warn them against that danger.

As they now had reached the highest point, Peter took off his knapsack and placed it carefully in a little hollow where it would be sheltered from the wind, which blew often in strong gusts up so high on the mountain. This Peter knew very well, and did not mean to see his knapsack, with the nice dinner, go rolling down the hillside. Having put this in a place of safety, he stretched himself full length on the sunny sod to rest after the steep ascent.

Heidi had also tucked her apron into the same hollow with the knapsack, after rolling it up with all the flowers in it. Then she seated herself beside Peter, and looked about her on every side. Below lay the valley in the full glow of the morning sun. Before her was a huge white snow-field rising toward the dark-blue heaven; to the left, an enormous mass of rocks was piled up, on each side of which stood a pillar of rock, bald and jagged against the blue sky. Heidi thought the pinnacles were looking down at her, and she sat there as still as a little mouse, and looked and looked on every side. All was still; only a light, soft breeze stirred the blue harebells and the shining yellow buttercups that grew all about and stood nodding to her on their slender stalks. Peter had fallen asleep after his exertions, and the goats climbed here and there, and up into the bushes.

Never had the child been so happy in all her life. She drank in the golden sunlight, the fresh air, the sweet perfume of the flowers, and longed for nothing but to stay where she was for ever.

Thus a long, long time passed; and Heidi gazed at the needles of rock above her so long and steadfastly that they seemed to her to have faces, and to be returning her gaze like old friends. Suddenly she heard above her a loud, sharp scream! As she looked up, a huge bird, such as she had never seen before, circled overhead. With widespread wings it soared through the air, and in great sweeps came back again and again, screaming loud and piercingly over Heidi's head.

"Peter! Peter! Wake up!" cried Heidi aloud. "See, the eagle is here; look, look!"

Peter roused himself at her cry, and the children gazed at the bird, which rose higher and higher disappearing at last in the blue ether over the gray rocks.

"Where is he now?" asked Heidi, who had watched the bird with breathless interest.

"In his home up there."

"Oh, how beautiful to live up there! But why

does he scream so?"

"Because he must."

"Let us climb up there to see his home," suggested Heidi.

"Oh, oh, oh!" cried Peter; and each "oh" was louder than the last. "Even the goats are not able to climb up there, and the Alm uncle said you must not fall over the precipice."

After this Peter began to whistle and call so loudly that Heidi did not know what had happened; but the goats knew well enough, and all came running and jumping, and were soon all gathered on the green field. Some nibbled at the sweet grass, others ran here and there, while some stood opposite each other a little way apart, and butted playfully with their horns. Springing to her feet, Heidi ran in amidst the goats, for she found it a new and indescribable pleasure to see the dear little creatures gamboling together so happily. She, too, jumped from one to another to make herself acquainted with each separately, for each had its own peculiarities and looked and behaved differently.

While Heidi played with the goats, Peter had fetched the knapsack, and arranged the four parcels in a square on the grass, the big ones on Heidi's side, and the little ones on his. Then he filled the mug with fresh milk from Schwänli and placed it in the middle of the square.

Then he called to Heidi to come. But he had to

call again and again, longer than to the goats, for the child was so delighted with the thousand movements and pranks of her new playfellows, that she saw and heard nothing further. Peter understood how to make himself heard. He shouted so very loud that he could have been heard up on the rocks, causing Heidi to run as fast as she could. The table looked so very inviting that she hopped about it for joy.

"Stop dancing about. It is time to eat," said Peter, seating himself and beginning.

"Is the milk for me?" asked Heidi, as she took her seat, surveying the four corners and the center ornament with pleasure.

"Yes," he replied, "and the two biggest packages are yours also. When you have emptied the mug, you can have another one full from Schwänli. When you have finished, 'tis my turn."

"And where do you get your milk?" asked the little girl curiously.

"From my goat, from Snail. Do begin."

Heidi began at last, with the milk, and when she had emptied the mug, Peter rose and filled it again. Heidi broke some of her bread into it, and then handed the rest of it to Peter. It was a big piece, twice as large as his, which he had already eaten, together with the rest of his dinner. She gave him also her big lump of cheese, saying, "You have it all. I have had enough."

Peter stared at Heidi with his big eyes in

speechless astonishment. Never in his life had he been able to say what she had just said, nor to give anything away. He hesitated a little, for he could not believe that she was in earnest, but the child held her pieces toward him again, and when he did not take them, she at last laid them on his knee.

When he saw that she was serious, he took his present, nodded for thanks and pleasure, and made forthwith the heartiest meal that had fallen to his share since he first tended the goats. While he ate, Heidi watched the flock.

"What are all their names, Peter?" said she. He knew them and could carry them in his head easily enough; for he had little else there. So he began and named them one after the other without hesitating, and pointed at each with his finger as he spoke. To this lesson Heidi gave all her attention. Soon she could also name them all, for each had its peculiarity, which was easily learned with a little trouble.

There was the big Turk with his strong horns, who was forever butting the others, so that they generally scampered away when he came toward them, and would have nothing to do with such a rough comrade. Only the bold and slender Thistlebird did not avoid him, but struck out sharply, once, twice, sometimes six times, until the great Turk stood still in astonishment, and did not try again soon. Thistlebird stood always ready for battle, and had sharp horns, too.

And often Heidi ran to the little white Snowball, who was always bleating beseechingly and took its head between her hands to comfort it. Even now the child sprang toward it again, for she heard its wailing cry. She put her arm round the little creature's neck, saying sympathizingly, "What ails you, Snowball? Why do you call for help so piteously?"

The animal nestled confidingly against the little girl, and was quiet again, and Peter called out from his seat, explaining Snowball's trouble between mouthfuls.

"She does that because her old one does not come with us any more. She was sold to Mayenfeld the day before yesterday and will not come any more to the Alm."

"Who is the old one?" asked Heidi.

"Pooh! Its mother," was the reply.

"Where is the grandmother?" asked the child.

"Has none."

"Or the grandfather?"

"Has none."

"Oh, you poor little Snowball!" said Heidi tenderly, pressing the goat softly to her side. "But now don't cry so any more. I will come here every day with you, then you will not be lonely; and if you are feeling very bad, you may come to me."

Snowball rubbed her head trustingly on Heidi's shoulder and bleated no more.

When Peter had finished his dinner, he came

again to look after his flock, which had already begun its researches.

By far the loveliest and cleanest of the goats were Schwänli and Bärli, who certainly behaved with greater decorum than the others, generally going their own way and avoiding all, particularly Turk, who was very forward. The animals had begun again to climb up toward the bushes, each in its own way, one springing lightly over every obstacle, others carefully searching all along the way for a good mouthful: Turk trying now and then to give some one a blow; Schwänli and Bärli climbing prettily and lightly, finding the best bushes, and eating in a delicate and dainty manner. Heidi stood with her hands behind her back, watching all that went on.

"Peter," said she to him, as he lay again stretched on the ground, "the prettiest of all are Schwänli and Bärli."

"I know that," was his reply; "the Alm uncle cleans them and combs them, gives them salt, and has such nice stalls." Suddenly the lad sprang to his feet, and was after the goats with great leaps, and Heidi after him, for something must have happened, and she could not stay behind.

Away went Peter through the flock toward the side of the Alp, where the rocks rose up steep and naked—where a heedless goat might easily fall and get its legs broken while climbing. He saw that the giddy Thistlebird had strayed in that direction, and he ran after her only just in time, for she had reached the very edge of the precipice. As he was about to seize her, he tripped and fell, catching her only by the leg as he came down. But he held her fast, though she bleated with surprise and anger to find herself held, and unable to go on with her frolicsome amusements, while she persisted in pressing forward.

Peter called loudly for Heidi. He was unable to rise, and seemed to himself almost pulling the little goat's leg off, she was so determined to go on. In a trice Heidi was there, saw the danger of his situation and of the goat's. Pulling quickly a sweet-smelling herb, she held it under Thistle-bird's nose, saying soothingly, "Come, come, little goat; come and be good, Thistlebird. See, now, you might have fallen and broken your leg, and that would have hurt you sadly."

The goat turned quickly about to nibble at the herb held out by Heidi, and was quite content. Peter, having regained his feet, hastened to seize the string that hung from her collar, while Heidi took the collar from the other side. Then they led the wanderer between them to rejoin the rest of the flock, which was peaceably feeding below.

Once Peter had his goat in safety again, he raised his rod and was about to whip her soundly. Thistlebird drew back in alarm, for she saw what was coming. Heidi, however, screamed out in terror, "No, Peter, no! You must not strike her. See how frightened she is!"

"She deserves it," said he angrily, and was about to strike, but the child seized him by the arm, calling out, "You must let her alone!"

Her companion stood staring in surprise at her commanding tones and flashing eyes, while he involuntarily dropped his arm, saying, "So, then, she may go, if you will give me some of your cheese tomorrow." He felt that he must have something to console him from his fright.

"You may have it all, tomorrow and every day, for I do not care for it," said Heidi, "and a big piece of bread also, as I gave you today; but you must promise me not to strike Thistlebird nor Snowball, nor any of the goats."

"It's all the same to me," said Peter. That was his equivalent for a promise, and he let the offender go. Away sprang the happy goat with great leaps, in amongst the others.

Almost unheeded the day had passed, and now the sun was beginning to sink behind the mountain. Heidi sat quietly on the ground, gazing at the harebells and bluebells, as they shone in the golden light, observing how the grass took a golden hue, and how the rocks above began to shimmer and flash, when suddenly she started to her feet, shouting, "Peter, Peter! it is burning, it is on fire! All the mountains flame, and the great snow yonder, and the sky. Look, look! the highest peak is glowing. Oh, the beautiful fire! Now look,

Peter, it has reached the eagle's nest. See the rock! See the pines! Everything burns!"

"It is always like that, but it is no fire," said Peter kindly.

"What is it, then?" cried Heidi, and ran about in every direction to look, for she could not see enough of it standing still, it was so beautiful everywhere. "What is it, Peter? what is it?" she asked again.

"It comes of itself," explained the lad.

"Look, look now!" she screamed in the wildest excitement. "Just this minute it is all as red as roses. Look at the snow and those high, pointed rocks! What are they called?"

"Mountains have no names," was the answer.

"Oh, the lovely, rosy snow! And all over the rocks are roses. Oh, now they are growing gray! It is going! It has all gone, Peter!" and little Heidi threw herself on the ground looking as unhappy as if there were an end to all beauty in the world.

"It will be just so again tomorrow," said the lad. "Get up. We must go home now." So, whistling the herd together, they set out on their homeward track.

"Will it be so every day, always when we go up to the pasture?" asked the child, longing for an assuring reply as she descended the Alm with the goatherd.

"Generally," he said.

"But certainly tomorrow?"

"Yes, tomorrow, of course."

This promise quieted the child, who had today received so many new impressions, and through whose little head such a multitude of thoughts was running, that she scarcely spoke a word until the Alm hut came in sight and she discerned her grandfather sitting on his bench outside, waiting for the goats.

Then she ran to him quickly, with Schwänli and Bärli at her heels.

Peter called out, "Come again tomorrow. Good night." He was very anxious for Heidi to go again. And the child ran to him, gave him her hand, promising to go tomorrow and bidding good-bye to the departing goats. She put her arm about the neck of little Snowball especially, saying, "Good night, Snowball. Sleep well. Don't forget that I am going with you again tomorrow and you must not bleat so sadly again."

The goat looked at her with friendly eyes and then sprang joyfully after the others.

Then Heidi came back under the pine tree, calling out before she could reach her grandfather, "Oh, it was so beautiful! The fire, and the roses on the rock, the blue and yellow flowers. Look what I have brought you."

She shook out all the flowers from her apron before her grandfather.

But how the poor little flowers looked! The child did not recognize them. They were like hay—not one was open!

"What is the matter with them, Grandfather?" cried she, frightened. "They did not look like that when I got them."

"They want to be out in the sun and not in your little apron," said the old man.

"Then I will not bring any more. But why did the eagle scream so?" she asked anxiously.

"Now you must go and wash yourself while I go to the goat's stall to fetch the milk. Afterward we will go into the hut for supper and then I will answer your questions."

Heidi obeyed, and later, when she sat on her stool, and ate her bread and milk, she began again, "Why does the eagle scream so, and scold so loud?"

"He is scornful about the people down below who huddle together in their villages and tease each other, and so he scolds at them. If they would separate, and each go his own way and climb up a mountain, as I do, it would be far better." Her grandfather said this in a half-wild way that reminded the child of the screaming eagle.

"But why have the mountains no names?" asked she, after a pause.

"They have names," he said. "If you can describe one to me so that I recognize it, I will tell you the name."

Heidi described the pile of rocks with the two pinnacles on each side, exactly as she saw it, and her grandfather replied, well pleased, "That is right, I know it. It is called Falkniss. Have you seen others?"

"There was another with the big snow-field, which looked as if it was on fire, and then grew pink, and was suddenly quite gray, and died out."

"I know that, too," said he; "that is the Cäsaplana. So you liked it up there on the pastures?"

Then Heidi told him all that had happened during the day: how beautiful it was, and particularly about the fire at sunset, and begged her grandfather to explain it to her, for Peter knew nothing whatever about it.

"Yes," said her grandfather, "the sun does that when he says good night to the mountains. He casts his most beautiful beams across them so that they will not forget that he is coming again in the morning."

This pleased the little girl, and she could scarcely wait until the morrow, she was in such haste to go again to see the sun bid good night to the mountains. But first she must go to sleep, and she did sleep through the whole night soundly in her little hay bed, and dreamed of pink mountains covered with roses, in the midst of which Snowball jumped gaily about.

Chapter 4
With the Grandmother

On the following day the bright sun came again, as well as Peter with the goats, and they all climbed up again to the pasture. Many days passed thus, and the life agreed so well with little Heidi that she became strong and brown, and had never an ailment, but was as merry as the merry birds on the trees in the green woods.

As autumn came on and the wind blew harder over the mountains, her grandfather would sometimes say, "You must stay at home today, Heidi. Such a little one as you might be carried off by the wind at one blast, down the valley."

When Peter learned this, he did not look happy, and foresaw all sorts of unpleasant things that would happen. He was so lonely that he did not know what to do without Heidi, and then he would not have his fine dinner. The goats were also very unruly when the child was not with them, and gave him twice as much trouble, for they were so accustomed to her companionship that they could not go forward properly without her, and ran about on all sides.

Heidi, for her part, was never unhappy. There was always something that interested and amused her. Best of all she liked to go with the herd and the herd-boy to the pasture, to be sure; for there were the flowers and the eagle, and always something new and exciting happening to the different goats. Still, in her grandfather's room there was always hammering and sawing that delighted her also. Once when he was making a new trough for the goats, she watched him working with his bare arms in the round tub, and he was so skilful that she was enchanted.

But Heidi's greatest joy came on the windy days, when the soughing and sighing in the big pines behind the hut began. Then she was always running to listen to the wind, and left anything she might be about to hear the deep, mysterious tones in the high branches. She would stand looking up, and never get tired of wondering at the swaying and rushing and moaning of the trees.

The sun was now no longer hot as in the summer, and the child was glad to get out her shoes and stockings, and her frock, for it was every day colder, and when she stood out under the trees she was blown about as if she were a little thin leaflet. But she always was scampering out and could never stay in the hut when once she heard the call of the wind.

At last it was very cold. Peter blew upon his fingers as he came up early, but he did not come much longer, for one night there was a deep snowfall, and in the morning the whole Alm was white and not a green leaf to be seen anywhere. Now the goatherd came no more with his flock; and Heidi sat looking through the tiny window, for it was snowing again, and the thick flakes filled the air, and the snow was piled up at last on a line with the window. Then it was higher still, so that they could not open it, and were quite boxed up in the hut.

Heidi found this very pleasant indeed. She was constantly running from one window to another to see the view from each, and wondering if they were to be quite buried, for then they would have to light a lamp in the daytime.

It did not get to be quite as bad as that, however. On the following day the old man went out, as it had ceased to snow, and he shovelled a path round the house, throwing up the snow in great shovelfuls till it was piled into big heaps, and formed a mountain here, and another there—all about.

Now at last the windows and the door were free, which was a good thing; for when Heidi and her grandfather sat at dinner together, each on a three-legged stool, suddenly there came a great knocking at the door, and some one struggled and kicked violently at it. Open it came at last, and there stood Peter, who had not indeed kicked and stamped so rudely without reason. It was to clear his shoes of the snow, for they were quite covered with it. In fact, the whole Peter was a mass of snow, for he had forced his way through the drifts, and great masses clung to him all over and were frozen on—it was so cold. He had persevered, however, for he wished to see Heidi. A whole week was too long for him to be away from her.

"Good evening," said he, and came as near to the fire as possible, and spoke not another word. His whole face, however, laughed for joy. He was so glad to be there. Heidi stared at him wonderingly, for now that he stood so near the fire the snow began to melt on every side, so that he resembled a waterfall rather than Peter.

"Well, general, how are you getting on?" said the old man. "Now that you have no army, you must gnaw your slate pencil, I suppose."

"Why must he gnaw his slate pencil?" asked Heidi curiously.

"He has to go to school in the winter," explained her grandfather. "There you must learn to read and write, which is difficult, and it helps a little, sometimes, to bite the slate pencil. Is not that so? Hey, general?"

"Yes, it is true," assented Peter.

By this time the little girl's interest was fully aroused. She asked such a vast number of questions about the school, what happened there, what one saw and did, that the time flew; and while they talked Peter became quite dry from top to toe.

It cost him always a great effort to explain himself clearly, so as to make his meaning plain. This time it was especially hard, for no sooner had he made one statement than Heidi had two or three more questions ready, and generally such as required a whole sentence for answer.

During this conversation the old man was quite silent, but often the corners of his mouth twitched with amusement, showing that he listened.

"Now, general, you have been under fire, and need some nourishment. You must call a halt now," said he; and rising, he brought what was needed for the supper from the cupboard and Heidi set the seats at the table.

A bench had been recently hammered to the wall, for now that the old man no longer lived alone, he had made all sorts of seats for two people, as Heidi had a way of following him about wherever he went or stood or sat.

So now they all three had comfortable seats, and Peter opened his round eyes very wide indeed when he saw what a big piece of beautiful dried meat the Alm uncle set before him on his thick slice of bread. It was long since the lad had had such a good time, but at last the agreeable meal was over, and he prepared to go home, for it was growing dark.

So he said good night, and God bless you, and stood already in the doorway, when turning back he said, "Next Sunday I shall come again, a week from today, and you must come see my grand-mother—she says so."

Now Heidi became possessed of an entirely new idea, that of going to make a visit herself. It took root in her mind at once, and on the very next day the first thing she said was, "Grandfather, now I must go to see Peter's grandmother. She expects me."

"There is too much snow," he replied evasively.

But the project had taken a deep hold of her, for the grandmother had sent her word and so it must be done. Not a day passed that she did not say at least five or six times, "Grandfather, now I must go, surely, for the grandmother expects me."

On the fourth day, although everything snapped and cracked from cold outside, and the snow all about was frozen hard, the sun shone beautifully through the window on Heidi, as she sat on her high stool at dinner. She began her little speech again, "Today I must certainly go to the grandmother, or it will seem too long to her."

Suddenly her grandfather rose from the table, went into the loft, and brought down the thick sack that had served Heidi for a coverlid all winter, saying, "Well then, come!"

Joyfully the child ran out after him into the

glistening snow. The old pines were quiet now, and the white snow lying heavily on their branches so sparkled and shone in the sunlight, that Heidi leaped into the air for joy, calling out repeatedly, "Come out, Grandfather, come out. It is all silver and gold all over the pines!"

The grandfather now appeared from the shed, with a very big sledge, that had a bar across the front, and from the seat, with his feet against the snow, any one could steer it in any direction. After the old man had looked at the pine trees with Heidi, he seated himself on the sledge, and taking her on his lap, wrapped her round and round in the sack, so that she was snug and warm. He held her with his left arm tightly to his side, which was a wise arrangement considering the journey they were to take. Then he seized the pole with his right hand, gave a shove with his feet, and away went the sledge down the Alm, with such rapidity that the child believed that they were flying, and shouted aloud for joy.

Directly in front of goat-Peter's door, the sledge all at once stopped. Heidi was placed on the ground by her grandfather after he had taken off her wraps, and bidden to go in; but she was told to come out as soon as it began to grow dark and to start for home. Then, turning back, he began to climb the mountain.

Heidi opened the door, and entered a small room. It looked very black inside. She could see a hearth, and some plates and dishes on the shelves. It was in fact a little kitchen. She opened another door, and came into another narrow little apartment, for the house was not a mountain cottage like the Alm uncle's, consisting of one large room with a hayloft above, but it was a little, old, very old, dwelling, where everything was narrow, small, and uncomfortable.

When our little girl stepped into the room, she came directly against a table at which sat a woman mending trousers—Peter's trousers. Heidi recognized them at once.

In the corner a bent little old woman was sitting at a spinning wheel. The child knew in a moment who that was. She went straight over to the spinning wheel, and said, "Good day, Grandmother. At last I have come to see you. Did you think it was too long that you had to wait for me?"

The grandmother raised her head, and felt for the hand that was stretched out toward her, and when she had held it thoughtfully in her own for a while, she said, "Is this the child who lives up with the Alm uncle? Are you Heidi?"

"Yes, yes, I am Heidi. I have just come down here with my grandfather on the sledge."

"How can that be? You have such nice warm hands. Tell me, Brigitte, did the Alm uncle come himself with the child?"

Peter's mother, Brigitte, who had been mending the trousers, stood up now, and looked at the child curiously, from head to foot.

"I do not know, Mother, whether the uncle himself came with her," she said. "It is not credible. The child may not know exactly."

Heidi looked fixedly at the woman, not in the least as if she did not know what she was talking about, and replied, "I know perfectly well who wrapped me in the coverlid and brought me down on the sledge in his arms. It was my grandfather."

"It must be true, what Peter has told us all summer, though we thought he was mistaken," said the old woman. "Who would have believed such a thing to be possible! I did not think that the child could live three weeks up there. How does she look, Brigitte?"

The latter had examined the little one so carefully all over that she was quite able to answer by this time.

"She is as finely built as Adelheid her mother was, but she has the black eyes and curling hair of Tobias and the old man up there. I think she looks like them both."

Heidi had not been idle all this time, she had looked about, observed everything in the room, and noticed each peculiarity. Now she said, "Look at the shutter, Grandmother; it is swinging to and fro. My grandfather would drive a nail into that at once to hold it fast. It will soon break one of the panes. Look, how it goes!"

"My good child," said the old woman, "I

cannot see it, but I hear it only too well, and much more besides. Not only the shutter, but everything creaks and cracks when the wind blows, and we feel the wind itself, too. Nothing holds together now, and in the night, when the other two are asleep, I am often very anxious lest the house should fall in upon us and we all be killed. Oh, there is no one to do anything to it, for Peter does not understand it at all."

"But why can you not see what the shutter is doing, Grandmother? Just look there, now, over there, right there!" and Heidi pointed carefully to the spot with her finger.

"Oh, child, I can see nothing at all! Not only the shutter, but nothing else," said the grandmother sadly.

"But if I go out and open the shutter wide so that it is quite light in the room, can you not see then, Grandmother?"

"No, not then, not even then. Nobody can make it light for me any more."

"But when you go out into the bright snow, then surely it is bright for you. Come out with me, Grandmother. I will show it to you"; and Heidi took the old woman by the hand to draw her out, for the child began to be terribly troubled that it could never be light again to her.

"Let me sit here quietly, you good little child. It will always remain dark for me, in snow and in sunshine. The light can never pierce my eyes again."

"But in summer," said the child, who was seeking more and more anxiously for some point of comfort, "in summer, when the sun gets hot again and then says good night to the mountains, until they glow as if they were on fire, and all the yellow flowers glisten, then it will be light again for you."

"My child, I cannot see the fiery mountains nor the golden flowers. It will never be light for me on the earth, never again."

At this Heidi broke forth with tears and sobs. Full of grief she cried out, "Who can make it bright for you again? Can nobody? Is there nobody that can?"

The grandmother must now comfort the little one, but that was not easy. Heidi very seldom cried, but when she once began it was almost impossible for her to check herself. Everything was tried that could be thought of to distract her from her grief, for it went to the old woman's heart to hear the child sobbing so piteously. At last she said, "Come here, you good little Heidi. I have something to tell you. When one can see nothing, then listening becomes a pleasure, and I listen so gladly when you tell me something pleasant. Come, sit down by me, and talk to me. Tell me what you do up there, and what your grandfather does. I used to know him, but I have heard nothing about him for many a year, except what Peter tells me, and that is not much."

Now Heidi had an idea. She wiped away her tears as quickly as possible, and said consolingly, "Only wait a bit, Grandmother; I will tell my grandfather all about it. He can surely make it light again for you, and he will manage so that the cottage will not fall to pieces. He can bring everything right."

The old woman remained silent; and Heidi began to tell her, in the most lively manner, about her life up on the mountain with her grandfather, and about the days spent in the pasture, and the present winter life indoors; how her grandfather could make anything whatever out of wood, benches and chairs, and mangers into which he could put hay for Schwänli and Bärli; and how he had just finished a big new water trough for summer bathing, a new porringer, and some spoons. Heidi became more and more excited as she recounted the wonderful things that his skilful hand fashioned from a single piece of wood, and how carefully she had watched the processes, and how she meant to do all that some time herself.

To all this the grandmother listened with the greatest interest, only calling out now and then, "Brigitte, do you hear what the child tells me about the uncle?"

Suddenly there was such a stamping and noise at the door that the conversation was interrupted, and Peter burst into the room, and stood stock-still with his big round eyes wide open; but he made most friendly grimaces at Heidi when she cried out immediately, "Good evening, Peter."

"Is it possible that you are already let out of school?" said the grandmother. "I have not known an afternoon pass so quickly for many a long year. Good evening, Peterkin. How goes the reading?"

"Just the same," was the reply.

"Well, well; I thought perhaps that there would be a little change by this time. You will be twelve years come February," said the old woman, sighing a little.

"Why should there be a change then?" asked Heidi, full of interest.

"I only mean that perhaps he might have learned a little—to read, I mean," said his grandmother. "I have up there on the shelf an old prayer book, in which there are beautiful hymns. I have not heard them this long time, and can no longer remember them. So I hoped when Peterkin had learned to read, he could sometimes read me a good hymn, but it is of no use; he can't learn. It is too hard for him."

"I think that I must light the lamp, Mother. It is quite dark," said Brigitte, who had been working all this time at the lad's trousers. "The afternoon has flown away without my knowing it."

Heidi sprang up from her chair at this, and stretched out her hand to the grandmother, saying, "Good night; I must go straight home, for it is dark." And she shook hands with Peter's mother, and went toward the door.

"Wait a moment. Wait, Heidi," cried the grandmother anxiously. "You must not go alone. Peterkin must go with you; do you hear? And take care of the child. Do not let her fall, Peter, and she must not stand still, lest she get frostbitten. Has she a thick shawl?"

"I haven't any shawl, but I shall not be cold," said Heidi, and she was out of the house quickly, running on so nimbly that Peter could hardly overtake her, while the grandmother called out tremulously, "Run after her, Brigitte. Do run. That child will freeze; so near night, too! Take my shawl with you, and run!"

Brigitte obeyed. But the children had not gone far up the mountain when they saw the Alm uncle coming toward them, and with a few prodigious strides he stood beside them.

"That is right, Heidi. You have kept your promise," he said. And taking the child, whom he had wrapped carefully again in the coverlet, in his arms, he turned back toward home.

Brigitte went back with Peter to their cottage to tell her mother what they had seen. The old woman's surprise was great, and she said once, and again, "God be praised that the Alm uncle is so kind to Heidi! God be praised! I hope he will let the little one come to me again. It has done me so much good. What a good heart she has, and how she can tell about things!" So the poor old grandmother rejoiced, and kept saying until she went to bed, "If only she can come again! Now I have something to look forward to; something to make me happy."

Brigitte agreed with her mother heartily each time; and Peter grinned from ear to ear, saying, "I knew as much," while he nodded his head vigorously.

All the time that Heidi went up the mountain on her grandfather's arm she chatted incessantly; but as nothing could penetrate the covering so closely folded about her, he said at last, unable to distinguish a single word, "Wait a little, until we reach home, child, and then tell me."

So as soon as they reached the hut, and Heidi was free from her wrappings, she began, "Tomorrow we must take the hammer and the big nails and go down there, Grandfather; for the shutters shake so. We must make them fast, and we must drive in a good many other nails, too, for everything shakes terribly."

"Must we, must we, indeed? Who told you that?" asked the old man.

"Nobody told me. I know it myself. Nothing holds together there, and it makes the grandmother so uneasy and afraid, because she cannot sleep when there is such a noise, and she fears that everything will fall to pieces on their heads. And oh! No one can make it light for her again. She doesn't know how any one can do it, but you can, grandfather. Only think how sad it must be, always to sit in the dark, and how sorrowful it is for her! No one can help her as you can. Tomorrow we will go and help her, won't we, Grandfather?"

Heidi was clinging to her grandfather, and looking up at him with confident eyes. He looked at her for a long time in silence, then replied, "Yes, Heidi, we will make things fast for the grandmother, so that it will no longer clatter and keep her awake. We can do that, and tomorrow we will."

The child danced round and round the room for joy at these words, crying out, "Tomorrow we will go! Tomorrow! Tomorrow!"

And the old man was as good as his word. On the following afternoon they took their sledge ride as before. Again he placed the child on the ground before the cottage door, saying, "Now go in and when it is evening come out." Then he laid the sack on the sledge and went round about the cottage.

Heidi had scarcely opened the door, and stepped into the room, when the grandmother's voice from the corner was heard, "There comes the child! There is Heidi!" and the thread hung loosely on the wheel as she stretched out her arms for joy to embrace her little friend.

Pushing a little as closely to the old woman's knees as possible, Heidi seated herself, and had already begun narrating and questioning, when suddenly there resounded such a pounding and banging from the outside of the cottage, that the grandmother started up trembling, almost overturning her wheel in her fright.

"O heavens!" she cried, "now it has come. Now the cottage is falling down!"

Holding her fast by the arm, Heidi said soothingly, "No, no, Grandmother! don't be afraid; it is my grandfather with his hammer. He is making things fast about the house, so that you need not feel uneasy nor frightened any more."

"Can it be true? Is it possible? Then the good God has not forgotten us," cried the old woman. "Do you hear, Brigitte? It certainly is a hammer. Go out, and if it is the Alm uncle, beg him to come in for a moment that I may thank him."

And Brigitte obeyed. Just at that moment the uncle was propping up an insecure place in the wall. She went up to him, saying, "I wish you good evening, Uncle, and the mother greets you also. We are much obliged to you for doing us such a good turn, and my mother would like to thank you herself in there. Certainly no one has ever done us such a kindness before, and we wish to thank—"

"You have said enough," interrupted the old man. "What your opinion of the Alm uncle is, I know well. Go now. What more there is to be done here I can find out for myself."

Brigitte retreated immediately, for the uncle had a way with him that made it difficult for any one to oppose his will. He pounded and hammered on all sides of the little cottage; then climbed the narrow steps to the roof, hammering here and there until he had used up every nail he had brought with him. By this time it was quite dark, and he had scarcely come down to fetch his sledge from behind the goat shed when there stood Heidi at the door, and her grandfather took her on his arm, and dragging the sledge behind him, up they went to their home. For had he drawn her sitting alone on the sledge, her wraps would never have stayed in place and she would have been quite frozen.

Thus the winter passed. Into the joyless life of the blind woman a ray of happiness had come after many years of sorrow. Her days were no longer dark and tedious, one just like the other. Now there was always something in prospect. In the early morning she began to listen for the tripping footsteps she loved so well, and when the little one came dancing in, she called out joyfully each time as the door flew open, "God be praised, she has come again!"

On her little stool at the grandmother's feet, Heidi would seat herself, chattering to her of all sorts of pleasant things, so that she felt well and happy, and the hours flew by without her asking as formerly, "Brigitte, is not the day almost over?"

Instead, each time that Heidi in departing closed the door behind her, she said, "How short the afternoon has been, hasn't it, Brigitte?"

To which the daughter would answer, "Yes, Mother, it seems to me as if I had just cleared away the dishes from dinner."

And the grandmother added, "Oh, I hope the good God will keep the dear child in health, and will preserve the Alm uncle's good will! Does the little one look well and strong?"

And the answer was always the same, "As strong and well as an apple."

Heidi had become sincerely attached to the grandmother, and when the recollection of the old woman's blindness came over her, and she thought that no one, not even her grandfather, could restore the lost sight, her heart was sad. But the grandmother's constant assurance that she suffered least from her misfortune when Heidi was with her, somewhat consoled the little girl, who came down to her on the sledge every fine winter's afternoon to do what she could to brighten her days.

Without anything more being said, the Alm uncle had each time taken his hammer and all the necessary tools with him on the sledge, and had pounded and mended, and put things in excellent condition on the outside of goat-Peter's cottage.

The effect was most satisfactory. It no longer rattled and banged the long nights through, and the grandmother declared that she had not had such comfortable nights and such good sleep for many years, and that she should never cease to be grateful to the Alm uncle.

Chapter 5

A Visit, and Another, and the Consequences

Quickly passed the winter, and still more quickly another summer, and yet another winter approached its end. Heidi was as gay and happy as the birds in the sky, and rejoiced daily in the coming of the spring, when the warm south wind would again blow through the pines, and sweep away the snow; when the bright sun would coax out the blue and yellow flowers; when the days for the pasture would come, which were for the child the most beautiful days that could be imagined. She was now in her eighth year, and had learned all sorts of useful things from her grandfather. She could take care of the goats, and Schwänli and Bärli ran after her like faithful dogs, and bleated loudly for joy when they so much as heard her voice.

Twice during the winter Peter had brought a message from the schoolmaster to the Alm uncle that he should send Heidi to school. She was more than old enough, and indeed should have come the winter before. The answer returned each time was that if the schoolmaster had anything to say to him, he would always be found on the Alm, but there was no thought in his mind of sending the child to school. Peter had delivered the message correctly.

Now that the March sun began to melt the snow everywhere, the white snowdrops peeped up in the valley, and on the Alm the pines had shaken off their burden and the boughs waved merrily in the wind once more. Heidi began to scamper back and forth with delight, from the house to the stalls, then to the pines, and again into the hut to tell her grandfather how much larger the strip of green had become under the trees; for she could not wait, in her impatience, for the summer to cover the mountain with grass and flowers. One sunny morning, as the child was running about and had just bounded for the tenth time over the threshold, she almost fell backward for fright, for before her stood an old man all in black, who gazed at her earnestly.

Seeing her fear, however, he said in a kindly tone, "You must not be afraid of me, for I love children very much. Give me your hand. You must be Heidi. Where is your grandfather?"

"He is sitting at the table cutting round spoons out of wood," explained the child, and opened the door wider.

It was the good pastor from Dörfli, who had known the uncle long ago, when he lived down below, and they had been neighbors. He now went into the hut, approached the old man, who was stooping over his work, and said, "Good morning, neighbor!"

The latter looked up in surprise, and rising, said, "Good morning, Pastor!" and immediately placed his own chair for the guest adding, "If the pastor does not object to a wooden seat, here is one for him."

"It is a long time since I saw you, neighbor," said the pastor.

"Yes, it is a long while since we met," replied the Alm uncle.

"I came here today to speak to you about something," began the pastor afresh. "I think that you already surmise what I allude to, what I wish to talk over with you, and learn your intention about."

The good man stopped, and looked toward Heidi, who was now standing in the doorway, examining him with attention.

"You may go to the goats, Heidi," said her grandfather. "Take a little salt with you and stay until I come."

Heidi disappeared at once.

"That child ought to have gone to school this year, if not a year ago," said the pastor. "The teacher sent you word to that effect and you have not replied. What do you mean to do about it, neighbor?"

"I mean not to send her to school," was the reply.

The pastor stared in astonishment at the old man, who sat with folded arms upon his bench, and certainly did not look like yielding.

"What do you mean to do for the child?" he asked again.

"Nothing. She grows and thrives with the goats and birds. With them she can learn no evil. She is safe."

"But she is not a goat, nor is she a bird. She is a human child. If she learns nothing evil from such company, she learns, on the other hand, nothing at all. But she should learn, and it is high time, too, that she began. I have come to warn you, neighbor, so that you can be thinking it over, and making your arrangements during the summer. This must be the last season that the child passes thus, without instruction. Next winter she must begin to go to school, and go every day."

"I shall not do it," replied the other, unmoved.

"Do you mean to say that there is no way of bringing you to your senses? How can you be so obstinate in your foolishness?" said the pastor, now getting roused. "You have been about a great deal, and must have learned much. I thought that you had more wisdom than this, neighbor."

"Well," replied the old man, and his voice betrayed that he was no longer quite tranquil, "and does the pastor think that it really would be a wise thing for me to send such a tender child as this down the mountain every day next winter, in snow and wind, a two hours' journey? To say nothing of her coming up again every evening, when we ourselves can scarcely brave it? Perhaps the pastor remembers the child's mother, Adelheid. She was delicate, and had nervous attacks. Shall I let this child also become ill through overexertion? Just let some one try to force me. I will go with him before the judge to see if I *can* be forced."

"You are right, neighbor," replied the pastor in a friendly tone; "it would not be possible to send the little one down to school from here. But I can see that you are fond of her, so do something for her sake that you should have done long ago. Come down into the village and live again amongst us there. What sort of life is this that you lead up here, in bitterness with God and man? If anything should happen to you here in the winter, how could any help reach you? I cannot even understand how you can manage to get through the winter, with this tender child, without freezing."

"The child has young blood and good clothing, this much I can tell you, and this too, that I know where to get wood, and the best time to fetch it. If the pastor pleases, he can look into my shed. There is plenty of fuel there. On my hearth the fire never goes out all winter long. What the pastor proposes about moving down into the village will not suit me. The people down there despise me, and I them. We must remain apart, so it is best for all."

"No, no, it is not good for you! I know what is lacking with you, though," said the pastor earnestly. "As for the contempt of the village people, what does that amount to? Believe me, neighbor, seek to make your peace with God, ask His forgiveness in whatever way you need it, and then come and see how differently men will regard you, and how pleasant it will be for you."

The good man now stood up. He held out his hand to the Alm uncle, and continued cordially, "I shall count upon it for next winter to have you again amongst us. We are good old neighbors, and it would be very disagreeable to me to have any force used toward you, so give me your hand upon it, that you'll come back and live with us again, at peace with God and man."

The Alm uncle gave his hand to the pastor, but said also decidedly, "I know that the pastor feels kindly to me, but I shall not do as he wishes. I say it plainly, without circumlocution. I shall neither send the child to school, nor come myself."

"So may God help you!" said the pastor sadly, and passed out of the door and down the mountain.

The old man was out of humor, and when Heidi said, "Now shall we go to the grandmother?" he answered, "Not today," and did not speak again that whole day long. The next morning, when the child said, "Today shall we go to the grandmother?" he was short with her in word and tone, answering only, "We'll see."

But before there was time to clear the table after dinner came another visitor. It was no other than Dete. She had a fine hat with a feather, and a dress that swept up everything in its path, and in the mountain cottage all sorts of things lay on the floor that might have soiled a nice dress. The uncle looked at her from head to foot, but did not speak.

Dete, however, had the intention of making herself very agreeable, and began at once to praise what she saw, saying that Heidi looked wonderfully well, that she should hardly have recognized the child, that is was plain that the grandfather had cared well for her. She declared that she had always meant to take the child back again, for she fully understood that it must be very inconvenient for him to have the charge of her, but that there had never been a time, day or night, when she had been able to come for her or even to bring her anything. Today she came because she had just heard of something that might be of such advantage to Heidi that she herself could scarcely believe it possible. She had looked well into it at once, and now she could safely say that such a piece of luck rarely happens, perhaps once in a thousand times to any one.

Very rich relations of the family with whom she lived, who owned almost the handsomest house in Frankfort, had only one daughter, who was ill, and obliged to remain all the time in a rolling chair because she was paralyzed on one side. This girl was almost always alone, and had to study alone with her teachers, which was tedious for her. It was thought desirable to find a companion for her, to live in the house. Dete had learned all this, she said, from the family with whom she lived, and they wanted to find a child. When Dete heard the description of what they wanted—the housekeeper said she must be a perfectly unspoiled little girl, unlike all other children—she thought at once of Heidi. She went to the lady and told her about her little niece, and gave the child such a good character, the lady agreed at once that she was just what she wished for.

Nobody could realize, said Dete, what was in store for Heidi. Such luck! Such comfort! And when she once came to live with these people, she would have everything that the daughter had, and no one could tell, the daughter was so delicate—if the family should be left without a child, what wonderful piece of luck—

"Have you almost finished?" said the grandfather, who thus far had not spoken a word.

"Pah!" said Dete, and threw back her head. "You behave exactly as if I had brought you a commonplace piece of news, and there is not in all Prättigau a single person who would not have thanked God for such tidings as I have just given you."

"Take them, then, where you choose. I'll have none of them," said the old man dryly.

At these words off went Dete's tongue like a skyrocket.

"Well, if such is your opinion, I will tell you then, uncle, what I think. This child is now eight years old, and knows nothing, and can do nothing, and you will not let her learn, nor send her to school, nor to church. They told me down in Dörfli. She is my only sister's child, and I must be responsible for her, and what happens to her, and when such a chance falls to a child's share as this, there can be but one opinion about it, for no one has any particular interest in her, and no one feels disposed to do anything for her. I will not yield, that I tell you plainly, for I have everybody on my side. There is not one single person down in Dörfli who will not help me against you. And if you wish to come before the court, though you'd better think twice of that, there are things that can be brought up against you that you will not care to hear. When once an affair is brought before a court, much is raked up that has almost been forgotten."

"Hold your tongue!" thundered the old man, and his eyes flashed fire. "Take the child, and ruin her, but never let me see her with such a hat and feather on her head, and such words in her mouth as you have used today." And with great strides he went out of the house.

"You have made my grandfather angry," said Heidi, her sparkling eyes showing an expression that was far from friendly toward Dete.

"Oh, he will soon be all right again. Come along, now. Where are your clothes, child?"

"I am not going," said Heidi.

"What did you say?" said Dete. Then changing her tone a little, she continued, half in friendly, half in angry fashion, "Come, come, you do not know what you are talking about. It will be far pleasanter for you there than you can even imagine."

She went to the press and took out Heidi's things, and packed them together. "Come, now, get your hat. It does not look very nice, I must say, but it will pass for the present. Put it on, and let us get off."

"I am not going," repeated Heidi.

"Do not be stupid and obstinate like a goat. You must have learned it from them. Think a little, child! Your grandfather is angry; you saw that yourself. You heard him tell us not to come before his eyes again. He is quite determined that you shall go with me. Do not anger him still more. You have no idea how delightful it is in Frankfort, nor what you will see there, and if you don't like it, you can come back here again, and by that time your grandfather will have recovered his temper."

"Can I turn right about and come home this evening?"

"What? Come along, now. Did I not tell you that you could come back whenever you wished? Today we go as far as Mayenfield, and early tomorrow morning we take our places in the railway, and in that you can come back here in a twinkling. It is like flying."

Aunt Dete had taken the little girl's hand in hers, and with the bundle on her arm, they went down the mountain side together.

As it was not yet quite time to take the goats to pasture, Peter still went to school in Dörfli, or rather, should have gone, but he now and then took a holiday, for he thought, "It is not of the least use for me to go to school. I cannot learn to read, and to go about a little, searching for big sticks, is of use, for they can be burned."

So it happened that he was in the neighborhood of his cottage, with most unmistakable evidence of his day's occupation on his shoulder, for he carried an enormous bundle of sticks of hazel wood. He stood still, and stared at the pair as they came toward him. When they drew near, he said, "Where are you going?"

"I must go straight to Frankfort with Aunt Dete," said Heidi; "but first I will run in to see the grandmother."

"No, no! No stopping to talk. It is already too late!" said Dete, anxiously, and held the child, who was already hastening away, fast by the hand. "You can come back again to see her soon, but now come with me."

And she drew Heidi quickly along, and did not release her again. She was afraid that it might again come into the child's head not to go with her, and that the grandmother might also induce her to remain.

Into his cottage went Peter at one leap, and flung his whole bundle of sticks down on the table with such violence that everything quivered, and his grandmother started from her spinning, and cried aloud. Peter had to give vent to his feelings.

"What is the matter? What has happened?" asked the old woman.

And his mother, who had been sitting quietly at the table, almost flew into the air at the noise, crying, "What is it, Peterkin? Why are you so wild?"

"Because she has taken Heidi away with her," exclaimed Peter.

"Who? Who? Where, Peterkin?" cried the grandmother. She must have soon guessed what had happened, however, for Brigitte had told her, a little while before, that she had seen Dete going up the mountain to the Alm uncle's. Trembling all over with haste, the old woman opened the window, and called beseechingly, "Dete, Dete! do not take the child away! Do not carry Heidi off."

The fugitives were still within sound of her voice: and Dete must have heard perfectly what she said, for she held the child faster, and increased her speed to a run. Heidi resisted, saying, "The grandmother is calling me. I must go."

Now Dete forced Heidi along, lest they should not be in time to take the train for Frankfort, she said; and once there, Heidi would not want to return, but if she did, there might be something to bring to the grandmother that the old woman would like.

This idea pleased the little one, and she began to run of her own accord.

"What can I bring the grandmother?" she asked, after a while.

"Something good," said Dete. "Some beautiful, soft, white bread, for she can scarcely eat the hard, black bread. That would be nice for her."

"Yes, yes! She always gives it to Peter, and says it is too hard for her. I have often seen her do that. Let us go quick, Aunt Dete, and perhaps we can get to Frankfort today, so that I can come back at once with the white bread."

And now it was Heidi who urged her aunt

along, and ran so quickly that Dete found it hard to follow with the bundle. But she was glad to hasten, for they were near the first houses in Dörfli, and there might begin a new set of questions and remonstrances that would bring Heidi again to another mind.

Through the village they raced along, therefore, and the child dragged her aunt by the hand, and Dete reflected with satisfaction that everybody might see that she was hurrying along in this way for the child's sake. So she called to all who would stop her, from the houses, "You see, I can't possibly stop. Heidi is in such a hurry, and we have still far to go."

"Are you taking her with you?" "Are you running away from the Alm uncle?" "It is a miracle that the child is living!" "And so rosy-cheeked too!" Such remarks reached her from all sides; and she was glad that she could get off without hindrance and not be obliged to give explanations; also, that Heidi spoke not a word, but urged forward in the greatest haste.

From this day forward the Alm uncle looked more and more wicked. When he chanced to be in Dörfli he spoke to no one, and looked so repulsive that the women said to the little children, "Take care! Get out of his way, or the Alm uncle will harm you."

The old man held no intercourse with any one in Dörfli but went through the little town and deep down into the valley, where he exchanged his goat cheese for provisions of bread and meat. When he passed through Dörfli, the people gathered together in little groups behind his back, and each one had something strange to tell about the old man: how he looked wilder and wilder, and how he never even exchanged a greeting with anybody. All agreed it was very fortunate that the child had escaped, for it was easy to see that the little one ran as if afraid that her grandfather was pursuing her to carry her back.

Only the blind grandmother stood up for him always, and whoever came to her cottage to bring her stuff to spin, or to take away something that she had done for them, were told how good and careful the Alm uncle had been with the child, and how he had worked on her cottage for many an afternoon, and had mended it, and made it safe, or it would certainly have fallen in pieces long ago. This information had come also down to Dörfli, but most of those who heard it said that the grandmother was too old to understand rightly, for she probably did not hear very well just as she could no longer see. At any rate, the Alm uncle never appeared again at the goatherd's cottage, but it was true that he had mended it very thoroughly, for it held together for a long time, and was perfectly safe.

Chapter 6

A New Chapter, and Altogether New Things

In the house of Mr. Sesemann, in Frankfort, lay his little sick daughter. In the comfortable armchair she reclined all day, and was rolled from one room to another. She was in the so-called study, which adjoined the big dining room, and in which all sorts of pretty things were arranged, and disposed in such a way as to make it look attractive, and prove that it was the place where the family usually lived. A large, handsome bookcase with glass doors showed whence the room derived its name, and here the lame daughter of the house had her daily lessons.

Klara had a small, pale face, out of which looked two gentle blue eyes, which were fixed at this moment on the face of the large wall clock, whose hands seemed today, especially, to move slowly. For Klara, who was seldom impatient, was certainly so now, and said with decided symptoms of irritation in her voice, "Will the time never come, Miss Rottenmeier?"

The lady so addressed sat bolt upright by a little worktable, embroidering. She wore a mysterious kind of wrap, half collar, half mantle, which invested her person with a majestic appearance, heightened by a kind of built-up cupola upon her head.

Miss Rottenmeier had lived in the house ever since the death of Mrs. Sesemann. She directed the housekeeping, and had the management of the servants. As the master of the house was almost always away travelling, he gave up the entire care of everything to this lady, with the understanding, however, that his daughter should be consulted, and that nothing should be done contrary to her wishes.

As Klara asked for the second time, with every sign of impatience, if it was not getting late for the arrival of those whom they were expecting, Dete, with Heidi's hand in hers, stood below before the house door and asked of John the coachman, who had just driven up with the carriage, if it was too late to venture to disturb Miss Rottenmeier.

"That is no affair of mine," said John gruffly. "Go into the hall, and ring for Sebastian."

Dete did so, and the house servant came downstairs. He had big round buttons on his coat, and almost as big eyes in his head.

"I should like to inquire if at this hour I might

venture to disturb Miss Rottenmeier," launched forth Dete.

"That is not my business. Ring for Miss Tinette. That is her bell over there." And without other information Sebastian disappeared.

So Dete rang again, and presently Miss Tinette made her appearance on the stairs, with a dazzling little white cap on the top of her head, and a very mocking expression on her face.

"What is wanted?" said she from the top step, without coming down.

Dete repeated her demand.

Miss Tinette disappeared, but came quickly back again, saying, "You are expected."

They now mounted the stairs, following Tinette, Dete still holding Heidi by the hand, and entered the study. Dete stood politely near the door, but never let go of Heidi, for she did not know what the child might do in this strange place.

Miss Rottenmeier rose slowly from her seat, and came nearer to examine the newly arrived playmate of the daughter of the house. The sight did not seem to please her. Heidi had on her simple woolen dress, and her old defaced straw hat was on her head. The child looked, in the most innocent way, round about her, and examined the turret on the lady's head with astonishment.

"What is your name?" asked Miss Rottenmeier, after she had looked at the child searchingly for several minutes, during which Heidi never dropped her eyes.

"Heidi," was the answer, given distinctly in a clear, ringing tone.

"What? That is certainly no Christian name. You were not baptized by that name. What name was given you at your baptism?" asked the lady.

"I don't know that now."

"Is that a proper reply?" said the housekeeper, slowly shaking her head. "Is the child simple, or pert, Miss Dete?"

"If the lady will allow me, and with her consent, I will reply for the child, for she is very inexperienced," said Dete, while she gave her niece a secret push for her inappropriate answer. "She is certainly not simple, nor is she impertinent—of that she knows nothing. She means everything just as she says it. Today is her first appearance in the presence of gentlefolk, and she has no knowledge of good manners, but she is a docile child, and willing to learn, if the lady will teach her, and show her what to do. Her name at baptism is Adelheid, after her mother, my late sister."

"Good, now! That is something like a name that one can say," replied Miss Rottenmeier; but added, "Miss Dete, I must say to you that the child strikes me as very strange, considering her age. I had informed you that the companion needed for Miss Klara should be about the same age as she is in order to follow her lessons, and share the same general occupations. Miss Klara has passed her twelfth year. How old may this child be?"

"With your leave, madam," began Dete again, "I am not exactly sure about the age—how old she is. She is really somewhat younger than that; not much, however. I cannot say with precision—perhaps in her tenth year, or thereabout, as I believe."

"I am just eight years old. My grandfather told me so," said Heidi.

"What do you say? Only eight years old? Four years too young! What does this mean? And what have you learned? What books have you studied?" broke forth Miss Rottenmeier.

"None," was the answer.

"What? How then have you learned to read, child?"

"I have not learned to read, nor Peter either."

"Merciful heavens! You cannot read? Cannot really read at all?" cried Miss Rottenmeier in great surprise. "Then what have you learned?"

"Nothing," replied Heidi truthfully.

"Miss Dete," said the housekeeper after a pause, in which she strove to regain her composure, "I find nothing here that accords with our agreement. How could you bring me such a creature?"

Dete, however, had no idea of allowing herself to be frightened off in this manner. She replied with confidence, "If the lady will pardon me, the child exactly agrees with what is wanted. The lady told me that she sought for some child utterly unlike any other children, and I chose this little one, for bigger children are no longer so simple and truthful, and she seemed to me to answer the description as if made to order. But now I must be going, for my employers expect me. I will come again as soon as they can spare me, and inquire how it is with her."

With a curtsy Dete was away, out of the door and down the stairs very quickly. Miss Rottenmeier stood still a moment, then ran after Dete, for it occurred to her that there were many things still of which she must speak, if the child were to remain, and she plainly saw that Dete's intention was to leave her with them.

Heidi stood still in the same place by the door. Klara had until now remained a passive observer in her chair, and noticed all that took place without interfering. Now she beckoned to Heidi. "Come here to me."

Heidi approached the rolling chair.

"Do you prefer to be called Heidi rather than Adelheid?"

"My name is Heidi, and nothing else," said the child.

"Then I will always call you so. The name pleases me for you. I never heard it before, and I have never seen a child like you. Have you always had such short curly hair?"

"Yes, I think so."

"Were you glad to come to Frankfort?" pursued the older child.

"No, but tomorrow I am going home again, to carry the grandmother some white rolls," said Heidi.

"Well, you are a strange child," replied Klara. "You have been sent for expressly to Frankfort to take lessons with me, and now it turns out that you cannot read. It will be great fun for me! Now there will be something new during the lessons. It has always been so dreadfully tedious. The mornings seem to have no end. Just think! Every morning at ten o'clock the professor comes, and then the lessons begin, and continue until two o'clock. That is so long! Often the professor holds his book before his face quite near, as if he were suddenly nearsighted, but it is really to yawn. He yawns frightfully; and Miss Rottenmeier also takes out her handkerchief, and holds it over her whole face, as if she is very much amused at something that we are reading, but I know well enough that she too is yawning horribly behind it. And then I should like to yawn too, but I have to smother it, for if I once yawn outright, Miss Rottenmeier would say that I was weak, and would fetch the cod-liver oil at once, and of all things I hate to take that stuff, so I much prefer to swallow my yawns. But now that you are here, it will be much more pleasant, for I can listen while you learn to read."

Heidi shook her head very thoughtfully when the question came of learning to read.

At this moment Miss Rottenmeier came back into the study. She had not been able to call Dete back, and felt very much excited, as she had many things to ask her and to tell her that seemed absolutely necessary. She had undertaken this business on her own responsibility, and now that it did not seem likely to prove satisfactory, she was anxious to get out of it. So she ran, in her agitation, from the study to the dining room, and back again, turning immediately about, to go again through the same process, when lo! There was Sebastian, and she ran plump against him. He was casting his round eyes anxiously over the table, which he had just set for the dinner, to see if anything was missing.

"This train of thought can be followed out tomorrow, but today dinner may be served at once."

With these words Miss Rottenmeier pushed past Sebastian, and called for Tinette with such a disagreeable tone that the lady's maid tripped forward with much shorter steps than ever, and stood before the housekeeper with such a mocking expression on her face that Miss Rottenmeier did not venture to attack her, but tried, instead, to control herself.

"The room for the child must be made ready," said the lady, with a great effort at calmness.

"Everything is there. It is only necessary to dust the furniture."

"Well, that is worth while," said Tinette ironically, and went away.

Sebastian now threw back the folding doors between the dining room and the study with a decided bang. He, too, was very much excited, but dared not show it before Miss Rottenmeier. So he walked into the study to roll Klara's bath chair to the table. Whilst he was adjusting the handle at the back into its proper position, Heidi placed herself in front of him, and regarded him fixedly. Suddenly, as he could bear it no longer, he shouted out, "Well, what do you find so wonderful about me?" and returned the child's stare in a way he would not have dared to do had the housekeeper been present, but she already stood on the threshold, and heard Heidi's answer, "You look exactly like goat-Peter."

Horrified, Miss Rottenmeier could only clasp her hands. "Now that child is talking to the servants as if they were friends," said she half aloud. "The creature passes all understanding."

The chair being rolled to the table, and Klara carefully placed in her seat, the housekeeper took that next to her young mistress, and Heidi was directed to take the opposite chair. As there was no one else at the table, Sebastian had plenty of room for the service, the seats being far apart.

Near Heidi's plate lay a beautiful white roll.

The child looked at it with delight. The resemblance to Peter that she had discovered must have inspired her with confidence, for she sat perfectly still and did not stir until Sebastian came round to her with the big dish, to help her to baked fish. Then she pointed to the bread, and asked, "May I have that?"

The servant nodded assent, casting meanwhile a little glance at Miss Rottenmeier, for he was curious to see the effect it had on her. In a moment the child had seized the roll, and stuffed it into her pocket. Sebastian made a wry face, for the desire to laugh overtook him, but he knew that it would not be tolerated. Stolid and unmoved he stood before Heidi, as he dared not speak, and still less leave the room, until the service was over.

Heidi stared at him for some time, and then asked, "Shall I eat some of that?"

Sebastian nodded again.

"Then help me," she said, and looked quietly at her plate.

Sebastian's grimaces now became alarming, and the dish in his hand began to shake ominously.

"The dish may be set upon the table, we are served for the present," said Miss Rottenmeier with severity.

Sebastian vanished instantly.

"I see, Adelheid, that I must instruct you in everything from the beginning," said the housekeeper, with a deep sigh. "In the first place I will tell you what is proper when you are at the table," and a minute description followed of all the etiquette required while being served. "Then you must particularly remember not to talk to Sebastian while he is waiting on us at table, and indeed never to speak to him unless you have a message to deliver, or a necessary question to ask, and then only as *you* or *he*. Do you hear? Never let me again hear you address him otherwise. Tinette, too, should be addressed as *you*, Miss Tinette. You must address me as all the others do. Klara will tell you herself what she wishes to be called."

"Klara, of course," said the latter.

Now followed a quantity of instructions and rules about getting up and going to bed, entering and quitting a room, about being orderly, and closing the doors. In the midst of it all, Heidi fell fast asleep, for she had risen that morning at five o'clock, and had made a long journey. The poor child leaned her head back in her chair, and slumbered. At last the lady had finished her directions. "Now think it over, Adelheid," she said. "Have you understood it perfectly?"

"Heidi has been asleep this long time," said Klara, smiling with delight. Certainly, for the lame girl, this dinner had been the most diverting that she had ever known.

"I have never imagined anything like what one must endure with this child," said Miss Rottenmeier very angrily; and she rang the bell with such violence that Sebastian and Tinette came running in together. The child did not waken, in spite of all the noise, and it was with the greatest difficulty that they could get her sufficiently roused to lead her to her bedroom. They had to go through the dining room, the study, Klara's room, and Miss Rottenmeir's, before they reached the corner chamber which was hers.

Chapter 7

Miss Rottenmeier Has a Day of Troubles

When Heidi opened her eyes on her first day in Frankfort, she could not in the least understand what she saw. She rubbed her eyes very hard, and looked and looked again, and saw the same things each time. She was sitting in a high white bed, and before her she saw a large, wide room, and where the light entered, hung long white curtains. Near them stood two chairs, with great flowers thereon. Against the wall was a sofa, also covered with flowers, before which stood a round table. In the corner was the washstand, with things upon it such as Heidi had never seen.

Now she remembered that she was in Frankfort, and the whole of the day before came to her mind, and lastly the instructions given by the lady, as well as she had heard them. Heidi sprang down from her bed, and got herself dressed. She now went to one window, then to the other. She must see the sky, and the earth outside, it seemed as if she were in a cage behind the big curtains. As she could not draw them aside, she crept under them to get to the window; but this was so high that she could only just look, nor did she find what she wanted. She ran from one window to another, and then back again, but the same things were always before her eyes, walls and windows, and another wall and more windows. The child began to be troubled.

It was still early, for Heidi was accustomed to rise early on the Alm, and to run out at once before the door to see what the weather was, if the wind sang in the pines, and if any little flowers had opened their eyes. Like a bird that for the first time finds itself in a beautiful glittering prison, and runs here and there, trying on all sides to regain its freedom, so the child ran from one window to another, trying to open them, for she felt that she must see something besides walls and windows. There must be green grass on the earth beneath, and the last traces of melting snow on the precipices, and Heidi longed for the sight.

All the windows were tightly fastened down,

and no matter how the child lifted and tugged, and tried to get her little fingers under the sash, in hopes to get hold enough to force it open, it was in vain; everything was as firm as if made of iron. After a long time she became convinced that her efforts were useless. She gave up trying, and wondered if she could not perhaps get out of the house door, and run around the corner until she found the grass, for she remembered that when they came, on the preceding evening, they had passed over stones all the way. But just then some one knocked on the door. Miss Tinette's head appeared, and she uttered the words, "Breakfast ready!"

Heidi had no idea that this meant she was to go to breakfast, and on the scornful face of the lady's maid the child saw a warning not to approach too nearly rather than anything of a friendly nature, and read the face too truly to wish to try familiarities.

She now took a little footstool from beneath the table, set it in the corner, and taking her seat there, waited patiently to see what would happen next. After a while, something came with a good deal of noise. It was Miss Rottenmeier, who was again in great excitement, and came hurriedly into the room, saying, "What is the matter with you, Adelheid? Don't you know what breakfast means? Come at once!"

This Heidi understood, and followed into the

dining room where Klara had long been seated. She greeted her little friend with pleasant words, and had a far more cheerful expression than usual, for she anticipated all sorts of adventures in the day that had just begun.

Breakfast, however, proceeded without accident. Heidi ate her bread and butter very properly, and when Klara was rolled into the library, Miss Rottenmeier gave the child to understand that she was to remain with Klara until the professor came.

As soon as the children were alone together, the little girl asked at once, "How can one look out, Klara, and see quite down to the ground?"

"You open the window, and peep out, of course," said the other, much amused.

"But these windows won't come open," said Heidi very sadly.

"Oh yes, they will," was Klara's reassuring answer. "You cannot open them, nor can I help you. But when you get a chance to speak to Sebastian, he will open one at once."

It was a great relief to our little mountain girl to know this, for she had felt as if she were in prison.

Soon Klara began to question Heidi concerning her life at home, and Heidi told with pleasure all about the Alm, and the goats, the pasture life, and all that she loved up there.

While the girls talked, the professor arrived, but he was detained by Miss Rottenmeier in the dining room before she allowed him to go to the study.

There she seated herself before him, and began excitedly to explain the dilemma she was in, and how it had all happened: how she had written to Paris a while ago to tell Mr. Sesemann that his daughter had long wished for a companion, and that she herself was convinced that were some one to join Klara in her studies, it would act as a spur to her learning. Miss Rottenmeier felt that it would also be most agreeable to herself to be released from the necessity of being always with her young mistress.

Mr. Sesemann had replied that he should gladly comply with his daughter's wish, only making the condition that such a playfellow should be treated in every way as if she were a daughter of the house, for he would have no tormenting of children in his home, which indeed was a most unnecessary remark, said Miss Rottenmeier, for who would wish to be cruel to a child? Now the professor must hear how very unlucky she had been in her choice, and there followed a detail of every instance of ignorance that Heidi had shown. Not only must the child's education begin with the alphabet, but every point of good breeding must be taught her from the very rudiments.

Out of this unbearable position she could see but one hope of escape, which was for the professor to declare that it would be very unprofitable for two children who were in such different stages of advancement to study together, especially for the more proficient. Such a statement would afford Mr. Sesemann a plausible ground for withdrawing from the bargain, and he would agree that the child should be sent back to her home. This step she herself dared not take, now that the master of the house was aware that the child had arrived. But the professor was cautious, and never one-sided in his decisions. He comforted Miss Rottenmeier with many words, and with the prospect that if the little girl were so backward on the one side, she might be as forward upon others, and that a well-regulated method of teaching would soon bring things to a proper balance.

At last the housekeeper became aware that she could hope for no support from the professor, but that he intended to begin with teaching the alphabet. She opened the study door for him and shut it behind him quickly; for of all things she dreaded to be obliged to listen to the teaching of A B C. Walking up and down the dining room with great strides, she now tried to decide the momentous question of how the servants were to address Adelheid. Mr. Sesemann had certainly written that she must be treated as if she were his daughter, and this order must particularly have reference to the conduct of the servants, thought Miss Rottenmeier.

She was not, however, allowed to pursue her train of thought without interruption, for suddenly a startling crash as of something falling was heard in the study, followed by a call for Sebastian. She hastened in. On the floor, in the greatest confusion, lay the whole collection of school books, copy books, inkstands, and other aids to study, and over all the tablecloth, from beneath which a black rivulet ran down the whole length of the room. Heidi had vanished.

"Now we have it!" cried Miss Rottenmeier, wringing her hands. "Carpet, books, workbasket, everything in the ink! Never has the like happened before. This is the work of that wretched child, without doubt."

The professor stood, much disturbed, and looked at the wreck, a wreck which certainly had only one side, and that a very distressing one. Klara, on the other hand, was regarding the whole thing with a pleased look, and now explained: "Yes, Heidi did it, but not intentionally. Indeed she must not be punished. She was so dreadfully quick in her movements that she dragged the tablecloth with her, and so everything fell down. A number of carriages drove by, one after the other, and that made her fly off. She has probably never seen a coach."

"There! Is it not just as I told you, Professor? Not one proper idea has the creature; not the least suspicion of what a lesson is, nor that she should give attention, and keep still. But where has the mischievous child gone? If she should have run away, what shall I tell Mr. Sesemann?"

Miss Rottenmeier hurried downstairs. There in the open house door stood Heidi, looking up and down the street quite puzzled.

"What is the matter? What are you thinking of? How dare you run off in this way!" cried out Miss Rottenmeier to the child.

"I heard the wind in the pines; but I don't know where they stand, and now I do not hear it any more." And she stood staring with disappointment toward the side from which the sound had come. It was the sound of rumbling of heavy carriages, which seemed to her unwonted ears to be the rushing of the Föhn in the pines, and which had filled her with the greatest delight.

"Pine trees! Are we in the forest? What kind of notions are these? Come upstairs with me, and see the mischief you have done!"

Miss Rottenmeier went upstairs again, followed by Heidi, who looked on the heap of things that she had spilled on the floor in consternation, for in her joy at hearing the wind she had thought of nothing but getting to the pines.

"You have done this once. A second time it must not happen," said the housekeeper, pointing to the floor. "In order to learn, one must sit still, and pay attention. If you cannot do it of yourself, then I must bind you fast to your chair. Can you understand what I say?"

"Yes," answered Heidi, "but indeed I will sit

still." She understood now that it was a rule that during study hours she was to sit quiet.

Sebastian and Tinette came in to put things in order again. The professor withdrew, for there could be no more lessons that day. There had certainly been no yawning.

It was Klara's habit to rest for a while in the afternoon, and Heidi was to choose her own occupation for that time, as the housekeeper had that morning explained to her. So when Klara had settled herself to rest in her bath-chair, and Miss Rottenmeier had withdrawn to her own room, the child realized that she was free to do as she liked. She was glad enough, for she had something in her mind that she longed to accomplish. For this, however, she needed assistance, so she stationed herself in the corridor, before the entrance to the dining room, in order that the person to whom she wished to speak could not escape her.

In a short time, up came Sebastian with a tray, bringing the silver from the kitchen, to put it away in the sideboard in the dining room. As he reached the topmost step, there stood Heidi before him, and very distinctly she said, "You or he!"

Sebastian's round eyes opened to their utmost capacity, and he said rather sharply, "What do you mean, mam'selle?"

"I want to ask you something, but it is nothing naughty, like this morning," she said deprecatingly, for she thought he was angry, and she supposed it was because of the ink on the carpet.

"Oh ho! But why must I be called you or he? First tell me that," said the man still sharply.

"That is what I must always say, for Miss Rottenmeier has ordered it so."

At these words Sebastian burst out laughing so loudly that Heidi stared at him in surprise, for she saw nothing to laugh at. The man, however, understood at once what it all meant, and said, "All right; now go on, mam'selle."

"I am not mam'selle; I am Heidi," said the child, now somewhat nettled in her turn.

"That is true enough, but the same lady has ordered me to say mam'selle."

"Has she? Well, then, I must be called so," said Heidi resignedly, for she had learned that everything in the household must be as Miss Rottenmeier wished.

"Now I have three names," she added with a sigh.

"But what did the little mam'selle wish to ask?" asked Sebastian at last, as he went into the dining room to put away the silver.

"How can one open these windows, Sebastian?"

"So, just so," and he opened one of the great windows.

The child ran to look out, but she was too small, she reached only to the sill.

Sebastian brought a high wooden stool to the window. "Now the little mam'selle can look out," he said, as he helped her up on to it.

But the child withdrew her head quickly, with a look of keen disappointment on her face. "There's only the stone street, and nothing else," said she sadly. "But if you go all round the house, what can you see on the other side, Sebastian?"

"Just the same."

"Is there no place where you can see the whole valley far down and away?"

"To do that you must climb up a high tower, a church tower, like that one over there with the golden ball on the top. You can look down from that and see about on every side."

In a twinkling Heidi had clambered down from her high stool, was off to the door, out into the street, and away. Things did not happen as she expected, however. When she saw the tower out of the window she thought that she could go to it by simply crossing the street; it seemed directly before her. She went the whole length of the street, but did not come to it, nor could she see it anywhere. She turned a corner, going farther and farther; still no tower to be seen.

A great many people passed her by, but they all seemed in such haste that the child thought they would not find time to give her any information. But on the next corner she saw a boy standing, who carried a small hand organ on his back, and on his arm a queer-looking animal. Running up to him, the child asked, "Where is the tower with the golden ball at the top?"

"Don't know."

"Whom can I ask to tell me?"

"Don't know."

"Do you know of any other church with a high tower?"

"Yes, I do."

"Then come and show me."

"Tell me first what you will give me."

The boy held out his hand. Heidi searched in her pockets, and drew out a little picture of a pretty wreath of red roses. She looked at it rather regretfully, for Klara had given it to her that very morning, but to look down into the valley, to survey the green precipices!

"Here," she said, and held the card toward the lad, "will you take this?"

He withdrew his hand, and shook his head.

"What do you want, then?" asked she, tucking her picture away gladly.

"Money."

"I have none, but Klara has. She will certainly give you some. How much do you want?"

"Threepence."

"Well, then, come along."

They wandered down a long street, and the child asked her guide what he carried on his back. He explained that there was a beautiful organ under the cloth, that made charming music, if he turned the handle. All at once he stood still before an old church with a high tower. "This is it," he said.

"But how can I get in?" asked Heidi, as she discovered that the door was fastened.

"Don't know."

"Do you think I could ring, as they do for Sebastian?"

"Don't know."

The child had discovered a bell, at which she pulled with all her might.

"When I go in, you must wait for me here, for I do not know my way back, and I want you to show me."

"What will you give me for it?"

"What do you want?"

"Another threepence."

The creaking lock was turned from within, the creaking door was opened, and an old man stepped out. He stared somewhat curiously at first at the children; then in surprise and anger demanded, "What do you mean by ringing me down, you two? Can't you read what is written here over the bell? 'For those who wish to climb the tower.'"

The lad pointed to Heidi with his forefinger, and said nothing. Heidi said at once, "That is just what I want to do."

"What business have you up there? Did any one send you?"

"No. I want to go up so that I can look down."

"Make haste and get you home, and do not try this joke again, for you will not get off so easily the second time!" The tower-keeper turned away, and was going to shut the door, but Heidi held him by the coat, and begged, "Only just once."

He looked round, and Heidi's eyes gazed up at him so beseechingly that he was moved, and took the child by the hand, saying kindly, "If you've so very much set upon it, come with me."

The boy had seated himself on a stone seat beside the door to show that he did not wish to accompany them.

They climbed many, many steps, Heidi holding the tower-keeper's hand. Soon the stairway became much narrower, and at last it was only the smallest passage, and they were at the top. The tower-keeper raised her in his arms, and held her at the open window. "There, now! Look down," said he.

Heidi looked down over a sea of roofs, towers, and chimneys. She drew back quickly, saying, quite downcast. "It isn't anything like what I thought it would be."

"Now you see how it is. How could such a little girl understand about a view? Come now, and ring no more tower bells."

He set the child again on the floor and led the way back down the narrow stair. Where the passage grew wider, they came to the keeper's room. Near the door the floor extended under the steep roof, and there stood a big basket. A large gray cat sat there growling, for her family lived in the basket, and she warned everybody who passed not to meddle with her household affairs. Heidi, who had never seen so huge a cat, stopped to admire her. Armies of mice lived in the old tower; and Mrs. Puss fetched every day without trouble a good half-dozen for dinner.

Seeing Heidi's interest, the keeper said, "She will not hurt you while I am here. You may look at her kittens."

Heidi drew near the basket, and broke out into exclamations of delight. "Oh, the pretty little creatures! The beautiful kittens!" she cried again and again, and ran round and round to see all the funny movements and gambols that the seven or eight little things were making, as they rolled about in the basket, springing, crawling, and tumbling over each other.

"Would you like to have one of them?" asked the keeper, who was regarding the child with pleasure, as she jumped about for joy.

"For myself? For always?" said she excitedly, and could not believe in such happiness.

"To be sure. You may have more, you may have them all, if you have room for them," said the man, who was glad to get rid of his kittens without being obliged to kill them.

Heidi's delight was at its climax. In that big house the kittens could have so much room, and how surprised and pleased Klara would be when she saw the dear little things!

"But how can I take them home with me?" Heidi now asked, and put out her hand to take one immediately. But the big cat sprang on to her arm, spitting at her so angrily that she drew back afraid.

"I will bring them to you, if you will tell me where."

The keeper said this while he stroked the old cat to quiet her. She was his good friend, and they had inhabited the tower for many years.

"To Mr. Sesemann's big house," answered Heidi. "There is a golden dog's head on the door, holding a thick ring in his mouth."

It was not necessary to give all these directions to the tower master, who had lived all his life in the tower, and knew every house far and near, and was also an old friend of Sebastian.

"I know the house well. But to whom shall I bring the little things? For whom shall I ask? You do not belong to Mr. Sesemann."

"No, but Klara. She will be delighted when the little kits come home."

The child could scarcely tear herself away from the enchanting basket, though the keeper said it was time to go down.

"If I could only take one or two of them with me! One for myself, and one for Klara! Oh, may I?"

"Wait a moment," said the keeper, and drew the

old cat cautiously into his little room. He set her down to a dish of milk, shut the door upon her, and came back, saying, "Now take two."

Her eyes dancing with joy, Heidi chose a white one and a yellow one striped with white, and stuck one into her right-hand and the other into her left-hand pocket. They then went down.

The lad still sat on the steps where they had left him, and when the keeper had closed the door and gone away, Heidi asked, "Which way must we take to go to Mr. Sesemann's house?"

"Don't know."

She described the house, the door, the steps, and the windows, but her companion only shook his head. He knew nothing about all these.

"Now look!" said she, with a new idea. "From one of the windows can be seen a big, big gray house, and the roof goes *so*," and she drew great notches in the air with her finger.

Up jumped the boy at this. These were the signs that he needed. Now he knew the way. Off he started, and the little girl after him, and soon they stood before the door with the big metal dog's head. Heidi pulled the bell. Sebastian quickly appeared, and seeing the child, cried out, "Come at once, as fast as you can!"

In sprang Heidi, the door slammed to. The servant had not even noticed the boy, who stood abashed outside.

"Quick, mam'selle!" urged Sebastian again.

"Run into the dining room. They are already at table, and Miss Rottenmeier looks like a loaded cannon. What possessed the little mam'selle to run away?"

Heidi entered the room. Miss Rottenmeier did not look up. Klara also took no notice. The silence was rather oppressive. Sebastian placed Heidi's chair for her. As the child took her place, the housekeeper began, with a severe expression and a very solemn voice, "Adelheid, I wish to speak to you later. I will only say now that you have misbehaved yourself greatly, and deserve punishment for having left the house without asking permission, or letting anybody know, and for running about until this late hour. It is most unheard-of-conduct."

"*Miew!*" came for reply.

At this the lady's anger rose to a terrible pitch. "How is this, Adelheid?" she cried, speaking louder and louder. "Do you dare, in addition to your misbehavior, to make game of me? Beware what you are about! I warn you!"

"I am not—" began Heidi. *Miew! miew!*

Sebastian now almost flung his dish on the table, and fled from the room.

"It is too much!" This is what Miss Rottenmeier tried to say, but her voice was quite gone from excitement. "Rise, and leave the room," she stammered.

Very much frightened, the child rose, trying

once more to explain.

"I truly am not—" *Miew miew! miew!*

"But, Heidi," interposed Klara, "when you see that it makes Miss Rottenmeier so angry, why do you keep on making that noise?"

"I am not making it. It's the kittens," Heidi at last found chance to answer.

"How? What? Young cats!" screamed the lady. "Sebastian! Tinette! Find the horrid things. Get rid of them." With the words she ran into the study and bolted the door, to make herself more secure, for of all created things young cats were the most terrible to her.

Sebastian stood outside, where he was obliged to have his laugh out before he again entered. He had seen, while he was serving Heidi, a small feline head, and then another, peeping out of her pockets on either side, and foresaw the trouble that was brewing. When the storm fairly broke, he could contain himself not another moment, hardly long enough even to set his dish on the table.

At last he went again into the room, but not until the terrified lady's cries for help had been repeated over and over again. Everything now seemed quiet and tranquil enough. Klara held the kittens in her lap, Heidi knelt on the floor by her side, and the children were playing most happily with the tiny, graceful creatures.

"Sebastian," said Klara to him as he entered,

"you must help us. You must find a nest for the kittens where Miss Rottenmeier will not see them, for she is afraid of them, and will send them away. But we do want to keep the little darlings, and have them here to play with whenever we are alone. Where can you hide them?"

"I will take care of them, Miss Klara," said Sebastian willingly. "I will make a nice little bed for them in a basket, and put it somewhere so that the lady who is afraid of them shall not find it. Leave it all to me."

Sebastian went at once to work, and sniggered to himself as he thought, "There will be some fun out of this"; for he was not sorry to see the housekeeper stirred up now and then.

The particular scolding that Miss Rottenmeier intended to administer to Heidi passed over till the following day, for she felt herself too much exhausted, after all the emotions of anxiety, anger, and fear, that the child had so unintentionally caused her, to do anything that evening. She withdrew early, and the little girls followed in perfect contentment, knowing that the kittens were safe.

Chapter 8

In the Sesemann House Things Do Not Go Smoothly

When Sebastian had opened the door for the professor on the following morning, and had shown that gentleman, as usual, into the study, suddenly the door bell rang again, and with such violence that the servant flew downstairs again as if shot, for he said to himself, "It must be Mr. Sesemann himself, who has returned unexpectedly."

When he opened the door as quickly as possible, a ragged boy with a hand organ on his back confronted him.

"What do you mean? I will teach you to pull the door bell hard enough to tear it out! What do you want here?" cried the angry servant.

"I must see Klara," was the answer.

"You dirty street boy, you! Can't you at least say Miss Klara, as the rest of us do? What business can you have with Miss Klara?" asked the man, still more roughly.

"She owes me sixpence," said the lad.

"There is something wrong with your head, I think. How do you know, in the first place, that there is a Miss Klara?"

"I showed her the way yesterday. Comes to three: and then the way back again, comes to six."

"Now what stuff you are making up! Miss Klara never walks out, can't even do it. Be off now! Go home, where you belong, before I help you!"

But the lad was not intimidated by these threats. Standing his ground, he said stolidly, "I saw her yesterday in the street. I can tell you how she looks. She has short hair that curls, and is black. Her eyes are black, too, and her frock is brown. She does not talk as we do."

"Oh ho!" thought Sebastian, and sniggered to himself. "That is the little mam'selle. She has started something new!"

He told the lad to follow him inside, then to wait at the study door until allowed to enter, and once in, to begin to play his organ immediately, that would please Miss Klara.

Knocking at the study door, Sebastian was told to come in. "There is a lad here who insists that he has something to say to Miss Klara herself," he announced.

Klara was delighted at this unusual occurrence.

"Let him come in at once," she said. "May he

not, Professor?"

The lad had already stepped into the room, and, as directed, had begun to play.

Now this morning Miss Rottenmeier had found all sorts of things to attend to in the dining room, in order to avoid hearing the teaching of the alphabet. Suddenly she stopped, and listened. Did those sounds come from the street? Yet they sounded so near! Could there be a hurdy-gurdy in the study? Yes, yes; in there it certainly was. She flew through the long dining room, and tore open the door. There—incredible! There, in the middle of the study, stood a ragged boy, turning the handle of his instrument with the greatest diligence! The professor seemed standing as if about to speak, but could not get a chance. Klara and Heidi were listening, entranced.

"Stop! Stop at once!" cried Miss Rottenmeier, coming into the room, but her voice was drowned by the music. She ran toward the lad, when suddenly something came between her feet, and she stooped to look on the floor. A grayish, blackish animal was crawling under her feet; it was a tortoise. Miss Rottenmeier made one spring into the air, such as she had not made for many a year. Then she screamed with all her might, "Sebastian! Sebastian!"

The organ grinder stopped suddenly, for this time the voice was louder than the music. Sebastian stood behind the half-open door, all doubled up with laughter, for he had seen the leap Miss Rottenmeier had made. At last he came in. The housekeeper had sunk down into a chair. "Drive them out! Man and beast ! Get rid of them, Sebastian, at once!"

The servant obeyed, drew the lad, who had quickly caught up his tortoise, out of the room, pressed something into his hand, saying, "Sixpence for Miss Klara, and sixpence for the music. You did it very well"; and shut the house door.

In the study it was now quiet again; the lessons were resumed, and this time Miss Rottenmeier remained stationary, to prevent, if possible, any new outbreak. She had determined to investigate the matter after lessons, and to punish the wrongdoer so that it would never be forgotten.

But soon another knock was heard at the door. Sebastian appeared again, with the announcement that a great basket had come, to be delivered to Miss Klara.

"To me?" asked Klara in surprise, and very curious. "Let me see at once how it looks. What can it be?"

Sebastian brought in a covered basket, and withdrew as quickly as possible.

"I think we will first finish our lessons, and unpack the basket afterward," said Miss Rotten-meier.

Klara could not imagine what had been sent to

her. She looked longingly toward the basket.

"Professor," she said, interrupting herself in her declension, "may I not take one look, just to see what there is in it? Then I would go on with my lessons."

"From one point of view there is reason for your request, and from another against it," replied he. "In its favor, lies the fact that as long as your whole attention is concentrated on this object—"

The professor's speech was never finished; for the covering of the basket was quite loose, and behold! out leaped one, two, three, and again two kittens upon kittens, till the whole room seemed full of these creatures, they were everywhere with such inconceivable rapidity. One jumped over the professor's boots, and bit at his trousers. Another crawled over Miss Rottenmeier's feet, and clambered up her dress, while a third sprang upon Klara's chair. They scratched, they clawed, they mewed. It was a perfect turmoil!

Klara cried out, in the greatest delight, "Oh, what darlings! What little beauties! How they jump! See, Heidi! Look at this one! Oh, at that!" Heidi ran after them, here and there, into all the corners. The professor stood much embarrassed by the table, lifting first one foot, then the other, out of the way of the unpleasant little skirmishers.

At first the housekeeper sat speechless from terror, glued to her chair. Soon she recovered voice, and began to scream with all her might,

"Tinette! Tinette! Sebastian! Sebastian!" It would have been impossible for her to rise from her seat, with all these little horrors around her.

At last the servants came in, caught the kittens, one after another, and stuffed them into the basket, and carried them off to the attic, to their companions of the previous evening. During today's study hours, as yesterday's, there had been no desire for yawning.

In the evening, when Miss Rottenmeier had recovered sufficiently from her alarm, she called Sebastian and Tinette into the study, and instituted a thorough investigation into this most objectionable occurrence. It now came to light that Heidi, during her excursion of the day before, had arranged the whole affair. The housekeeper sat perfectly white with dismay, and could find no words to utter after this disclosure. She made signs with her hand for them to leave. After a while she turned to Heidi, who was standing by Klara's chair with but slight idea of what crime she had been guilty.

"Adelheid," she began in a severe tone, "I know of only one punishment that would touch you in the least, for you are a barbarian, but we will see if you do not get tamed down in our cellar with the rats and lizards, until you are cured of your taste for such things."

Heidi listened in quiet surprise at her sentence, for she had never been in a frightful cellar. The room adjoining the mountain cottage that her grandfather called the cellar, where the cheese was kept and where the milk pans stood, was a pleasant and attractive place, and as for rats and lizards, she had never seen any.

Klara, however, raised a loud protest. "No, no, Miss Rottenmeier! We must wait until papa comes. He will soon be here, and then he will decide, after I have told him all about it, what is to be done to Heidi."

Against this there could be no objection, as the master was really coming in a few days. Miss Rottenmeier rose, and said somewhat wrathfully, "Very well, Klara, very well! I shall also have a few words to say to your father," and sailed out of the room.

Several quiet days now passed by, but the housekeeper did not recover her composure. She hourly felt her disappointment about Heidi, and it seemed to her as if, since the child's arrival, everything had been out of joint, and could not be adjusted again.

Late one afternoon, Klara having rested for the usual time, Heidi sat beside her, and told her yet more about her life on the Alm, and as she talked about it, the desire to return became so great that she said at last, "Now I certainly must go back tomorrow!"

She had often said so, and Klara had always been able to quiet her, and to persuade the child that it would be better to wait until her father came, then they would hear what he said about it. Heidi always yielded, and was content, being helped by the secret thought that every day she stayed, the heap of rolls for the blind grandmother would become larger. Morning and evening she added to her collection the beautiful white roll that lay beside her plate. She stuffed them quickly into her pocket, and could not have eaten them herself, because the thought of how the poor old woman could not eat the hard black bread rose always in her memory.

After luncheon, Heidi sat always alone in her room for two long hours, and did not move. She understood now that she was not allowed to go out alone in Frankfort, as if she were on the Alm, and she never tried again to do so. She was also forbidden to go to the dining room to talk to Sebastian; while to have any conversation with Tinette never occurred to the child, who always got out of the way of the lady's maid as quickly as possible, because she spoke to her only in a mocking tone, making fun of her.

So the little girl sat alone and had plenty of time to imagine how the Alm was again green, how the yellow flowers glistened in the sunshine, and how everything shone in the bright light, the snow and the mountain, and the whole valley, until she could scarcely wait another moment, so great was her longing to be back there again. Her aunt had assured her that she could go home whenever she wished, and so it came to pass that the child one day restrained herself no longer. She packed up all her rolls in the great red kerchief, put her old straw hat on her head, and started off.

No farther than the house door, however, Heidi encountered an insuperable obstacle, in the shape of Miss Rottenmeier, just returning from a walk. She stood still in blank amazement, and stared at the child from head to foot, her gaze resting especially on the red kerchief evidently full of something. At length she burst forth:

"What sort of costume is this? What does the whole thing mean? Have I not strictly forbidden you to go running about the streets any more? Now you are doing so again, and looking like a tramp into the bargain!"

"I am not going to stroll about the streets. I am only going home again," answered Heidi, a little frightened.

"How? What? Go home? Do you wish to go home?" Miss Rottenmeier clasped her hands in her agitation. "Do you mean to run away? If Mr. Sesemann were to know of this! Running away from his house! Never let him hear of it! Pray, then, what does not suit you here? Have you not been far better treated than you deserved? Do you miss anything? Have you ever in your life had a dwelling, or food, or service, as you have had here? Speak, I say!"

"No," replied Heidi.

"I am sure of that," continued the housekeeper angrily. "You want for nothing. You are an entirely incomprehensible, thankless creature, and for sheer well-being, you do not know what mischief to be at next."

At last there rose up in Heidi's heart all that had been surging within her, and she broke out, "I must and will go home, for if I do not, Snowball will always be crying, and the grandmother will get no white bread, and Thistlebird will be whipped because goat-Peter will have no more cheese. And here you can't see the sun say good night to the mountains, and if the eagle was to fly over Frankfort, he would scream a good deal louder to see so many people living close together, and making each other wicked, instead of living on the mountain, and being happy."

"Heaven help us! The child has gone crazy!" screamed Miss Rottenmeier, as she rushed up the stairs in terror, running not at all gently against Sebastian, who was just descending.

"Carry that wretched child upstairs at once," she said to him, while she rubbed her head ruefully; for she had hit herself very hard.

"Yes, yes, at once. Many thanks," muttered Sebastian, while he, too, rubbed his pate, for he had suffered most in the encounter.

Heidi stood all the while in the same place, with flashing eyes, and trembling all over with emotion.

"What! Have you been up to more mischief?" asked Sebastian gaily of her. But seeing that Heidi did not move, he looked at her more closely for a moment, then, patting her kindly on the shoulder, said consolingly, "Fie, fie! The little mam'selle must not take it so much to heart. Only be gay, that is the best thing. She has just run against me, and almost made a hole in my head, but we must not be frightened. What! Are you going to stay in that one spot? We must go upstairs. She has ordered it."

Heidi went upstairs, but slowly and heavily, not at all in her usual way. It made Sebastian sorry to see her, and as they went he spoke encouragingly to her, "Now don't give way! Be brave! Don't be sad! She has always been such a good little mam'selle, never crying once since she has been with us. Generally children cry a dozen times a day at her age, I know that. The kittens are all so jolly upstairs in the attic, and act so droll! We'll go up there soon, when she is out of the way, shall we?"

Heidi nodded a little in reply, but was so sorrowful that it went straight to Sebastian's kind heart, and his eyes followed her very sympathetically as she moved away to her own room.

At dinner-time the housekeeper did not say one word, but kept casting wrathful glances at Heidi, as if she expected something extraordinary to break out even while she ate her dinner. But the child sat as still as a mouse, and did not stir, nor eat, nor drink, only stuck her roll quickly in her pocket as usual.

The next day, as the professor came upstairs, Miss Rottenmeier beckoned him into the dining room mysteriously, and proceeded to confide to him her anxiety lest the change of air, and the new way of life and strange surroundings, should have affected the child's brain. She told him about Heidi's attempt to run away, and go home, also repeating to him as much of her conversation as she could. The professor, however, comforted her with the assurance that he had convinced himself, by observation, that although Adelheid was certainly on the one side very eccentric, yet on the other she was perfectly sane, and that little by little, by a carefully considered education, the necessary balance might be established, which was what he had in his mind to effect. He found the situation somewhat difficult only because he could not, thus far, get beyond the A B C.

Miss Rottenmeier felt calmed by this conversation, and released the professor to his duties. Later in the day she thought of the strange costume in which Heidi appeared when arrayed for her journey, and she decided to alter some of Klara's dresses for the child's use, that she might look properly dressed when Mr. Sesemann returned. Klara, whom she consulted about this new plan, readily fell in with it, and gave at once a quantity of dresses, jackets, and hats for Heidi's use.

The housekeeper now repaired to Heidi's bedroom to inspect her wardrobe, and decide what should be kept and what rejected. In a few minutes she returned, with strong signs of disgust on her countenance.

"What have I discovered now, Adelheid? Something that was never before in a clothes-press! A clothes-press is for clothes, Adelheid. But what do I find in the bottom of yours? A heap of white rolls! Bread! Bread, I say, Klara, and such a pile in under the clothes! Tinette!" she cried, "carry away all that old bread out of the press in Adelheid's room; and the old straw hat that lies on the table."

"No, no!" exclaimed Heidi. "I must keep the hat, and the rolls are for the grandmother!" and she tried to run after Tinette, but was stopped by Miss Rottenmeier.

"You must stay where you are," was the severe order; "and the rubbish must be thrown away where it belongs."

Heidi threw herself passionately on the floor by Klara's chair and wept, louder and yet louder, sobbing out in her distress, "Now I have no rolls at all for the grandmother. They were all for her; and now they are thrown away, and the grandmother won't get them!" And she cried as if her heart would break.

Miss Rottenmeier ran out of the room, leaving

Klara very much frightened at the distress of her little friend.

"Heidi! Heidi!" she said entreatingly, "do not cry so. Listen to me! I will give you just as many rolls for the grandmother, and even more, when you go home, and they shall be fresh rolls, soft and nice. Yours would have become quite hard; they were so already. Heidi, listen, and do not cry any more!"

But it was a long time before the torrent of grief could be checked. Heidi understood what Klara said, and believed in her promise, or she would have gone on for much longer. As it was, she had to be reassured many times before she was quite tranquil, and asked every now and then, "You will give as many, just as many as I had, for the grandmother?"

And Klara repeated kindly, "Yes, Heidi! As many, and more, if only you will be happy again."

At table that evening Heidi's eyes were red from crying, and as she caught sight of her usual roll, she began again to sob. But this time she controlled herself with all her might, for she understood the rule that she must be quiet at table. Throughout the meal Sebastian made the most wonderful gestures every time that he came into Heidi's neighborhood. He pointed first to her head, then to his own, and nodded and winked, as if to say, "Don't be downhearted! I have looked out for things, and it is all right."

When the child went to her room, and was about to climb into bed, she found tucked away under the coverlet her old crumpled straw hat. She pulled the beloved thing out, and hugged it for joy, adding thereby another dent, then she wrapped it in a pocket-handkerchief, and stuffed it in the farthest corner of her press.

It was Sebastian who had rescued the hat for his little friend. He had been in the dining room with Tinette at the moment when she was called upon, and had heard Heidi's cry of anguish. When Tinette passed through the room with the pile of rolls, and the hat on the top of all, he had snatched the latter, saying, "I'll take care of this!" and had saved it for Heidi. And that was what his pantomime at supper meant.

Chapter 9

The Master of the House Arrives, and Hears All Sorts of Things Not Heard by Him Before

Several days later the arrival of Mr. Sesemann caused a great commotion in the house. There was much running up and down stairs, and carrying big parcels and boxes here and there, for Mr.

Sesemann always brought with him a quantity of beautiful things upon his return home.

He himself went first of all into his daughter's room, to get his kiss of welcome, and found Heidi sitting beside her, for it was late in the afternoon, when they were always together. Klara greeted her father very tenderly, for she loved him dearly, and her good papa returned her kisses with equal affection. Then he stretched out his hand toward Heidi, who had quietly withdrawn into a corner, saying in a friendly tone, "And this is our little Swiss, is it? Come here, let us shake hands. That is right. Now tell me, are you and Klara good friends together? No quarrelling, no ill temper, no crying and making up, and then beginning all over again?"

"No. Klara is always good to me," said Heidi.

"Heidi never loses her temper, papa," added Klara quickly.

"Now that is good. That pleases me," said Mr. Sesemann as he rose. "But now you must allow me to have something to eat, as I have had nothing today. I will come in later, and you shall see what I have brought you."

Mr. Sesemann went into the dining room, where the housekeeper was superintending the preparations for his noonday meal. He took his seat, and she placed herself opposite, with a countenance of such dismal import, that presently the master of the house said, after waiting for her to begin, "Really, my dear Miss Rottenmeier, I do not know what to think. You have received me with such a doleful face, as if there were a misfortune about to happen! Pray, what is amiss? Klara seems quite cheerful."

"Mr. Sesemann," began the lady with an air of importance, "this affair concerns Klara as well as myself. We have been fearfully deceived."

"How is that?" asked the gentleman, while he sipped his wine very unconcernedly.

"We had, as you know, decided to take a playmate for Klara, some one to live with us. Knowing how particular you are to have only good and noble companionship for your daughter, Mr. Sesemann, I had set my mind on finding a young Swiss, hoping to secure a being such as we read of in literature, sprung from the pure mountain breezes, who would conduct herself as if she had no contact, so to speak, with our earth."

"I have always believed, for my own part, that the children of Switzerland walk on the ground if they wish to go about," said Mr. Sesemann quite seriously. "Otherwise, would they not have been provided with wings instead of feet?"

"Oh, Mr. Sesemann, you know what I wish to say! I was thinking of those inhabitants of the higher regions who are raised above us, and seem to be purer, like the breath of an ideal creation."

"But what could my Klara want of an ideal

breath?''

"No, no! I am not joking. Indeed, this is a much more serious affair than you have any idea of. I have been fearfully, really fearfully, deceived."

"But where is there anything fearful? I see nothing in the child to answer to that description," said Mr. Sesemann calmly.

"You must know one thing, Mr. Sesemann, and one is enough. The child has introduced the strangest men and beasts into your house during your absence, as the professor can attest to you."

"Beasts! How am I to understand this, Miss Rottenmeier?"

"It is not to be understood. The whole conduct of this girl is incomprehensible, except upon the supposition that she has attacks of insanity."

Up to this point, Klara's father had regarded the matter as of slight importance. But attacks of insanity!

Joining his daughter in the study, and seating himself beside her chair, he turned toward Heidi. "Here, little one," he said, "run and fetch me—stop a moment!—run and get"—Mr. Sesemann wished nothing but to get the child out of the way for a while—"oh, get me a glass of water!"

"Fresh water?" asked Heidi.

"Yes, yes; nice and fresh."

Heidi disappeared.

"Now, my dear little Klara," said her papa, bending over his daughter, and taking her hand fondly, "tell me clearly, and in a few words, what kind of animals has your playfellow brought into the house, and what makes Miss Rottenmeier think that the child is sometimes not right in her mind."

Klara knew all about it, for the frightened lady had repeated to her some of Heidi's bewildering speech, a speech which to herself was quite intelligible. So she explained, quite to her father's satisfaction, and told him about the tortoise, and the kittens, and Heidi's outburst on the doorsteps, until Mr. Sesemann laughed heartily.

"Then you do not wish the child to be sent away, Klara? You are not tired of her?"

"Oh, papa, no, indeed! Do not think of sending her away! Since Heidi came, there has been something new happening every day, and it is so pleasant, quite different from what it used to be— *then* nothing every happened. And Heidi tells me so much that I like."

"Very well, my child, very well. And here comes your little friend again. Well, have you brought me nice fresh water?"

"Yes, fresh from the fountain," replied the child.

"Did you fetch it all the way from the fountain yourself, Heidi?" asked Klara.

"Yes, I did. It is quite fresh, but I had to go a long way to get it. There were so many people at the first fountain that I went up the street, and then there were too many by the next one. Then I turned into another street, and there I got the water. And a gentleman with white hair sends his compliments to Mr. Sesemann."

"Well, now, the expedition was a successful one," laughed Mr. Sesemann. "But who was the gentleman?"

"He was passing the fountain, and he stopped and said, 'Since you have a glass, will you give me some water to drink? Pray, for whom are you fetching the water?' And I said, 'For Mr. Sesemann.' Then he laughed very hard, and said he hoped you would enjoy it."

"Well, who was it that wished to be remembered to me? How did he look?"

"He looked pleasant, and he had a thick gold chain, and a gold thing hung from it with a big red stone, and on his stick is a horse's head."

"That is the doctor"—"That is my old doctor," said Mr. Sesemann and his daughter in the same breath. And Mr. Sesemann laughed quietly to himself over his friend's reflections as to his new way of getting his supply of water.

In the evening, as Mr. Sesemann sat in the dining room alone with Miss Rottenmeier, talking over some matters relating to the household, he took occasion to explain that Heidi was to remain in his house as Klara's companion. He found the child in a perfectly normal condition, while his daughter was much pleased with her society, and preferred it to any other.

"I also wish," continued Mr. Sesemann with still more decision of manner, "that this child should from this time forth be most kindly treated, and that none of her peculiarities should be considered as misconduct. If you cannot manage her alone, Miss Rottenmeier, there is a very great help in prospect for you. In a short time my mother will be here to make her usual visit, and my mother can manage anybody if she attempts it, as you know very well, I think."

"Ah, yes! I know that, Mr. Sesemann," replied the housekeeper, but not with an expression as if the prospect of such assistance were very welcome.

Mr. Sesemann's stay this time was to be a very short one. He was obliged to go back to Paris at the end of the fortnight. But he consoled his little girl with the prospect of the speedy arrival of her grandmamma.

Soon after his departure a letter came from Holstein, where the grandmamma lived, saying that she would arrive on the following day.

Klara's joy at this was great. She told Heidi so much and so minutely about her grandmamma, that the child began to speak of her by the same name, which called down upon her the sourest looks from Miss Rottenmeier. This, however, had no effect on Heidi, who felt herself to be under the continual displeasure of that lady. When she went later to her bedroom, she was called first into the housekeeper's, and there told never to use the word grandmamma again, but always to address Mrs. Sesemann as "Gracious lady."

"Do you understand?" asked Miss Rottenmeier, seeing that Heidi looked rather doubtful. She gave her at the same time so determined a look, that Heidi did not dare to ask for an explanation, though she had no idea what the title meant.

Chapter 10
A Grandmamma

Busy preparations went on the day that Mrs. Sesemann was to arrive. It was easy to perceive that the expected guest had a decided control over the household, and that every one felt the greatest respect for her. Tinette had a fine new white headdress for the occasion, and Sebastian got together a multitude of footstools, and put them in every possible place, so that the lady might find one ready wherever she should choose to be seated. The housekeeper went round through the rooms, setting everything in order, as much as to say, that although another person with authority was about to appear, she was not to be extinguished.

At last a carriage rolled up before the house. Tinette and Sebastian ran down the stairs. Slowly, and with dignity, Miss Rottenmeier followed, for she knew that she must receive Mrs. Sesemann.

Heidi had been ordered to withdraw into her own room, to wait until she was sent for, as the grandmamma naturally would hasten to Klara, and wish to be alone with her. Seating herself therefore in her bedroom, she repeated over and over again the strange way in which she was to address Mrs. Sesemann. She did not understand it, for she had always heard the title placed before the name and not after. So she presently conceived that Miss Rottenmeier had but tripped in her speech, and she turned the words about accordingly. She had not long to wait, however; for Tinette soon appeared, and said shortly, as usual, "You are wanted in the study."

As Heidi opened the door, she was greeted by the friendly voice of Mrs. Sesemann, "Ah, there comes the child! Come here to me, and let me take a good look at you." Heidi entered, and in her clear voice said very distinctly, "Good day, Mrs. Gracious."

"That is not bad," said the grandmamma, laughing. "Do they say so where you live? Have you heard that at home on the Alp?"

"No, there is no one of that name where I live," said the child seriously.

"Nor here, that I know of," said Mrs. Sesemann pleasantly, and patted the child on the cheek. "In the nursery I am always grandmamma. You must call me so too. Can you remember that?"

"Yes, yes, indeed! I was going to say so," said Heidi.

"Oh, I understand now!" the grandmamma said, and nodded her head, much amused.

Then she looked steadily at the little girl for some time, nodding again as if in sign of approval, and Heidi looked straight into the kind eyes that were regarding her, and felt quite happy. She could not turn away, indeed. Mrs. Sesemann had such soft white hair, and round her head a beautiful lace was twisted with two wide ribbons that hung down from the cap, and that were always moving a little, as if a light breeze stirred about the grandmamma, to Heidi's infinite delight.

"And what is your name, my child?" was the next question.

"My name is Heidi, but if I must be called Adelheid, I will pay attention," said the little girl, and choked a little, for she felt guilty, as she did not always answer promptly when Miss Rotten-meier called her by that name, which she could not rightly recognize as hers.

With the words the housekeeper had entered the room. "Mrs. Sesemann will undoubtedly agree with me," said she, "that I must choose a name that can be spoken without annoyance, were it only on the servants' account."

"My good Rottenmeier," said Mrs. Sesemann, "if any one is called Heidi, and is accustomed to the name, I use it, and no other."

It was very disagreeable to the housekeeper to be called by her surname, without a preceding title, but there was no help for it. The grandmamma had her own way of doing things, and it was a way not to be opposed. In full possession of her five senses, sharp and healthy ones too, was Mrs. Sesemann, and the moment she saw the child she knew what was amiss with her.

When Klara, on the day after her grandmamma's arrival, disposed herself for her daily rest, the old lady took an armchair near her, and closed her eyes, too, for a few moments. She soon rose again, however, for she was quickly refreshed. She went into the dining room; no one was to be seen. "Oh! all asleep," she said to herself, and went to the housekeeper's room, and knocked loudly. After a little while Miss Rottenmeier appeared, and started back in alarm at this unexpected visit.

"Where does the child stay at this time, and what does she do? That is what I wish to know," said Mrs. Sesemann.

"She sits in her bedroom, where she might employ herself if she knew how, or had the slightest idea of anything useful. But Mrs. Sesemann ought to know what mad projects the child gets up one after another, and often carries out too, things that in polite society can scarcely even be mentioned.

"That is just what I should do if I were obliged to sit alone there as that child does, then you might see how you would speak of my goings-on in polite society. Go now and fetch the child to me in my room, where I have some pretty books that I have brought with me."

"That is the most miserable thing about it! That is just it!" cried Miss Rottenmeier, and clasped her hands together. "What can that child do with books. In all this time she has not learned her alphabet. It is impossible to give her the least idea of reading. The professor can tell you all about that. If that man did not possess the patience of an angel from heaven, he would have given up the lessons long ago."

"Now, that strikes me as strange," said Mrs. Sesemann. "The little girl does not look like one who could not learn her letters. Go and fetch her. She can at least look at the pictures."

Miss Rottenmeier had still more to say, but Mrs. Sesemann was already moving briskly toward her own room. She was greatly surprised at this account of the child's backwardness, and determined to find out what it meant, but not from the professor, whose excellent character she prized highly, and to whom she always extended a friendly greeting when they met, but whose presence she fled for fear of being entangled in conversation with him, for his way of expressing himself was a little tiresome to her.

Heidi came into the grandmamma's room, and opened wide eyes when she saw all the beautiful pictures in the big books on Mrs. Sesemann's table. Suddenly she cried out as a leaf was turned, and looked with eager eyes at the picture before her, then broke forth into tears and heavy sobs. The grandmamma examined the picture. It was a beautiful green field, where all sorts of animals were feeding, and nibbling at the green bushes. In the midst stood the shepherd leaning on his crook, and surveying his happy flocks. Everything was flooded with a shining, golden radiance, for the sun was just sinking behind the horizon.

Taking the child kindly by the hand, the grandmamma said soothingly, "Come, come, my child, do not cry. This has probably reminded you of something. But look, there is a pretty story all about the picture. I will tell it to you this evening. There are all sorts of nice stories in this book, that one can read and tell over. Now let us have a little talk together. There, dry your eyes, and put yourself here right in front of me, so that I can look at you. Yes, that is right, now we are happy."

It was some time, however, before Heidi was tranquil again. Then the grandmamma said, "Now tell me, my child, how do you like your lessons with the professor? Do you learn easily, and have you got on well?"

"Oh no," answered Heidi, sighing, "but I knew beforehand that I could not learn."

"Why can't you learn child? What do you mean?"

"That some people cannot learn to read. It is too hard."

"Indeed! And where did you pick up this wonderful piece of news?"

"Peter told me so, and he knows very well. He has to keep trying, but he never can learn. It is too hard."

"Well, that must be a queer kind of Peter! But really, Heidi, you must not take for granted what such a Peter as that says, but must try for yourself. Perhaps you have not given close attention to what the professor says, and have not looked at the letters."

"It is no use," said the child, in the tone of one thoroughly convinced of the uselessness of trying.

"Heidi," said Mrs. Sesemann gravely, "I am going to tell you something. You have not learned to read because you have believed what your Peter said. Now you must believe me, and I tell you, without doubt, that you can learn to read, and in a short time too, as all children do who are like you, and not like Peter. And now hear what will come next, when you have learned to read. You saw the shepherd in the beautiful green meadow? Now, as soon as you have learned to read, you shall have that book, and then you can understand the whole story just as if some one told it to you, all about what he does with his sheep and goats, and what wonderful things happen to him and them. That you would like to know, I am sure."

The child had listened with sparkling eyes to all that had been said, and now replied, with deep-drawn breath, "Oh, if I only could read!"

"That will soon come. You will not have to wait long, my child, I see you will only have to try. But now we must go to Klara. Come, we will take the pretty books with us."

A great change had taken place in Heidi since the day when Miss Rottenmeier had stopped her on the steps in her flight toward her home. The housekeeper had told her that she was very ungrateful, and that Mr. Sesemann must never know about it. She understood that she could not go home again whenever she wished, as her Aunt Dete had assured her she could, and that Mr. Sesemann would be displeased with her for wishing to go, and she reasoned in her own mind that Klara and her grandmamma would think the same. So she did not dare to tell any one of her longing, for fear of making the grandmamma, who was so kind to her, and whom she loved dearly already, as angry as Miss Rottenmeier had been. The thought of that, the child could not endure.

So the burden within Heidi's heart became heavier and still heavier. She could not eat, and she grew paler every day. At night it was often a long time before she could get to sleep; for as soon as everything was quiet, the Alm and the sunshine upon it, and the flowers, came so vividly before her eyes. And when she at last slept, the red pinnacles of Falkniss, and the fiery snow-field on Cäsaplana, came to her in her dreams, and she awoke full of joy, ready to spring out of bed, and then—oh, it was the big bed in Frankfort, far, far away from home, and she could not get back! Then she would hide her face in her pillow, and cry for a long time, but quietly, so that no one could hear her.

Her unhappy condition did not, however, escape the vigilant eyes of Mrs. Sesemann. She let several days elapse, to see if the depression did not pass, but this not being the case, and the child's eyes betraying often in the early morning that she had been weeping, she took Heidi one day into her room again and said, with great kindness, "Tell me, Heidi, what is your trouble?"

But this good grandmamma must not know what an ungrateful child she had before her, thought Heidi, and feared to lose her love. So she said sadly, "It isn't anything that I can tell."

"No? Cannot you tell Klara?"

"Oh no. Not anybody!" and Heidi looked so miserable all the while that Mrs. Sesemann's heart ached for her.

"Then I will tell you something, my child. When one has a sorrow that cannot be told to anybody on earth, it must be confided to the good God, and He must be asked for help and comfort, for He can make our sorrows lighter, and teach us to bear them. You understand, do you not? You pray every evening to the dear Father in heaven, to thank Him for all that he sends you, and ask Him to protect you from evil?"

"No, I never do that," said Heidi.

"Have you ever learned to pray, Heidi? Don't you know what it is?"

"With my first grandmother I did, but it is so long ago that I have forgotten about it."

"Now I see, Heidi, why you are so very unhappy. It is because you do not know of any one who can help you. Just think how happy it is for those who have heavy hearts to be able to go to the good God at all times, and beg Him for help! And He can help us, and make us happy again."

Through Heidi's eyes flashed a joyful light. "Can we tell him everything? *Everything?*"

"Everything, Heidi, everything."

Drawing her little hand out of the grand-mamma's, the child asked breathlessly, "May I go?"

And the little one ran quickly to her room, seated herself on her footstool, folded her hands, and told all the sorrow of her heart to God, begging and beseeching Him to help her to get away to go home to her grandfather on the Alm.

It may have been something more than a week

from this time that the professor one day asked permission to pay his respects to Mrs. Sesemann, as he had an important communication to impart to her. He was invited to her room, and kindly greeted by Mrs. Sesemann, who extended her hand cordially toward him, saying, "My dear professor, I am glad to see you. Be seated, pray!" and she gave him a chair. "There now, tell me what brings you here. No bad news, I trust? No complaints?"

"On the contrary, gracious lady, something has taken place that I did not expect, and that no one who had been cognizant of what has gone before could have foreseen. For judging from the past, it would have been considered an impossibility, and yet it has taken place, and that, too, in a most remarkable way."

"Has Heidi begun to learn to read, Professor?"

The astonished gentleman stared at Mrs. Sesemann in speechless surprise.

"It is truly wonderful," said he, at length finding his voice, "that this girl, who notwithstanding all my pains has not been able to learn the alphabet, has all at once, and just as I had decided to give up as impossible of achievement the attempt even of bringing the simple letters before her—this girl all at once, overnight, so to speak, has begun to read, and that too with a correctness that is rare in beginners. But it is almost as wonderful to me that the gracious lady should have divined this obscure fact."

"A great many wonderful things take place in this world, Professor," said Mrs. Sesemann, with a smile of satisfaction. "Two things sometimes take place at the same time—a new desire to learn, say, and a new method of teaching. Neither of them is bad, my dear professor, and we will rejoice that the child has begun so well, and hope for continuance in well-doing."

With these words she accompanied the professor to the door, and went straight to the study, to confirm with her own eyes the pleasant news.

It was true. There sat Heidi by Klara's side, reading a story, astonished even at herself, and penetrating with constantly increasing interest the new world that had opened before her, as suddenly the black letters turned into men and things, taking life, and revealing wonderful stories.

And on that very evening, when Heidi took her seat at table, there, on her plate, lay the beautiful book, and when she glanced inquiringly toward Mrs. Sesemann, the latter said kindly, "Yes, yes; it is yours."

"Forever, even when I go home?" asked Heidi, quite red with joy.

"Yes, certainly, forever. Tomorrow we will begin to read it."

"But you will not go home for many years yet, Heidi," said Klara. "When my grandmamma goes away then you will really begin to live with me."

Once more, before going to sleep, Heidi looked at the new book in her own room, and always after, it was her favorite occupation to read and reread the stories that belonged to the beautiful colored pictures. If the grandmamma said in the evening, "Now, Heidi, read something to us," then the child was perfectly happy. It was now quite easy for her to read, and when she read aloud she understood better, and then Mrs. Sesemann could explain so much, and added so much that was new.

The favorite picture was always the green pasture, with the shepherd in the midst of his flock, leaning on his crook, and looking so happy. He took care of the sheep and goats because they were his, and he loved them. But the next picture was where he had run away from his father's house, and was in foreign lands, and was forced to feed swine, and had grown thin over the husks, for he got nothing else to eat. And in this picture the sun did not look golden, and the land was gray and misty. One other picture belonged to the story. There the old father came with outstretched arms from the house, and ran toward the repentant son to receive and welcome him, as, ragged and famished, he drew near his home.

This was Heidi's favorite story, that she would read again and again, aloud and to herself, and she never tired of the explanations that Mrs.

Sesemann gave of it to the children.

So the time drew near, all too quickly, when the dear grandmamma's visit must come to an end.

Chapter 11

Heidi Loses on One Side and Gains on the Other

During Klara's afternoon rest, Mrs. Sesemann always seated herself beside her, and closed her eyes also. Miss Rottenmeier had a way of disappearing at the same time, probably also needing repose. But the grandmamma's nap was very short, and she always called Heidi into her room, and either talked with the child or occupied her with work of various kinds. She had brought a variety of pretty little dolls with her, and showed Heidi how to make dresses and aprons for them. Without realizing it the child had learned to sew, and could make for the little women the prettiest dresses and mantles. For the grandmamma had also provided bits of cloth, of the loveliest colors.

It was now the last week of Mrs. Sesemann's stay in Frankfort, and one day, as Heidi came into the room with her book under her arm, the grandmamma motioned her to put it down and come nearer to her, and said gravely, but kindly, "Now tell me, my child, why you are not gay. Have you still that trouble in your heart?"

"Yes," said the little girl.

"Have you prayed to God to help you?"

"Yes."

"And do you pray to Him every day, that He will make it all right for you, and let you be happy?"

"No, I do not pray any more now."

"What do you say, Heidi? Do I hear right? Why do you not pray any longer?"

"It did not do any good. The kind Father in heaven did not listen. I can understand," continued she, in some excitement, "that if so many people pray every evening in Frankfort, all at the same time, of course the good God cannot listen to them all, and so He must have forgotten me."

"And why are you so sure of that, Heidi?"

"I have asked every day for the same thing many weeks together, and the good God has not given it to me."

"But that will not do at all, my child. That is not the right thing to do. The good God is a dear Father to us all, and always knows what is best for us, though we may not know ourselves. If we pray to Him to give us something that is not good for us, He does not grant it, but sends us something better, that is, if we continue to pray to Him, and do not run off, and lose all confidence in His goodness. You must believe that the thing you prayed for is not good for you now. God heard you. He can hear everybody at the same time, because He is the good heavenly Father, and not a mere mortal like you and me. And as He knows what is best for you, He thinks: Yes, Heidi shall sometime have what she is praying for, but not until it is good for her, not until she can really enjoy it, and be happy over it, for if I do it for her now, and she sees later that it would have been better if I had not granted her prayers, then she will still cry more, and say, 'Oh, I wish that God had not given me what I prayed for! It was not so good as I thought.'

"And now, while your Father in heaven was looking down on you, to see if you really trusted in Him, and prayed to Him in your trouble, all at once you have stopped praying, and have forgotten Him and His goodness. But if the good God hears no longer the voice of any of His children praying, He too forgets them, and lets them go their own way. And if things go wrong with them, and they complain, 'No one will help us!' then, indeed, nobody does pity them, and everybody says, 'Why, then, did you run away from the good God, who is the only one who can help you?'

"Will you be like these, Heidi? Or will you go again to God and pray for forgiveness, and continue to pray every day, and put your trust in Him, that He will do what is good for you, and make you happy again?"

The child had listened intently. Every word that the grandmamma said fell deep into her heart, for Heidi had perfect faith in her kind friend.

"I will go this instant," she said, "and beg the good God for forgiveness, and I will never forget Him again."

The end of Mrs. Sesemann's visit had come, and a sad time it was for the two little girls. The grandmamma made it as merry as possible, until she was fairly off in the carriage. Then such a feeling of loneliness fell on the children that they sat still, feeling lost and forlorn, and did not know what to do with themselves.

After lessons the next day, when the hour came for the children to be together, Heidi brought her book under her arm, and said, "Now I will always read to you. May I, Klara?"

Klara agreed to the proposal, and Heidi set herself with zeal to her task. But the pleasure did not last very long. Heidi began, unfortunately, with a story about a sick and dying grandmother, and she began to cry in distress, for she thought everything she read must be true, and that it was the blind grandmother in Dörfli who was dying, and her distress increased the more she thought of it.

"Now the grandmother is dead," she sobbed, "and I cannot go to see her, and she has never had a single roll of white bread!"

Klara tried to comfort her, and to explain that the story had nothing to do with the grandmother on the Alm, but was about another person altogether. But she did not succeed in calming Heidi's excitement. The thought had entered the child's mind that her aged friend might die while she was far away, and her grandfather even, if she stayed in Frankfort for a long time. And she thought how still and dead everything would be on the Alm, and that she would have to live there alone, and never again see anybody whom she loved.

With all this, moreover, she lost her appetite, grew pale and thin, and Sebastian could hardly bear to see how she allowed the daintiest morsels to go away untasted, for she ate almost nothing. He often whispered encouragingly to her as he passed a dish, "Take a bit, little mam'selle; it is delicious, it really is! A good big spoonful, just one." But such fatherly advice availed nothing. Heidi could not eat; and when she lay down on her pillow at night, she saw before her eyes that which she was longing for all day, and lay there and cried herself to sleep for homesickness.

So the winter went by, and the sun shone so warmly and so dazzlingly upon the white walls opposite, that Heidi knew that the time was come when Peter went up to the mountain pasture with the goats, and where the golden buttercups glistened in the sunshine, and in the evening everything glowed with rosy light. Then she would seat herself in a corner of her lonely bedroom, and hold her two hands over her eyes so that she could not see the sunshine on the wall, and sit there motionless, stifling her speechless homesickness, until Klara sent for her.

Chapter 12

The Sesemann House Is Haunted

About this time Miss Rottenmeier developed a habit of wandering silently, sunk in thought, about the house. And if she went in the twilight from one room to another, or through the corridors, she looked round about her toward the corners, and then quickly behind, as if she thought some one might come quietly along and pull her dress without being seen. But she did not go about alone except in the rooms where the family lived. If she had business that called her upstairs, where the handsomely-furnished guest rooms were, or had anything in the lower part of the house to attend to she always called for Tinette to come with her, in case, she said, there should be anything to carry up or down.

Tinette in her turn, did the same. When she had any business upstairs or down, she called Sebastian to accompany her, in case there were something to be moved that might be too heavy for her strength.

Strangest of all, Sebastian did the same. If he was sent to a distant part of the house, he begged John to come too, and for the same reason, lest he might not be able to produce what was wanted. And each responded to the other's call, although there was really nothing to bring up or down. It was as if each knew that similar help might be needed in his own case. And while all these things were happening above stairs, the old cook stood amidst her pots and pans, saying thoughtfully, with many sighs and shakings of her head, "To think that I should live to see such goings-on!"

Certainly something very strange had taken place in the Sesemann house for some time. Every morning when the servants came downstairs the house door stood wide open, but no one was to be seen, far or near, who could have any connection with the fact. When this happened the first time, every hole and corner was searched throughout the house in fear that something had been stolen, for of course everyone thought that a thief had hidden himself in the house, and carried off his plunder in the night. But nothing had been stolen.

Nothing in the whole house was missing. At night the door was not only double-locked, but fastened with wooden beams. It did no good. In the morning it stood wide open, and no matter how early the servants in their excitement might come downstairs, there stood the door open, though everybody in the neighborhood was asleep, and all the other houses were fastened securely.

At length Sebastian and John took courage, and prepared themselves, in accordance with the urgent request of Miss Rottenmeier, to pass the night below in the room that opened into the big hall, and there to wait and watch for what might take place. The housekeeper got out several weapons of Mr. Sesemann's, and gave them a big flask of spirits, so that they might have means of refreshment as well as defense.

On the appointed night the pair seated themselves and began at once to partake of the refreshment, which soon made them very sleepy; whereupon they both lay back in their armchairs and went fast asleep. When the old tower clock struck twelve, Sebastian roused himself, and called his comrade, who was not so easily awakened. As often as Sebastian spoke to him, so often he turned his head to the other side of his chair, and still slept on.

Sebastian listened intently. He was now very wide awake. All was still; not even in the street was anything stirring. Sebastian did not go to sleep again, it was too uncomfortable there in the silence. He aroused John, but only with a smothered voice, and shook him now and then a little. At last, about one o'clock, John awoke, and remembered why he was in a chair, and not in his bed. Suddenly he felt very brave, and said, "Now, Sebastian, we must out of this, and see what is going on. You needn't be afraid. Come behind me!"

John opened the door of the room, that had been only partly closed, and went out. At the same moment a sharp draught, coming from the open house door, put out the light that he had in his hand. He started back, knocked Sebastian, who stood behind, into the room, shut the door quickly, and turned the key in the lock rapidly as many times as it would go round, then he pulled out his matches and lighted his lamp.

Sebastian did not rightly know what had happened, for he had been sheltered, standing as he did behind the stout John, from the draught. When, however, he saw his comrade by the lamplight, he gave a cry of alarm, for John was as white as chalk, and shook like an aspen leaf.

"What was there outside?" asked Sebastian anxiously.

"Wide open stood the door," whispered John, "and on the steps was a white figure, Sebastian, just going down, and whist! It disappeared."

Sebastian felt creepy down his whole back. Now

the two men seated themselves close together, and did not stir again until it was bright daylight, and the streets began to be filled with movement. Then going out together, they closed the front door, that had stood wide open all this time, and went to tell Miss Rottenmeier what had happened to them.

As soon as she heard what they had seen, she seated herself, and wrote to Mr. Sesemann such a letter as he had never before received, saying that he must come home at once without delay, for unheard-of things were taking place. She recounted then what had occurred; that the house door was found wide open every morning; that nobody in the household felt secure, as it was impossible to foresee what events these mysterious signs might portend.

Mr. Sesemann replied that it was impossible for him to drop everything and come away at such short notice. The ghost story he found very absurd, and hoped that the excitement would soon pass over. If it did not soon quiet itself, he begged Miss Rottenmeier to write to Mrs. Sesemann, who would undoubtedly come at once. He was sure that she would quickly put a stop to all spectral apparitions, and so effectually that they would not dare to show themselves in his house again.

Miss Rottenmeier did not feel pleased at the tone of this letter. The thing was not considered of enough importance. She wrote, as directed, to Mrs. Sesemann, and did not get more comfort from that lady's answer, which contained some very unpleasant remarks. Mrs. Sesemann stated that she had no intention of travelling from Holstein to Frankfort because the Rottenmeier saw ghosts. Formerly there were no such things as ghosts to be seen in the Sesemann house. If any were wandering there now, they must be living creatures, with whom the Rottenmeier might easily settle. If she were not equal to that, then she could call the watchman to her aid.

The housekeeper was not inclined to pass her days in terror, and knew very well how to help herself in an emergency. Up to this time she had refrained from telling the children about the apparition, for fear that they would not be willing to remain alone day or night, which would inconvenience herself exceedingly. Now she marched straight to the study where they were sitting together, and told them, in a mysterious whisper, of the nightly appearance of an unknown being.

Klara declared at once that she would not be left alone for a moment. Her papa must be sent for, and Miss Rottenmeier must come to sleep in her room, nor must Heidi be left alone, for fear the ghost should come to hurt her. They would all sleep in one room, and the light must be left burning all night, and Tinette must also sleep near by, and Sebastian and John must come down and pass the night in the corridor, to call out and frighten the ghost if they saw it coming.

Klara was very much excited, and the house-keeper had much trouble in making her listen to reason. She promised to write to Mr. Sesemann, as well as to bring her bed to Klara's room, and not to leave her alone at night. She decided, however, that they should not all sleep in Klara's room. If Adelheid were afraid too, Tinette could go to sleep with her. But Heidi was far more afraid of Tinette than of ghosts, of which, indeed, she had never before heard. She said at once that she was not afraid, and would much rather sleep alone in her room.

Miss Rottenmeier hastened to her writing desk and sent off a letter to Mr. Sesemann, to the effect that the unnatural condition of affairs in his house, recurring as it did every night, was likely to have a bad influence on the health of his delicate daughter. The worst consequences might follow, instances being known of epileptic attacks or Saint Vitus's dance being brought on by such excitement as his Klara was now under, owing to these nightly alarms.

This letter was successful. Two days later, Mr. Sesemann stood before his house door and pulled the bell with such violence that the servants all stood looking at each other, with the fear that now the ghost had become bolder, and begun to play its tricks in broad day. Sebastian peeped out through a half-open shutter cautiously, but such a determined clang now resounded through the hall, that the servant suspected a man's hand to be the cause, and a hand that he recognized too. So he hurried downstairs headlong.

Mr. Sesemann greeted Sebastian but shortly, and went straight to his daughter's room. The joyful welcome that he received from her, and her face of gladness, soon smoothed the wrinkles that had gathered on his forehead, and they vanished entirely when she assured him that she felt perfectly well, and that it did not matter, now she had him fast, if a ghost did walk at night, for without the ghost she should not have had her father.

"And pray, how is the specter getting on, Miss Rottenmeier?" asked Mr. Sesemann, the corners of his mouth twitching a little.

"I assure you, sir," was the earnest reply, "it is not a joking matter. Tomorrow morning Mr. Sesemann will not think of laughing, for what nightly takes place in this house now, points clearly to something terrible that has taken place here at some former time, and been concealed."

"There I am ignorant," replied the gentleman; "but I must beg of you not to make my entirely respected ancestors appear in the characters of persons under suspicion. Now call Sebastian into the dining room, that I may speak with him."

In the dining room the master of the house acted on the observation that he had made concerning the little love that existed between Sebastian and the housekeeper.

"Come here, my man," he said, and beckoned his servant to approach. "Tell me honestly, has there not been some trickery here to put Miss Rottenmeier about a little?"

"No, upon my truth, the gracious master must not think that. I do not feel at all comfortable about the thing myself," replied the man with unmistakable veracity.

"Very well, if that is the case, I will soon show such brave fellows as Sebastian and John how ghosts look by daylight. Shame upon you, Sebastian, a strong young fellow like you, to run away from a ghost! Now take my compliments to my old friend Dr. Classen, and ask that he come to me without fail at nine o'clock this evening. I have travelled from Paris expressly to consult him. He must watch tonight with me, so very bad is the case, and must make his preparations accordingly. Am I understood?"

"Perfectly, perfectly. The gracious master may be sure that I shall repeat the message correctly."

Punctually at nine o'clock, just as the children and Miss Rottenmeier withdrew for the night, appeared the good doctor, who under his gray hair had a fresh complexion, and a pair of bright, kindly eyes. His anxious looks soon gave place to merriment after the first greeting, and tapping his friend gaily on the shoulder, he said, "Well, well!

You do not look as if you were in need of a watcher, old friend.''

''Only be patient awhile, old fellow. The person for whom we are to watch will look ill enough when we have captured him.''

''What is this? A sick person in the house, and one who is to be caught?''

''Far worse, far worse. A ghost in the house! We are haunted!''

Dr. Classen laughed outright.

''That is a pleasant way of taking my news! It's a pity my friend Rottenmeier can't enjoy it with you. She is convinced that some old Sesemann is wandering about here, to expiate some horrible crime.''

''Where has she made his acquaintance, pray?'' asked the doctor, still much amused.

Mr. Sesemann now told his friend the whole story, and added that he had made preparations for whatever might be discovered. He had two loaded pistols, for the affair was either one of a very objectionable kind of joke that some of the servants' acquaintances had played upon them during his absence, and in this case a shot or two in the air would do no harm, or there was really a thief, who wished to establish the idea of a specter in order to pursue his depredations undisturbed, in which case also a good weapon would be useful.

While talking this over, the gentlemen descended the stairs, and entered the room where

John and Sebastian has passed their eventful night. On the table stood some bottles of good wine. Refreshment would not come amiss, if the night were to be spent in watching. The revolvers lay beside the bottles, and a couple of branched candlesticks, shedding a clear light around, stood there too. Mr. Sesemann had no idea of waiting for the ghost in partial darkness.

Now the door was pushed to, to prevent too much light from penetrating into the corridor, which might make the ghost feel shy. The two gentlemen seated themselves comfortably in their armchairs, and entertained themselves with all sorts of stories, taking now and then a sip of wine, until twelve o'clock sounded. They had not thought it to be so late.

"The ghost has got wind of us, and will not show itself tonight," said the doctor.

"It does not walk till one," said his friend.

The talk began afresh. One o'clock sounded. It was perfectly still, not a sound to be heard. Suddenly the doctor raised his finger.

"Do you hear nothing, Sesemann?"

They listened intently. Softly, but distinctly, they heard the bar from the house door removed, and the key turned twice in the lock. Then the door was opened.

"You are not afraid?" asked the doctor, and rose.

"It is well to be cautious." whispered Mr. Sesemann, and took a candlestick in one hand and a revolver in the other. The doctor had preceded him, similarly equipped. They stepped into the corridor. A white figure, lighted up by the moonlight, stood motionless on the threshold of the wide-open outer door.

"Who goes there?" thundered the doctor, and with weapons and lighted candles both gentlemen approached the figure. It turned about, and uttered a low cry. There stood revealed little Heidi, with naked feet, in her white nightgown, staring with dazzled eyes at the bright lights and flashing revolvers, and quivering like a leaf in the wind from head to feet.

"I really believe it is your little water carrier," said the doctor.

"Child, what does this mean? What are you doing? Why have you come down here?" asked the master of the house.

White as snow from fear, Heidi answered almost inaudibly, "I do not know."

Now the doctor stepped forward. "Sesemann," said he, "the case belongs to my province. Go seat yourself in your armchair. I will first of all carry this child back where she belongs." So saying, he laid his revolver aside, took the trembling child by the hand, and with a fatherly tenderness led her upstairs.

"Do not be afraid. There is nothing to fear," he said kindly, as they ascended. "Now be quiet, there is nothing to be troubled about."

Having reached Heidi's room, and set down his light, he took the child in his arms, put her in her bed, and covered her up carefully, then, seating himself on a chair by the bedside, he waited patiently until her tremors had subsided. At last, taking Heidi's hand in his, he said soothingly, "Now that everything is right again, just tell me where you were going."

"I was not going anywhere. I did not go down there myself—I was all at once there."

"Well, well! Did you dream anything in the night? Do you remember seeing or hearing anything?"

"Yes, every night I dream the same thing. I think I am with my grandfather, and I hear the wind in the pines, and the stars are shining in the sky. And I jump up quick, and open the door of the hut, and oh, it is so beautiful! But when I awake, I am always in Frankfort." And Heidi began to sob, and fight with the trouble that swelled her little throat almost to bursting.

"H'm. And have you no pain, nowhere? None in your back or head?"

"No, only it hurts me here like a big stone all the time."

"As if you had eaten something, and wished to throw it off?"

"No, not that; as if I *must* cry."

"And then do you cry very hard?"

"Oh no, I try not to cry, for Miss Rottenmeier

has forbidden it."

"So you swallow it down till the next time? That is the way? Yes, I understand. And you like it here in Frankfort, do you?"

"Oh yes!" But the reply sounded as if it meant "Oh no!"

"H'm. And where did you live with your grandfather?"

"Always on the Alm."

"That couldn't have been so very agreeable? Tiresome, was it not?"

"Oh no! It was beautiful! So beautiful!"

Heidi could contain herself no longer. The flood of longing, the agitation of the last half-hour, the long-restrained tears, overpowered her strength, and she burst forth into violent weeping.

The doctor stood up, smoothed the child's pillow, and said kindly, "Yes, cry a little now, it will do you good. Then go to sleep, go to sleep quietly, and tomorrow everything shall be right." Then he left the room again.

Once again downstairs, the doctor seated himself in the armchair opposite to his anxious host.

"In the first place, Sesemann," he said, "I must tell you that your little protégé is moonstruck. In total unconsciousness she has played the ghost, and opened your house door every night, and frightened your servants. In the second place, she is suffering from homesickness so that she is reduced almost to a skeleton, and soon will be one, if this goes on. An immediate remedy is necessary. For the first trouble, and the extremely excited state of her nerves, there is only one cure, and that is to send the child back to her native mountains, for the second, naturally, the same thing is needed, her home. My prescription is that she must leave Frankfort tomorrow."

Mr. Sesemann sprang from his chair, and began walking rapidly up and down the room. At last he broke out. "Moonstruck! Sick! Homesick! Reduced to a skeleton in my house, Classen! All this within my doors, and nobody has attended to her, nobody knew anything about it! And you, doctor, you wish that this child, who came to us fresh and strong, should be sent back to her grandfather ailing and famished? No, you cannot ask that. I will not do it—I cannot! Take the little one in hand, cure her; do what you think best, only cure her. Then I will send her back whenever she wishes. You must help us."

"Sesemann," replied Dr. Classen impressively, "bethink yourself! This condition is not an illness to be cured by pills and powders. The child is not of a naturally strong constitution, but if she is allowed to return to the strengthening mountain air which she is accustomed to, and which she needs, she will be perfectly strong again. Sesemann, you would not have her return to her grandfather incurably ill, or return no more?"

From sheer alarm Mr. Sesemann stood still, and stared at the solemn doctor.

"Of course, if you talk so, Classen, there is no choice. It must be as you say."

He took his friend's arm, and they walked back and forth, talking the case thoroughly over, and making plans, until it was morning. When the master of the house opened the door to let his friend out, the bright sunlight streamed in.

Chapter 13

A Summer Evening on the Alm

After his friend's departure, Mr. Sesemann ascended rapidly to the housekeeper's room, at which he knocked loudly. Miss Rottenmeier uttered a cry of alarm. Outside she heard the master's voice, saying imperiously, "Be kind enough to make haste, and come to the dining room without delay. Preparations for a journey must be made at once."

It was only half-past four in the morning. Miss Rottenmeier had never been out of bed in her life so early. What could have happened? Moved by curiosity, and much agitated, she took up the wrong thing continually in dressing, and therefore got on very slowly, or when she had put an article of dress on her person, she began to search in the room to find it.

In the meantime Mr. Sesemann went through the hall, and pulled every bell with all his might, to call each separate servant. In each room a frightened man or maid sprang out of bed, hurrying to dress pell-mell. All believed that the specter had laid violent hands on the watchers, and that it was a call for help. Down they came one after the other, each looking worse than the last, and stood in surprise before their master, who looked fresh and lively, and not as if suffering from a fright. John received an order to get horses and carriage in readiness to go out. Heidi was to be awakened and dressed by Tinette, and prepared for an immediate journey. Sebastian was dispatched to the house where Dete lived, to bring her without delay to Mr. Sesemann.

At last Miss Rottenmeier appeared. Her clothes were all in good order at last, except her headdress, which was put on the wrong side before, presenting from a distance the strange and alarming suggestion that the housekeeper's head was turned. Mr. Sesemann, rightly ascribing this puzzling aspect to her early rising, went on with his business unconcernedly, requesting her to prepare a trunk for the little Swiss (so he always spoke of Heidi, whose unusual name continually escaped his memory), and to place in it a good portion of Klara's clothing, so that the child should carry away with her whatever was fitting. This was to be accomplished at once, and not a moment wasted.

Beyond this, no word of explanation was vouchsafed, much to Miss Rottenmeier's disappointment; and leaving her to follow his directions, Mr. Sesemann went to his daughter's bedroom. As he expected, he found Klara wide awake, listening anxiously to the sounds that reached her from every side, and trying vainly to divine what was going on in the house at this unusual hour. Seating himself on her bed, her father gave her a detailed account of what had happened in connection with the ghost story, and how little Heidi had in Dr. Classen's opinion undergone a serious strain, and would probably continue her nightly wanderings until she sometime mounted to the roof, which would be very dangerous. It was necessary to send the little girl to her native air, for he could not take upon himself the consequences if he kept the child in Frankfort. He appealed to Klara's good feeling and good sense to see that it must be.

At first, naturally, Klara could not believe in the necessity that would deprive her of her dear little companion, and tried, as her father had done at first, to find all sorts of remedies rather than a parting. But her father was inflexible. He promised, if Klara were able, to travel with her to

Switzerland the following summer, if she would only be quiet now. So Klara resigned herself to the inevitable, only begging as recompense that Heidi's trunk should be brought to her room, and there packed, in order that she could place in it anything she pleased, or that she thought would please her little friend. This plan her father heartily agreed to, encouraging her to provide for the little Swiss a handsome outfit.

While all this was going rapidly forward, Aunt Dete came with Sebastian, who left her in great suspense in the ante-chamber, since her being summoned at this unusual hour must indicate that something remarkable was about to happen. Going to her, Mr. Sesemann explained why it was necessary to send the child, her niece, immediately back to her grandfather, and requested Dete to accompany her at once.

Much disappointed Dete felt and looked at this unexpected turn of affairs. She remembered too well the parting shot of the Alm uncle, warning her against ever showing herself before him again, and she hardly deemed it prudent to return with Heidi now, having once brought her, and then removed her, each time without his permission. Her mind was promptly made up and expressed. Today it was utterly impossible for her to make the journey. Neither was it to be thought of for the morrow. The day after would be the least convenient of all, owing to work that must be done, and farther on she could do no better.

Mr. Sesemann understood her drift by this time, and dismissed her without comment. He sent for Sebastian and bade him prepare for a journey. He was to conduct Heidi to Basle today, and continue with her to her home the day after, then return to Frankfort without delay. Mr. Sesemann would give him a letter to Heidi's grandfather, to explain everything.

"One other thing Sebastian is not to forget," pursued Mr. Sesemann. "I am well known at the hotel at Basle. I have written directions on my card, and when this is given to the landlord a good room will be provided for the little Swiss. Sebastian can look out for his own comfort. All the windows in the little girl's room must be carefully closed and securely fastened, so that they cannot be opened with the greatest strength. The door must also be locked and fastened from the outside, when the child is quiet, for she wanders about in her sleep, and might chance to be in danger in a strange house if she got out of her room, and tried to open the house door. Does Sebastian understand what is said?"

"Ah! ah! ah! Was that it? Was that how it was?" cried Sebastian, on whose brain a great light broke suddenly concerning the ghost.

"Yes, that was it! That was how it was. And there is a coward, too, who can tell John that he also is a coward, and as much for the whole

ridiculous household." And in anger Mr.
Sesemann strode off to his own room to write to
the Alm uncle.

Crestfallen stood the doughty Sebastian in the
middle of the room, and repeated to himself
several times, "If I only hadn't let that cowardly
John push me back into the room, and lock the
door, I should certainly have gone after the white
figure. I would do it this very minute!" As, in fact,
he well might, for every corner of the room was
flooded with light.

Meanwhile Heidi stood arrayed in her Sunday
frock in the middle of her chamber, with no idea of
what had happened, or was to happen. Tinette
had shaken her awake, taken her clothes from the
press, and helped her to dress, without speaking to
her, as usual. The lady's maid declared she found
the little Swiss child's ignorance too debasing
when she tried to converse with her.

"Where is the child?" called out Mr. Sesemann,
coming into the dining room with his finished
letter in his hand.

Heidi appeared. She came toward Mr. Sesemann
to say good morning. "And now, what have you to
say about it, little one?" said he, examining her
face attentively.

In amazed silence Heidi looked up at him.

"So you really know nothing about it?"
continued he, smiling. "Today you are going
home, going at once."

"Home!" murmured the child, and turned perfectly white. She could scarcely breathe for a while, her heart seemed to stand still in her breast.

"And do not you wish to know something more about it?"

"Oh yes, indeed, I wish to very much!" she said, and grew crimson.

"That is better," said Mr. Sesemann, and made a sign for her to seat herself at the table, while he did the same. "Now eat a hearty breakfast, then into the carriage and away," he said encouragingly.

In vain Heidi tried to eat, though she would have liked to show her obedience. Such a commotion was taking place within her that she did not know if she were awake or asleep. She half dreaded to find herself in her nightdress on the house doorsteps.

"Let Sebastian take a good luncheon with him," said Mr. Sesemann to the housekeeper, who entered at this moment. "The child cannot eat, which is not surprising. Go into Klara's room, and sit with her until the carriage comes," he added in friendly wise, turning to Heidi.

That was just what Heidi was longing to do, so away she ran. A big trunk stood in the middle of Klara's room, the lid still open.

"Come, Heidi, come! See what I have packed for you. Is it not nice?" said Klara, showing her a great quantity of things, dresses and aprons, handkerchiefs and sewing implements, and—greatest treasure of all for the little Swiss, the sight of which made her leap for joy—a basket of twelve beautiful white round rolls for the grandmother in Dörfli. In their delight over these gifts the children forgot the coming separation, until a call from the other room startled them. "The carriage is ready," shouted Mr. Sesemann, and there was no time to grieve over the parting. Heidi rushed into her room for the beautiful book given her by the grandmamma, from which she never parted day or night. She knew that was not packed, for she kept it at night under her pillow. She opened the press wide; another precious thing must go home with her. There it was, and the old red shawl, which Miss Rottenmeier had esteemed too shabby to be put into the trunk. Heidi wrapped it round her other treasure, and put it on the top of the basket of rolls, so that the red parcel was very conspicuous. Then, placing her pretty hat on her head, she left the room.

The good-bye was quickly said. Mr. Sesemann was waiting to put Heidi into the carriage, and Miss Rottenmeier stood at the head of the stairs to take leave of her. But when she caught sight of the extraordinary red shawl, she took the bundle quickly from the top of the basket, and threw it on the floor.

"No, Adelheid," she said reproachfully, "you must not travel away from this house in this style, you have no occasion to carry back this stuff, at any rate. Now farewell."

After these severe words Heidi did not dare to take up her little bundle again, but she looked up at the master of the house with beseeching eyes, as if to tell him that she was losing her most valued possessions.

"No, none of this, Miss Rottenmeier. The child shall take home with her whatever she wishes, should it even be kittens or a tortoise. There is no need to become excited over it."

Mr. Sesemann spoke in so decided a tone that there was no more doubt either in Heidi's or Miss Rottenmeier's mind as to what was to be done. The child lifted up her treasure from the floor, and joy and thanks shone in her eyes.

Below, at the carriage door, Mr. Sesemann took leave of his little Swiss, shaking her kindly by the hand, wishing her a good journey, and bidding her not to forget her friends in Frankfort. Heidi thanked him right bravely for all the kindness she had received at his hands, and added earnestly, "And to the good doctor, I send a thousand thanks, and my best wishes."

For the conversation of the previous night remained in her memory, and how the doctor had said, "Tomorrow everything shall be right." And now it was true, and Heidi ascribed it to the right cause.

Already the child was lifted into the carriage, and after her came the basket, the lunch bag, and

Sebastian. "A happy journey!" cried Mr. Sesemann, and they were gone.

All the time they were on the railway Heidi held her basket tightly in her lap. She would not risk its being on the seat, for the precious rolls for the grandmother were there, which she must guard carefully. She raised the lid every now and then, to assure herself.

In perfect quiet the child passed the long day. She only now began to understand that she was on her way to the Alm, to her grandfather, to goat-Peter, and her thoughts became busy with what was in store for her, how they all would look. Suddenly remembering her old fear, she said anxiously, "Sebastian, is it certain that the grandmother on the Alm is not dead?"

"We'll hope so," said he soothingly, "Yes, yes, she must be still alive."

Then Heidi fell back again into her old train of thought, and pictured how she would spread out her twelve rolls on the table before the blind woman, and again she peeped at them. After a long time she said again, "Sebastian, if one could only be quite sure that the grandmother is alive!"

"Yes, yes," murmured Sebastian, only half awake, "why shouldn't she be?"

Soon sleep overpowered the tired child, for she had passed an unquiet night, been awakened early, and was fairly exhausted. She was roused at last by Sebastian's grip upon her arm. "Wake up!

Wake up! We must go out. We are at Basle."

Their journey was continued hour after hour the following day, Heidi always holding the basket, from which she had never parted. Today she did not speak at all, and every hour her anxiety increased. At last, when she least expected it, the guard cried out, "Mayenfeld!"

Sebastian, as well as herself, sprang up hastily, being both taken by surprise. They were on the platform, the basket safe, and the train puffing away in the distance. Sebastian followed it sadly with his eyes. How much better, he thought, to travel by that, than to undertake a foot journey which must end in a climb up a mountain, and that, too, in a country where the inhabitants were half wild, and where dangers surrounded him on every side! Such was the Frankforter's idea of Switzerland.

Having looked about him cautiously, he determined to find out the safest way to Dörfli. Not far from the station stood a little cart, with a horse harnessed to it. A broad-shouldered man was lifting into the cart a couple of sacks of flour, which had been brought by the railway. Sebastian questioned him concerning the safest road to Dörfli.

"All the roads are safe here," replied the man shortly.

Sebastian, however, continued his inquiries as to the best way, where there was least danger of falling over the precipices, also how a trunk could be conveyed thither. The man looked at the trunk, measured it awhile with his eye, and said that if the thing was not too heavy he would take it himself to Dörfli, as he was going there. So they fell into conversation, coming at last to the understanding that the child and her trunk should be put into the cart, and taken to Dörfli, and then Heidi could find some escort up the Alm.

"I can go alone," said Heidi. "I know my way up the Alm from Dörfli."

A great weight fell from Sebastian's heart, as he found himself relieved from the necessity of climbing up the mountain. He beckoned Heidi mysteriously aside and gave her a small but heavy parcel, and a letter for her grandfather, explaining that the parcel contained a present from Mr. Sesemann, and that it must be very carefully looked after, as his master would be very angry if it were lost. He advised that it should be put into the basket under the rolls, as there it would be safest.

"I will not lose it," said Heidi confidently, and buried the letter and the parcel far down amongst the bread. So Heidi, her trunk and her basket were put into the cart, Sebastian making many signs and mysterious movements to indicate that great care must be taken. As the driver stood near, he did not like to speak again of the last addition to the basket, but he made all the ado possible to quiet his conscience for not accompanying the child himself, as he was bidden. At last the driver climbed up to his high seat beside the little girl, and they rolled off toward Dörfli, while the servant went rejoicing on his way back, to await the train to go home to Frankfort.

It was the baker from Dörfli into whose cart Heidi had climbed. They were strangers to each other, but he knew her story, and how she had been brought up and left by her aunt with the Alm uncle. He had known her parents, and felt sure at once that the much-talked-about Heidi was now in his care. Why she was coming back again he could not understand, and as they jogged along he began to question her.

"You must be the child who lived with the Alm uncle, with her grandfather?"

"Yes."

"Have you had a hard time of it, that you are coming back again?"

"No, that is not so, nobody can be so well off as they are in Frankfort."

"Why, then, are you coming home?"

"Only because Mr. Sesemann has let me."

"Pah! Why didn't you stay there even if he did give you leave to come home?"

"Because I had a thousand times rather be with my grandfather on the Alm than anywhere else in the whole world."

"You'll think different when you are once up there again," muttered the baker. "I should like to know if she has heard how it is up there now.''

After this he began to whistle, and said no more. Heidi looked about her, trembling from excitement, for she recognized the trees on the roadside, and above she could see the great jagged peaks of Falkniss, which looked down on her, and greeted her like an old friend. Heidi returned the greeting, while with every step her excitement increased, it seemed as if she must spring from the cart, and run without stopping to the very top. She controlled herself, however, and did not move, though she trembled in every limb. As it struck five, they drove into Dörfli.

Suddenly they were surrounded by a crowd of women and children, and several men came toward them, for the trunk and the child attracted the attention of the inhabitants, and every one wanted to know whence she came, where she was going, and to whom she belonged. When the baker had taken Heidi down, she said quickly, ''My grandfather will soon come for the trunk. I thank you for the ride,'' and wanted to run on. But she was held fast on every side, and a vast number of questions asked by every one at once. She tried to press through the crowd, and her expression was so anxious that they made way for her involuntarily, and let her run on, while one said to the other, ''You see how frightened she is, and she has cause enough too.''

Then they all began to tell each other how for a

year past the Alm uncle had grown more and more morose, and would not now speak a word to any one, but looked as if he would like to kill all who crossed his path. If this child had any other place in the world to go to, she would certainly not venture into that old dragon's nest.

The baker, however, joined in the conversation, saying that he ought to know more than any one else about it. Then with great importance he related how a gentleman had brought the child to Mayenfeld, and had taken leave of her very affectionately, had also given him the price of the ride and something over without even bargaining. Above all, he could truly say that Heidi was happy in Frankfort, and had come back of her own accord to live with her grandfather. This news was received with a great deal of surprise, and spread through the village like wildfire. In every house they were all talking over the news that Heidi, leaving all sorts of comforts behind her, had returned of her own accord to her grandfather.

Heidi had all this time been scampering up the mountain as fast as she possibly could, but she was obliged to stand still now and then, for she was continually out of breath. The basket on her arm was rather heavy too, and it grew steeper and steeper as she went on.

One thought filled her mind: "Will the grandmother be sitting in the corner by her spinning-wheel? May she not have died in all this time?"

When at last she perceived the cottage in the hollow on the Alm side, her heart began to beat almost painfully, but she still ran on. Now she was there, yet could not open the door for trembling. At last she accomplished it. Into the little room she sprang, and stood there utterly breathless, and unable to speak a word.

"Oh," said a voice from the corner, "that is the way the child Heidi used to come running in to me! If I could once more in my life have her with me! Who was it that came in?"

"It is I, Grandmother! It is Heidi!" cried the child, and ran towards the corner. Falling on her knees, she seized the grandmother's hand, and laid her head upon the grandmother's lap, not being able to speak a word in her great happiness.

At first the grandmother was also silent from surprise, but soon began passing her hand caressingly over the little one's curly hair, repeating over and over, "Yes, it is the dear child's hair, and her voice. Oh, the dear God has let me live for this!" and happy tears streamed from her eyes. "Can you really be Heidi? Is it indeed you?"

"Yes, I am really here, Grandmother," said Heidi assuringly. "You must not cry any more. Here I am, and will come every day to you, and never, never, go away again. And here, Grandmother, now you will not have to eat hard bread for many a day. Here, Grandmother!" And the rolls were taken from the basket and placed one after another on the old woman's lap, till it was heaping full.

"Oh, child, child! what a blessing you bring with you!" cried out the grandmother, and there seemed to be no end to the bread which the child kept piling up. "But the greatest blessing of all is yourself." And again she passed her hand through the clustering curls, and stroked the hot little cheek, saying, "Speak, Heidi, only one word, that I may hear my child's voice." So the little girl told of her fears lest when she returned she should not find the grandmother alive, and that the white bread might not do her any good.

Peter's mother entered at this moment, and stood quite still for an instant from astonishment. Then she cried out, "It is surely Heidi! Can I believe my eyes?"

Heidi rose, and shook hands with Brigitte, who could not admire her appearance enough, and walked round and round the child, saying, "Oh, Mother, if you could only see the beautiful dress she has on! One can scarcely recognize her! Does the hat with the feather belong to you, Heidi— that one on the table? Put it on. I want to see how you look in it."

"No, I do not want it," said the child. "You can take it. I shall not wear it again. I have my old one."

So saying, she opened the red bundle and took

out her hat, which had acquired many more dents during the journey, in addition to the old ones. Little cared Heidi for that. She had never forgotten how her grandfather had declared, when she left the Alm, that in a hat with feathers he would never look upon her, and therefore she had always wished to keep the old hat, hoping always to wear it when she returned home.

Brigitte, however, reproved her for being so simple. It was a beautiful hat, she said; she could not take it, for it might be sold to the daughter of the teacher in Dörfli for a large sum of money if Heidi would really never wear it. Heidi held to her determination, and put the hat in the corner behind the grandmother, where it was quite hidden. Then taking off her pretty frock, and binding the old red shawl over her petticoat with its short sleeves, she was equipped for the Alm, and taking the grandmother's hand, she said, "Now I must go to my grandfather, but I will come again tomorrow to see you. Good night."

"You will surely come again, little one—come again tomorrow?" said the old woman, and held the little hand tightly in hers, and could hardly let the child go from her.

"Why have you taken off your pretty frock?" asked Brigitte.

"I must go up without it to my grandfather, for fear he should not know me. You said that you hardly knew me in that dress."

"Oh, you might have kept on your pretty dress. He would have known you. But pray be careful, for Peterkin says that the Alm uncle is cross all the time now, and never speaks a pleasant word."

Brigitte had gone out to the door step to give Heidi this parting warning. A good night was all the answer Heidi gave, as she began to mount the Alm with her bundle on her arm. The evening sun lighted up the green slopes, and up above the great snow-field on Cäsaplana was visible, and shone from afar.

Every few steps Heidi had to stop, stand still and turn about, for as she climbed, the highest peak lay behind her. The red light fell on the grass, reaching even to her feet. She stopped and rested, to enjoy it fully. It was even more beautiful than she had remembered or dreamed of it. The pinnacles on Falkniss flamed up to heaven, the white snow-field glowed, and rosy-red clouds moved across the sky. Even the grass looked aflame as the glowing reflection streamed from every peak, and below the whole valley was bathed in vaporous gold. Heidi stood in the midst of all this beauty, while in her happiness and rapture great tears rolled down her cheeks, and folding her little hands she looked up to heaven to give thanks to the good God who had brought her home again to find everything so beautiful, far more beautiful than ever before. It was all hers, Heidi felt, and was so happy in these exquisite possessions that she could not find words proper to express her deep thankfulness to the good heavenly Father.

Only when the light about her began to fade could Heidi tear herself away from the spot. Then she began to run at such a pace up the mountain that before long she espied the tops of the pine trees over the roof, then the hut itself, and on the bench her grandfather, who sat smoking his pipe, while the pine branches above were murmuring in the evening breeze. Heidi hastened yet more her steps, and before her grandfather rightly knew who was before him, the child had thrown her arms round his neck, clasping him tightly, and repeating in her intense happiness, "Grandfather, Grandfather, Grandfather!"

The old man was silent. His eyes were moist. It was the first time for many years that he had shed tears. Loosening Heidi's arms from his neck, he placed her on his knee, and looked at her for a moment. "So you have come home again, my child," he said. "How is this? Certainly they haven't furbished you up much. Have they sent you away?"

"Oh no, Grandfather," said Heidi eagerly, "you must not think that. They were all so good to me, Klara and the grandmamma and Mr. Sesemann. But do you see, Grandfather, I could not hold out any longer, but had to come home to you; and often I thought I should stifle, I felt so wretched, but I didn't say anything because it would be ungrateful. But one morning Mr. Sesemann called me very early—but I think it was what the doctor said—perhaps it is all written in the letter!" and Heidi jumped down, pulled the letter and the parcel out of the basket, which she had placed carefully on the ground by the bench, and gave both to her grandfather.

"This is yours," he said, and put the parcel beside her on the bench. He read the letter in silence, and put it into his pocket. "Do you feel as if you could drink a little milk with me, Heidi?" he asked, taking the child's hand in his to go into the hut. "But take your money, child. With that you can buy a new bed, and clothes enough for many years."

"I do not want money, Grandfather. I have a bed, you know, and Klara has given me so many clothes that I shall never have to buy any, I am sure."

"Take it, nevertheless, and lay it in the press. You may want it sometime."

Heidi obeyed, and danced into the hut behind her grandfather, where she was soon peeping into all the corners, delighted to be once more at home. From the loft, however, her voice came presently with a troubled sound, "O Grandfather, my bed is not here!"

"It will soon be there again. I didn't know you were coming back. Come down for your milk."

The little girl came down, seated herself on her

high stool in her old place, seized her mug, and drank with such avidity that her grandfather saw that she had not lost her old tastes. "There is no milk in the whole world so good as ours, Grandfather," she said, as she replaced her mug with a sigh of satisfaction.

A shrill, well-known whistle sounded without. Like lightning Heidi sprang through the door. Down from the heights came the little army of goats, in the midst Peter, who stood still as if rooted to the spot, and stared at Heidi in speechless surprise.

"Good evening, Peter," called out the child, and rushed in amongst the goats. "Schwänli! Bärli! Do you remember me still?" By their actions the little creatures showed that they recognized her voice, for they rubbed their heads against her shoulder, and began to bleat passionately for joy. One after another Heidi called them all by name, and they all ran at once, and pressed about her, the impatient Thistlebird jumping over two other goats to get near, while Snowball, forgetting her timidity, pushed aside the big Turk, who stood in her way. Turk, in amazement at her boldness, raised his long beard in the air to show that it was he.

Almost beside herself with joy at finding herself again amidst all these dear friends, Heidi put her arm about the gentle little Snowball, stroking her again and again, and patted the restless Thistlebird, and was pushed and shoved by all the herd, in their love and confidence, nearer and nearer to Peter, who had never stirred from the time he saw her.

"Come down here, Peter, and bid me good evening," said Heidi to him at last.

"You here again!" he blurted out, recovering his speech at last, and took the hand that Heidi had been for some time holding out to him. Instantly he repeated the old question, that he had so often asked in the evening when they came down from the pasture together, "Will you go with me again tomorrow?"

"No, not tomorrow, but perhaps the day after. Tomorrow I must go down to your grandmother."

"It's a good thing you've come back," said Peter, and twisted his face in every conceivable direction, in his great satisfaction.

He started now to go home, but it was harder than ever before to get the flock away. For when by coaxing and threatening he had collected them about him, and Heidi began moving toward the stalls with one arm round Schwänli's and the other round Bärli's head, then in an instant they all turned about and ran back to her. At last she went into the stalls out of sight with her two goats, and closed the door, or Peter might never have got his flock down the mountain.

On her return into the hut, Heidi found her bed

again arranged in the loft, beautifully high and fragrant, for the hay was quite fresh, and the great white linen sheet was carefully spread over it and tucked firmly under. Heidi laid herself down, and slept as she had not slept for an entire year.

At least ten times that night her grandfather left his bed and mounted the ladder to see if she slept quietly, and to try if the hay which he had stuffed into the round hole in the roof was fast, for now the moon must not shine on Heidi as she lay in bed. But there was no danger now for the child, whose great ardent longing was stilled. She slept without stirring, for had she not seen the mountains and the pinnacles glow in the light of the setting sun? Had she not heard the murmuring pines? Was she not at home on the Alm?

Chapter 14

On Sunday, When the Church Bells Ring

Heidi stood under the waving pine branches, waiting for her grandfather, who was going with her to fetch her trunk from Dörfli, while she visited the grandmother. The child could hardly wait to go down to find out how the rolls had tasted to her old friend. And yet the time did not seem long while she could listen to the beloved sound of the wind in the pines and drink in the perfume and beauty of the green pastures. She could never be satiated with these.

Her grandfather came at last out of the hut, looked about him with satisfaction, and said presently, "Now we can go down."

Today was Saturday; and the Alm uncle's custom had always been to put everything in order on that day, in and out the hut, the stalls, and the outhouses. This morning he had begun to work early, so that he might go down with Heidi in the afternoon. He well might look about him with contentment—everything was so fresh and clean.

They separated at the door of goat-Peter's mother's cottage, and Heidi darted in. She was expected, and received with joyous welcome. The blind woman grasped the child's hand, and held it tightly, as if fearful that her treasure might be again torn from her. The rolls had tasted delicious, and had so strengthened the grandmother that she declared herself quite another person. Brigitte added, that for fear they would be too soon gone, her mother had eaten only a single roll yesterday and today. Could she have one every day, it might really benefit her health.

Heidi stood plunged in thought for some time after this suggestion of Brigitte's. At last she hit upon a plan.

"I know what I can do. I can write to Klara, and ask her to send me as many more rolls, or twice as many. I had collected a great heap in my press, and when they were taken away from me, Klara promised to give me as many more, and she will do so, I am sure."

"Oh, that is a good idea," said Brigitte, "an excellent plan; but let us think, they would get very hard. If now and then we could have a fresh batch! The baker in Dörfli makes them, but I can only just manage to get black bread."

Now Heidi's eyes sparkled with joy. "Oh, I have a wonderful lot of money, Grandmother! Now I know what I will do with it. Every single day you must have a fresh roll, and on Sunday two. Peter will bring them from Dörfli!" And Heidi fairly danced in her delight.

"No, child, no! That cannot be. Your money was not given to you for that. You must give it to your grandfather. He will tell you what use to make of it."

But the little girl did not mean to have her happiness put aside in this way. She danced about, and shouted, and repeated, "Yes, Grandmother, you shall have a fresh roll every day, and get strong again. And perhaps when you are really strong," she added with fresh joy, "it will be light for you again. Perhaps it is dark only because you are so weak."

The good old woman was silent, for she would not disturb the child's happiness. But as Heidi was leaping and capering about the room, her eyes chanced to fall on the old hymn book, and with it a new idea came to her: "I have learned to read very nicely, Grandmother. Shall I read you something from the old hymn book?"

"O Heidi! Can you really read! Can you really?"

Down came the book from the shelf, where it had lain undisturbed for so long. Heidi wiped it clean, and seating herself on her footstool, said simply, "What shall I read?"

"What you please, child, what you please."

Almost breathless with expectancy the old woman sat, while Heidi turned the leaves and read here and there softly to herself a line or two. "I have found something about the sun. I will read that." And she began to read, more and more earnestly as she went on, and with greater emphasis:

"The sun's orb of gold
Brings joys untold;
Brings us the showers,
And the shining hours,
Brings heartfelt rejoicing and beautiful light.

"Heavy of heart,
I languished apart;
Now again I am strong.
Now I raise my loud song,

Praising the Lord with my strength and my
    might.

"I see, up above,
What God in his love
Has made to teach men,
Again and again,
How strong and how great is His kindgom on
    high.

"How one and how all
Who list to His call,
May gather in peace
Where all sorrows cease,
When from this earthly prison they fly.

"All things go past;
God only stands fast,
Stands firm as the rock,
Scorns tempest's rude shock;
His word and His will must forever endure.

"His blessing and grace
Make holy each place;
Heal in the heart
The aching and smart;
He raises the dying, the sick He can cure.

"Sorrow and pain
Will ne'er come again;
The storm and the wind
Are all left behind,
For the heavenly sun shows his beautiful face.

"Purest delight,
Peaceful and bright,

I now await
At the heavenly gate;
My heart and my soul are all flooded with grace."

The grandmother sat and listened with folded hands, and with a look of transcendent happiness such as Heidi had never yet seen on any face, while tears coursed freely down her cheeks.

"That makes it light for me, my child. That makes it light in my heart. The good you have done me no one knows." The face of little Heidi was irradiated with pure pleasure as the grandmother thus spoke, for the grandmother's countenance seemed as if the blind woman really saw the heavenly peace that awaited her.

At the moment some one knocked upon the window. It was the Alm uncle, who was there to take his little granddaughter back with him.

She followed quickly, but not without assuring her blind friend that she would come again on the morrow, even if she went with Peter to the pasture, she would come again in the afternoon. For being able to make life bright for the grandmother and restore her to happiness was the very greatest happiness that Heidi herself could know, far better than being in the sunny pasture on the Alm, with the flowers and the goats.

Brigitte followed Heidi to the door with the frock and hat Heidi had left, begging the child to take her things home with her. The dress she did take, for as her grandfather had already recognized her, there was nothing to fear in that direction, but the hat she persistently refused to touch. Brigitte should keep it, for Heidi would never, never again put it on her head.

Going up the Alm the child recounted to her grandfather, as in the old times, all that had happened in the cottage, about the rolls that could be bought in Dörfli, and about her reading, how she had made the grandmother look happy, and returned at length to the first proposition, saying, "Truly, Grandfather, even if the grandmother will not take it, you will give it all to me, all the money? Then I can give a piece every morning to Peter, to buy a roll with, and on Sunday two."

"But the bed, Heidi," said the Alm uncle. "A proper bed would be good for you, and there would still be money enough for a good many rolls."

The child would let him have no peace, assuring him that she slept far better on her bed of hay than she ever did in Frankfort on her bed of down, and begging so earnestly and persistently that at last he said, "It is your money. Do with it what you will. You can buy rolls for the grandmother for many long years."

"Good, good!" shouted Heidi. "Now there is no more need of her eating hard black bread! Oh, Grandfather, now everything is beautiful. It was never so beautiful before, never, since we were born!" and she danced along, holding her grandfather's hand, and singing like a bird carolling in the sky.

All at once, however, she became thoughtful, and said, "If the good God had granted my prayer at once, when I begged Him so hard, then I should have come home long ago, and brought the grandmother only a few rolls, and could not have read to her. The good God has arranged everything far better than I could have done. It has all come true, as the grandmamma told me it would be. I am thankful that He did not grant my prayer when I begged and complained. Now I will always pray as the grandmamma told me, always thanking Him, for even if it is not granted as I ask, I shall remember how it was in Frankfort. We will pray together every day, Grandfather, we will not forget it, and then the good God will not forget us."

"And if any one should forget it?" murmured the old man.

"Oh, then very bad things happen! Then He lets him go his own way, and if he complains, nobody has pity on him, but they all say that he forsook the good God first, and now he is forsaken of God, who alone could help him."

"That is true, my child. How did you find it out?"

"From the grandmamma. She explained it all to me."

They walked on for a while in silence. Presently

Heidi heard these words from her grandfather, who was following out his own thoughts: "And when this is once so, it remains so. There is no going back. If God has forgotten a man, he is forever forgotten."

"Oh no, Grandfather, he can go back! I know that, too, from the grandmamma, and from the beautiful story in the book she gave me. You never saw that book, but we are almost at home, and I will show it to you. You will soon see what a beautiful story it is."

Up the steep the child hurried, and rushed into the hut in all haste to fetch her precious book. The grandfather loosened from his back the basket in which he had brought the half of Heidi's things up to the Alm. The trunk would have been too heavy for him. Then he seated himself thoughtfully on the bench.

With her big book under her arm came Heidi. "That is nice, Grandfather, that you are all ready"; and the book seemed to open of itself at the oft-read place. In her own earnest way the child read of the son, how comfortable he was at home herding his father's flocks, dressed in a beautiful cloak, leaning on his staff, watching the sunset, as represented in the picture. But at last he wanted to have his property all to himself, and be his own master. He demanded it of his father, and went away and spent it all.

So when he had nothing left, he was obliged to

go to serve a peasant, who had not beautiful animals as his father had, but only swine. These he had to take care of and was in rags, and had only the husks to eat that they gave the swine, and of this food but little. When he thought of his father's house, he wept for homesickness and remorse, and he said, "I will go to my father, and beg his forgiveness, and say to him, I am not worthy to be called your son, but let me be as one of your hired servants."

And as he came near his father's house, his father saw him, and came running toward him.

"What do you think, Grandfather?" said Heidi, interrupting herself in her reading. "Do you think that his father was angry, and said to him, 'I told you so'? Listen, now to what is coming: 'And the father saw him and pitied him, and ran and fell on his neck, and kissed him. And the son said, "I have sinned before heaven and in thy sight, and am no more worthy to be called thy son." But the father said to his servants: "Bring the best dress, and put it on him, and put a ring on his hand, and shoes on his feet, and bring the fatted calf, and kill it, and let us eat, and be merry: for this my son was dead, and is alive again; he was lost, and is found." And they began to be merry.'

"Is not that a beautiful story, Grandfather?" said the child when she had finished, and felt sadly disappointed that the old man sat silently by her side, instead of being pleased, as she had expected.

"Certainly, the story is beautiful," he said, but his face was so serious, that Heidi sat perfectly still and looked at her pictures. Presently she gently pushed her book before her grandfather, saying, "See how happy he is!" and pointed to the picture of the prodigal, where he stood beside his father in fresh garments, and was recognized as his son.

Some hours later, when Heidi had long been sound asleep, her grandfather climbed the little ladder. He placed his lamp near Heidi's bed, so that the light shone on the sleeping child. She lay there with folded hands, for she had not forgotten to pray. On her face was an expression of peace and trust that must have appealed to her grandfather, for he stood a long, long time, and did not move, his eyes fixed upon her.

At last he too folded his hands, and half-aloud he said, with bowed head, "Father, I have sinned against heaven and in thy sight, and am no more worthy to be called thy son," and two great tears rolled down his cheeks.

Not many hours thereafter, at dawn of day, the old man stood before his hut, and looked about him with sparkling eyes. The sunlight of the beautiful Sunday morning flickered and played over hill and dale. Here and there the sound of an early bell rose from the valleys; the birds were singing their happy songs in the old pines.

The old man went back into the hut and called to Heidi, "Come, little one; the sun is up. Put on a tidy frock. We will go to church together.''

Heidi did not keep him long waiting. That was a new call from the grandfather, and one to be followed without delay. In a few minutes she came running down in her pretty Frankfort dress, and stood spellbound at the sight of her grandfather, in his coat with silver buttons, which she had never seen before. ''O Grandfather,'' she broke forth at last, ''how handsome you are in your Sunday coat!''

The old man looked with a pleased smile at the child, and said, ''And you also in yours. But come.'' He took Heidi's hand in his, and they wandered down the mountain together. On every side sounds of the sweet bells came towards them, fuller yet and richer, and Heidi listened in ecstasy, saying, ''Do you hear, Grandfather? It is like a great festival.''

Down in Dörfli all the people were already gathered in the church, and the singing had begun when Heidi and the Alm uncle entered together, and took seats on the last bench behind the others. But in the midst of the singing, the villager next to them touched his neighbor with his elbow, saying, ''Have you seen the Alm uncle? The Alm uncle is in the church.'' They passed it along from one to another, until it was whispered about even in the corners, ''The Alm uncle! The Alm uncle!'' And the women were obliged to keep turning round every minute, and most of them fell out a little in their singing, so that the leader had the greatest difficulty in keeping them together.

But when the pastor began his sermon, the disturbance was quieted, for there was such warmth of praise and thanksgiving in his words that all the congregation was impressed, and it seemed as if a great blessing had passed over them all.

When the service was at an end, the Alm uncle, holding his granddaughter by the hand, went out of the church and over to the parsonage; and everybody who came out with them, or stood already outside, looked after them, and the greater number followed, to see if he was really going into the pastor's house, which he did. They gathered in groups, and talked in the greatest excitement over the fact that he had at last appeared in the church. And they watched the door of the pastor's house, to see if when he came out he would look cross and angry, or seem in peace with the clergyman, since no one knew what had brought the old man down, nor what it really might mean.

A new feeling had sprung up among not a few, however, and one of these said to the others, "He cannot be so bad after all, as they say. Did you not see how carefully he held the little one by the hand?" And another said, "I have always said so, and he would not go to the pastor's if he were so out and out bad, for he would be afraid. People stretch things so." And the baker added, "Did not I say from the very first, who ever heard of a little child that had all she wanted to eat and drink, and everything she could wish, running home from a long way off to a grandfather who was harsh, and who made her afraid of him?" And gradually an affectionate feeling arose toward the Alm uncle, which gathered strength as the women joined in, and told how much they had heard from goat-Peterkin and his grandmother that placed the Alm uncle in quite a different light, till at last they all began to believe it was so, and that they were waiting there before the parsonage to welcome back an old friend whom they had long missed.

In the meanwhile the Alm uncle had stepped to the door of the study and knocked. The pastor opened the door and admitted the visitors at once, not seeming surprised, as he well might, but as if he had been expecting them. Undoubtedly their appearance in the church had not escaped him. He seized the hand of the old man and shook it many times most heartily, and the uncle stood there, and could not speak at first from emotion, being unprepared for such a reception.

At last collecting himself, "I came," he said, "to beg the pastor to forget what I said to him on the Alm, and not to lay it up against me that I was so obstinate concerning his well-meant advice. The pastor was perfectly right, and I was wrong. I will now follow his advice and find a lodging for myself for the coming winter in Dörfli. The winter is far too severe for this little one up there. She is too delicate. Even if the people down here do look a little askance at me, I deserve it, and the pastor will stand by me, I am sure."

The kindly eyes of the pastor shone with joy as he took the old man's hand and pressed it, saying, much moved, "Neighbor, you have been in the right church before you came down to mine. I am very glad of this, and if you will come among us again to live, you shall not have cause to repent, but always find in me a good friend and a good welcome. I shall look forward to many pleasant evenings in your society, which has always been agreeable and valuable to me. We will also find some good friends for your little grandchild."

So saying, the pastor laid his hand on Heidi's curly head, then taking her by the hand he led her out while he accompanied the grandfather, and only took leave of him outside before the house door. So all the people standing about saw how the pastor held the Alm uncle's hand, and kept shaking it, as if he were his dearest friend, from whom he could not bear to part.

Scarcely had the door closed when they all came crowding round the Alm uncle, and each one wished to be first, and so many hands were stretched out that he did not know which one to take. This one said, "I am very glad, Uncle, that you have come amongst us again"; and another, "I have long wished to exchange friendly words with you, Uncle"; and so it went on from all sides. When he told them that he thought of coming down to live amongst them in the winter, there was so much ado that one would have thought some old friend was returning to Dörfli, whose absence had been sorely felt by all.

A good way up on the Alm were the grandfather and the child accompanied by many of the villagers, and many begged him, at parting, to call at their houses when he next came down their way. When the people had turned back down the mountain, the old man stood and looked after their retreating forms with such a glow on his face that it seemed as if the sun itself was shining forth from within him. Heidi said, quite overjoyed, "Grandfather, today you grow more and more handsome all the time. You never looked so before."

"Do you think so, Heidi?" said he, smiling. "Yes, today it is well with me, more so than I can understand or deserve. To be at peace with God and man, that is well-being indeed. The good God meant this when he sent you to the Alm, Heidi."

When they reached the goat-Peter's cottage, the old man opened the door and entered. "God bless you, Grandmother!" he cried. "Shall we go to the quilting together, before the autumn winds blow strong?"

"Oh heaven! That is the uncle," cried out the old woman in delighted surprise. "That I should have lived to see it! Now I can thank you for all the kind things you have done for us. May God reward you! May He reward you!" With trembling joy she pressed the hand of her old friend, and continued, "I have one request to make of you, Uncle: if I have ever done you any harm, do not punish me by letting Heidi go away again before I lie in the churchyard. You do not know what she is to me!" And she held the child fast, for Heidi had already nestled into her accustomed place.

"Do not be troubled, Grandmother. I will punish neither you nor myself in that way. We will all remain together, and heaven grant that it may be for long."

At this moment Brigitte drew the uncle away into a corner quite mysteriously, showing him the pretty hat and feather and telling him all the little story, and that of course she was not one to take such a thing from a child. Most approvingly the grandfather looked at his Heidi. "That hat is hers," he said, "and if she will not put it on again, that is all right, and if she gave it to you, you keep it."

Brigitte was delighted at this unexpected decision. "It is certainly worth more than ten shillings. Just look at it!" she exclaimed, holding the hat high above her head. "Just think what wonderful things the child has brought back from Frankfort! I have thought a great deal about sending my Peterkin there. What is your opinion, uncle?"

With a merry twinkle in his eyes the uncle declared that in his view it could not do Peter any harm, but it would be best to wait for a good opportunity.

At that moment the individual spoken of came in at the door, not, however, until he had almost broken his head against it, for in his haste he had struck it, making everything shake and jingle. Something unheard-of had happened, an event indeed—a letter with Heidi's name and address! Peter stood still in the middle of the room, and held it toward the child. He had got it in Dörfli from the postman.

The letter was from Klara Sesemann. All the little company seated themselves around the table, and Heidi read aloud, and without stumbling, that Klara had found the time very tedious since Heidi's departure, and that she had begged her father so hard to take her to Ragatzbad, that he had at last promised to do so in the coming autumn; and her grandmamma would come also, for she wished to visit Heidi and her grandfather on the Alm. This message the grandmamma sent Heidi; that it was quite right for her to wish to bring the rolls to the blind grandmother, and lest they should taste very dry she must have some coffee to moisten them, and some was already on the way. Also she hoped to visit the grandmother herself when she came to Dörfli.

Now came questions and wonderings, and all were so busy that even the Alm uncle did not observe how late it had grown, while they were all rejoicing in the coming pleasures, and still more in that they were all together again. At last the grandmother said, "The best of all is when an old friend comes and gives you his hand, just as he did long ago; that is a blessed comfort. You will come again soon, Uncle, and bring me Heidi?"

The uncle promised, and gave his hand on it. Now, indeed, it was time to depart, and Heidi and her grandfather climbed together the Alm, and the sweet music that had called them in the morning to the valley seemed to float again about them as they returned to their dear mountain home, which lay shining so peacefully in the warm golden evening light.

Chapter 15
Preparations for a Journey

Our kind old Dr. Classen, who had decided so providentially that the child Heidi should be sent back to her grandfather, was walking slowly through the wide streets of Frankfort towards Mr.

Sesemann's house one sunny afternoon in September. The day was so bright and beautiful that it seemed as if all the world must rejoice, but the doctor's eyes were fixed on the stones beneath his feet, and he did not once raise them toward the blue heavens. His face wore an expression of deep sadness, and his hair had grown whiter since the spring, for the doctor had lost his only daughter, a lovely girl, who since her mother's death had been his most intimate companion. No wonder that the doctor's patients missed, in their sickrooms, the cheerfulness that had seemed unfailing.

At the stroke of the hall clock Sebastian opened the door with every demonstration of respectful sympathy, for the good doctor was looked upon as the friend, not only of the master of the house, but of the entire household. Sebastian's deep obeisance, however, as he followed the doctor upstairs, was naturally lost as an expression of good feeling, since the doctor possessed no eyes in the back of his head.

"I am most glad that you have come, Doctor," said Mr. Sesemann, as he grasped his friend's hand. "I must talk to you again and more about your last decision concerning Klara. To me she seems very much better, and I cannot agree with you exactly."

"I do not understand your conduct in this matter at all, my dear friend, I must confess," said the doctor, seating himself. "I really wish that your mother were here. With her everything is plain and simple. She sees things in their just bearings. With you there is no possibility of a decision. You have already sent for me three times, and I can only tell you the same thing each time."

"Yes, it must seem very foolish to you, Doctor," said Mr. Sesemann, laying his hand affectionately on his friend's shoulder. "But you can also understand that it is hard for me to deprive Klara of the pleasure she has been so eagerly looking forward to, the trip to Switzerland and the visit to Heidi, that she has been consoling herself with for so many long days and months. It is almost impossible for me to do it."

"Yet it must be done, Sesemann," said the doctor very decidedly; then, seeing how sad and dejected his friend still looked, he added: "Consider it rationally. For years Klara has not had such a bad summer as this one. It would be madness in you to undertake a long journey with her in this condition. It is almost the middle of September now, and though it may be still fine on the Alp, yet the days are growing short, and will soon be cold. Klara could not pass the nights on the mountain. She could stay there only a few hours of each day. The journey from Ragatzbad must require at least several hours to perform, and Klara would have to be carried up the mountain in a chair. In short, Sesemann, the thing is impossible.

"I will go in with you and talk with Klara. She is a sensible girl, and I will tell her of a plan I have made for her. With the coming spring she shall go to Ragatzbad, and take a course of baths there, until it is fairly warm on the mountain. Then she can be carried up from time to time, and her mountain visits will enliven and strengthen her, so that she can derive both pleasure and benefit from them, which would not now be the case. Do you quite understand, Sesemann, that the only reasonable hope for your child's ultimate recovery is through the most careful nursing and watchfulness?"

Klara's father, who had been listening in silence, rose now to his feet with characteristic impatience, saying, "Doctor, tell me truly, do you see any reason to expect soon a radical improvement in my daughter's condition?"

The doctor shrugged his shoulders. "Very little," he said softly. "But think a moment, my friend; contrast your position with mine. Your child is with you in your home. She longs for you in your absence, and welcomes you when you return. No lonely, empty house awaits you. You have a companion at the table, and a charming one. How much Klara can enjoy, surrounded as she is by every luxury and fostering care, sheltered from so much, if also deprived of a great deal! No, Sesemann, you cannot account yourself wholly unhappy, for you are not alone. Think of my house, how it is desolate."

As was his habit when excited, and when forced to an unpleasant decision, Mr. Sesemann now began to pace the room with great strides. At last he stopped, tapped his friend several times on the shoulder, and said kindly, "Doctor, I cannot bear to see you so depressed. It is not you. You must shake off this sadness, and come out of yourself a little. I have hit upon an excellent plan. You are to go up to the Alp, to visit the little Swiss girl and her grandfather in our name."

Greatly taken by surprise at this unexpected proposal, the doctor would have declined at once, had his friend given him time, but the latter was so enchanted with his brilliant project, that he seized the doctor's arm and almost forced him into the room where Klara was reclining.

The sick girl had always a cordial welcome for her old friend and physician, who had whiled away many an hour for her with his cheerful jokes and pleasant stories. This she did not look for now, but would gladly have cheered his sadness had she known how. She held out her hand to him, and he placed himself near her. Her father went round to the other side of her chair, and began at once upon the trip to Switzerland which had been promised, and from which Klara had anticipated so much pleasure. Now that must be given up. Her health was not equal to it at present, he said, and hastened—for he dreaded the coming tears—to introduce a diversion. How would it do for the doctor to go up in their stead? Was not that a good plan, a good change for their friend, if they could persuade him to it?

Klara choked down her tears, knowing well how the sight of them distressed her father, but she was almost overwhelmed with her sense of disappointment. To be called upon thus suddenly to relinquish all hope of the cherished Swiss journey, and the pleasure of seeing Heidi, which had sustained her through long hours of pain, was indeed hard. She did not need to be told, however, that her father deprived her of this indulgence only because it would be to her injury, and she resolutely addressed herself to the sole resource which remained to her.

"Will you really go, dear Dr. Classen," she said coaxingly, stroking the hand she had taken, "go to see Heidi, and how they really live up there on the Alp? And see her grandfather, and Peter, and the goats, that I've heard so much about? And you will take Heidi all the presents that I had arranged to take with me, won't you? I have something for the blind grandmother, too. If you will go, you dear doctor, I will promise to take all the cod-liver oil you wish me to while you are away."

We cannot be sure that this last argument was the determining one, but to this, at least, the doctor answered, "If that is your promise, I will certainly go, Klara, for you would become as

sound and firm as we wish you to be, papa and I.
Have you also arranged how soon I shall start?" he
asked, smiling.

"Tomorrow morning, if possible."

"Yes, she is right," added her father. "The sun
shines; the skies are blue; no time should be lost.
Such days as these you ought to be spending on the
Alp."

"The next step will be to find fault with me
because I have not already started," said the
doctor, laughing; "and to prevent this misfortune,
I will go off at once."

But Klara detained him yet a little longer. She
had many messages that she wished to send to
Heidi, and she begged him to take note of the
interior of the hut, and in fact of everything that
she had heard of again and again in her long talks
with her little friend. She said the bundle of
presents should be sent to the doctor at his house
as soon as Miss Rottenmeier returned to pack
them. Just now, indeed, she was out on one of her
shopping expeditions that might last all day.

Dr. Classen assured his friends, who were very
anxious to be rid of him, he said, that he would
carry out all their wishes. If he could not get off on
the morrow, it should certainly be postponed only
a day later, and as soon as he returned he would
hasten to give Klara an account of all he had seen
and heard.

The servants in a house have often a wonderful

knack of finding out what is taking place in a family before they are supposed to know anything about it. Both Sebastian and Tinette must have possessed this faculty to a remarkable degree, for while Sebastian was conducting the doctor downstairs, Tinette made her appearance in her mistress's room without being summoned.

"Take the box from the table over by the window, Tinette, and fill it with cakes quite fresh, such as we have with our coffee," said Klara, pointing to a box that had been procured for this very purpose.

The maid took the box contemptuously by the corner, swinging it as she left the room, and scarcely waiting till the door was closed to say, "This is worth while, indeed!" in her usual saucy style, for she knew for whom the fresh cakes were destined.

Sebastian, too, as he conducted the doctor to the door, betrayed himself thus: "Will Dr. Classen be so good as to give a kind greeting from me to the little mam'selle?"

"Hallo! Sebastian," said the doctor, not unkindly, "how did you know that I was going up there, pray?"

"I was—I had—I hardly know now—oh yes, I remember! I was just accidentally passing through the dining room when I heard the name of mam'selle spoken by some one, and as it so often happens, one thought led to another, and so—"

"Yes, yes. The more a man thinks, the more he finds out of what is going on. Is that it? Good-bye. I will take your message."

Already the good doctor was hurrying through the doorway, where he met with a decided obstacle. A strong wind had arisen, which deterred the housekeeper from pursuing further her shopping expedition. As she was quickly entering the house, a gust caught her shawl, extending it on each side until she looked like a ship under full sail. The doctor drew back somewhat startled at the apparition. Miss Rottenmeier, be it known, had long cherished a profound admiration, not to say affection, for Dr. Classen; and she also drew back with marked politeness, meaning to make way for him to pass. But the wind had other intentions, and with a tremendous puff sent her, with all her sails extended to the utmost, full against the physician. He drew back in time to prevent shipwreck, but the housekeeper was so near upon him that she had to fall off a little in order to make her curtsy.

She was much disturbed by this untoward occurrence, but the wily doctor soon smoothed her ruffled temper with soft words. He confided to her his project of going himself on the Swiss journey, instead of Klara, and begged her to pack carefully the case of presents for him to take to the little Heidi, for no one could pack so nicely and firmly as Miss Rottenmeier. On this the doctor made his escape.

Klara had been nerving herself for a contest with the housekeeper over the gifts to be sent off by the doctor, but to her surprise that lady was complaisance itself. The table was cleared at once, and the various packages arranged upon it, so that the best way to tie them up compactly could be seen before the work began. It was really a task of some difficulty, owing to the various sizes and shapes of the articles.

There was a long, thick mantle, with a warm hood attached, for Heidi to wear, instead of being wrapped in the sack, so that the little girl could walk by herself when she visited the grandmother. Then came a thick, soft shawl, for the blind woman to wrap about her in the cold weather, when the wind whistled so fiercely about the cottage. Then came the great box of fresh cakes, which also was intended for the grandmother, and following upon it, a huge sausage. This Klara had at first intended solely for Peter's consumption, because he never had any change from the black bread and cheese; but she decided, after further consideration, to send it to his mother, lest Peter should make himself ill by eating it all at once. Then there was a bag of tobacco for the grandfather, who was so fond of smoking his pipe on the bench in front of the hut in the afternoon. After these came a quantity of mysterious packages of all sorts, which Klara had prepared to surprise and please her little friend.

At last the great work was accomplished. Miss Rottenmeier stood awhile, deeply sunk in admiration at her own prowess as a packer. Klara looked at the bundle also, but her thoughts were far away, picturing the scene when the child should open it, and how she would spring into the air and shout for joy. Then Sebastian was called, who swung the big bale upon his shoulder, and carried it straightway to the doctor's house.

Chapter 16
A Guest on the Alm

The rose of dawn glowed on the mountain peaks; a fresh morning wind rustled through the pine branches, and swayed them back and forth. Heidi heard it, and opened her eyes. The sound, as ever, seemed to enter into the child's inmost being, and draw her irresistibly forth under the trees. She sprang quickly from her bed, and scarcely had time to get dressed for breakfast, but that had to be done, for the little girl knew well now that one's appearance ought always to be neat and orderly.

Presently she came down the little ladder. Her grandfather's bed was already empty. Out she ran. Her grandfather stood looking at the heavens, as he did every morning, to see what the weather was to be. Rosy clouds moved across the sky, and the blue increased constantly; the heights and the pasture-land were flooded with golden light, for at the moment the sun was climbing over the lofty peaks.

"Oh, how beautiful! How beautiful!" cried Heidi. "Good morning, Grandfather."

"Good morning to your bright eyes," said the old man, and gave her his hand.

Then Heidi ran under the pines, and danced to the sound of the wind in them, now leaping higher as the sound grew louder, now skipping gently as it fell to a murmur, and growing happier and more radiant as she went on.

Meanwhile her grandfather had gone to the stalls to milk the goats, and to wash and comb them. Presently he led them to the grass plot before the hut, ready for their morning trip to the pasture. Seeing her little friends, Heidi ran toward them, caressing them and speaking gently to them, with an arm round each. They, in return, bleated confidently, and pressed each one its head closer and closer to Heidi's shoulder, so that she was squeezed tightly between them. She had no fear of being hurt, however; for when the lively Bärli pressed too roughly with her head, the child had but to say, "Bärli must not strike like the big Turk," and in a moment the goat drew back her head and straightened herself quite decorously; and Schwänli, too, raised her head with a graceful movement, as if to say, "No one shall reproach me with behaving like the rough Turk;" for the snow-white Schwänli was a trifle more genteel than Bärli, who was brown.

Peter's shrill whistle was now heard, and the nimble Thistlebird, as usual, appeared in advance of the flock. With noisy greetings the goats all pressed round the little girl, each pushing her this way and that. She also pushed a little, for she wished to reach to where the timid Snowball stood apart; that little animal was always overmastered by the others in her efforts to reach Heidi.

Meanwhile Peter was waiting his turn, and gave a terrible whistle to startle his flock, and make them give way for him. "Today you can come with us again," was his somewhat brusque salutation.

"No, I cannot, Peter. At any moment they may come from Frankfort, and I must be here at home."

"That you have said again and again for a long time," grumbled the lad.

"And I shall keep on saying it again and again, until they come. Do you really mean it, that you think I ought to be away when they come from Frankfort to see me? Do you mean to say that, Peter?"

"They can stay with the uncle," said the lad snappishly.

"Why does not the army march?" said the powerful voice of the old man from the hut. "Is it the fault of the marshal, or his troops?" There was a sound in the voice that Peter, and his goats, it would seem, knew well, for off they scrambled together up the mountain.

Heidi now ran into the cottage. Since her visit to Frankfort many things fell under the child's observation in the hut that did not before strike her as out of the way. She could no longer see anything lying about, or hanging where it did not belong. She gathered together everything that made the room look disorderly, and put it into the press, and smoothed and patted her own bed in the loft for a long time every morning, to get it into proper shape. The stools and benches must be placed in order, and she wiped and polished the table so long with her cloth that it was quite white. Her grandfather often came in while she was at work, and looked on with a pleased air, saying, "My little maiden did not go away and learn nothing," or "Tis always Sunday with us here, since Heidi came back."

So today when Peter and his army had gone off, and she and her grandfather had breakfasted, she went straight to her housework. But she was not very ready therewith. It was so beautiful outside today. Every moment something happened that called off her attention from her work.

A bright sunbeam at last came through the window, seeming to say, "Come out! come out!" It was not to be resisted, and out she went. The sparkling sunshine lay all about her, the mountain was lighted above, and the valley flooded below with its warm beauty. Over on yonder grassy slope it looked so soft and enticing that the child scarcely could restrain her impulse to dash over there, to look out over the wide-stretched vale; but she remembered that the three-legged stool stood in the middle of the hut, and that the table was not yet cleared of breakfast. She went in with an air of resolution to her work. It was of no use. The music in the pines began, low music, that drew Heidi like enchantment. She must go, must dance with every moving twig, and keep time to the sweet sounds.

Her grandfather, too, left his work in the shed, drawn out to see his little girl's pretty gambols under the old trees. He stood watching her, laughing softly to himself, and turned away, and came again. As he was just entering the shed after one of these diversions, he heard her call out quickly, "Oh, Grandfather, come back! Come back!"

He turned, almost fearing she had hurt herself, and saw her darting toward the slope, calling out excitedly: "They are coming! They have come! And the good doctor first of all!"

Heidi rushed toward her old friend, who extended his hand to greet her. When she reached him she clasped tenderly his outstretched arm, and looking up at him said from the fullness of her heart, "Good day, Doctor, and thank you a thousand, thousand times!"

"God bless you, Heidi," was the answer. "But why do you thank me in advance?"

"Because I am at home again with my grandfather," said the little girl.

The countenance of the newcomer lighted up as with a ray of sunshine. This hearty greeting on the Alm he had not expected. Sadly, and oppressed with his burden of sorrow, he had climbed the mountain absorbed in his own thoughts, and giving no heed to the beauty about him, which increased with every step. He had scarcely expected a recognition from the little girl whom he had seen but seldom in Frankfort, and the knowledge that he came only to bring her disappointment made him dread that he would have no welcome. But he was welcomed, and joyfully too, and Heidi held fast the arm of her good friend, full of love and thanks.

"Come now, Heidi, and lead me to your grandfather, and show me where you live," said he at last.

Heidi stood still, gazing in amazement down the mountain side.

"But where are Klara and her grandmamma?"

"That is what I have to tell you, what will make you sorry, as I am. Heidi, I have come alone. Klara is ill and cannot travel, and so her grandmamma did not come either. But in the spring, when the days begin to be warm and long, then they will come certainly."

Poor little Heidi was disappointed indeed. She could not believe that the happiness she had so long looked forward to was not to be hers after all. She stood there motionless, as if confused at the unexpectedness of the blow. The doctor stood silently by her side, and no sound was heard save the soughing of the wind in the trees. Then Heidi suddenly remembered why she had run down the hill, and that the doctor was there.

She looked up at him. Such a look of sorrow lay in his eyes as he returned her glance, that she was startled. Surely it had not been so when in Frankfort the doctor had looked upon her. Heidi's tender heart was touched at once, for she could never see any one sad without suffering too, and the dear good Dr. Classen least of all. He must be feeling disappointed because Klara and her grandmamma could not come with him. So she set herself at once to find some consolation.

"Oh, it will not be so very long before the spring," she said, "and then they will certainly come! The time will quickly pass, and then they can stay much longer, and Klara will like that better, I am sure. And now we will go up to my grandfather."

Hand in hand the two good friends went up to the cottage. Heidi was so anxious to cheer the doctor, and took such pains to assure him that the time would not be long in passing, and that the long, warm summer days would soon come again, that in the end she believed it herself, and was quite consoled. When they reached her grandfather, she called out cheerfully, "They are not here now, but it will not be very long before they come."

Dr. Classen was no stranger to the Alm uncle, for Heidi had spoken of him very often, so the old man extended his hand to his guest, and gave him a hearty welcome. The two men seated themselves on the bench, and the doctor made room for Heidi by his side, and motioned her to sit down. Then he told them how Mr. Sesemann had begged him to undertake the journey, and how he himself had felt that it would be good for him, as he was not strong nor cheerful just now. Then he whispered in Heidi's ear that something would soon come up the mountain that had travelled with him from Frankfort, and that its arrival would give her much more pleasure than could the old doctor's.

The Alm uncle advised the doctor to come up every day, and stay as long as possible on the Alm. He could not invite him to pass the night there, as the hut contained no proper accommodations for such a guest, but he strongly urged him not to go all the way back to Ragatz, but to try the inn at Dörfli, which he would find simple, but clean and well kept. Then if the doctor would walk up the mountain every day, which the Alm uncle was sure would benefit him, they could make excursions in every direction, and find much that was beautiful and interesting. This was readily agreed to by Dr. Classen, who found the invitation in every way agreeable.

It was now high noon. The wind had ceased, and the pines were silent. A slight, refreshing breeze stirred about them as they sat on the bench, and the sun was not too warm. The Alm uncle brought the table from the hut.

"Now, Heidi," he said, "bring out what we need for dinner. Our guest must be indulgent, but if our fare is simple, our dining room, at least, is grand."

"Yes, that it certainly is," said the doctor, as he gazed down into the sunlit valley. "I gladly accept your invitation. Such keen air brings appetite."

Heidi ran back and forth as nimbly as a squirrel, bringing everything that she could lay her hands on from the press. It was a great delight to her to be able to serve the doctor. Her grandfather soon appeared from the hut, with the steaming jug of milk and the toasted golden cheese. He cut thin, almost transparent, slices of the rosy meat, prepared by himself, and dried in the pure mountain air. Their guest ate and drank heartily, declaring that nothing had tasted so good as this for a whole year.

"Yes, our Klara must come up here," he said enthusiastically. "She would gather new strength here, and should she eat for a while as I have done today, she would soon grow plump, and be sounder than she has ever been in her life."

Some one came toiling, at this moment, up the mountain, with a heavy load on his shoulder. As he reached them, he threw his burden on the ground and drank in the fresh mountain air in deep draughts.

"This is the package that was my companion from Frankfort," said the doctor, drawing Heidi toward the big bale, from which he quickly loosened the outside wrapper. "Now, child, go to work and discover the hidden treasures for yourself."

Heidi obeyed, and when everything was spread about, stood staring at her gifts with wondering eyes. At last the doctor came to her side, and removing the cover from the box, showed the cakes for the blind grandmother to eat with her coffee.

Now Heidi's joy found words. "Cakes, cakes for the grandmother!" she shouted, and danced with joy. All her other things were quickly piled together to put away. She would take the box at once down the Alm. Her grandfather persuaded her however, to wait until toward evening, when they would both go down to accompany their guest to Dörfli.

So the child pursued her investigations, and soon found the bag of tobacco for the grandfather, which she quickly brought him, and the two men sat smoking their pipes, which they filled at once. After further examination of her treasures, Heidi came and stood before her two old friends, as they sat puffing huge clouds of smoke into the cool air, and when there was a pause in their conversation, she said decidedly, "No, there is nothing that has given me more pleasure than the good old doctor."

The two laughed a little at this announcement, which the doctor said he had not at all expected.

At sunset the guest started to go down, to secure his night's lodging in Dörfli. Taking Heidi by the hand he went on, while the Alm uncle followed with the box of cakes, the shawl, and the big sausage. At the goat-Peter's cottage Heidi disappeared, and the two others went on to Dörfli. As Heidi entered the cottage she turned to ask, "Tomorrow will you go with the goats to the upland pasture?" for that was the most beautiful place to her in the world.

"Indeed I will, Heidi, if you will go too," he said, and bade her good evening.

In three trips Heidi carried her gifts into the cottage. Her grandfather had left them on the door step when he went on. The box of cakes was almost too heavy for the little hands, while the big woolen shawl and the huge sausage took each a separate effort. She carried them in quite to the grandmother's side, so that she could feel them at once, and the shawl she placed on her knees.

"From Frankfort they all come, sent by Klara and her grandmamma," she explained to the wondering women, for Brigitte was there, but so taken by surprise that she never thought of stirring to help the child, but let her carry all the heavy things unaided.

"But, say, Grandmother, do not the cakes make you ever so glad? See how soft they are!" cried Heidi over and over again. And the old woman each time replied, "What good people, Heidi! How kind they are!" and she felt constantly of the soft shawl, saying, "This is just splendid for the cold winter. I never could have believed that such a thing would come for me in this world!"

Heidi did not quite understand why the shawl gave more pleasure to her old friend than the cakes. Before the sausage stood Brigitte. That lay on the kitchen table, and Peter's mother regarded it with something approaching to awe. Such a giant sausage she had never seen in her life, and it really belonged to them, and they were to eat it! It seemed simply incredible to her, and she stood shaking her head and saying timidly, "We shall have to ask the uncle first, what it means."

But Heidi stoutly asserted that it was meant for them to eat, and for nothing else.

Peter now came stumbling in. "The Alm uncle is behind me. Heidi is to—" He could say no more; his eyes fell on the sausage, and he stood spellbound. But Heidi knew the end of the sentence, and gave her hand in parting to the grandmother at once. Generally now the Alm uncle came into the cottage when passing, to say a cheering word to its inmates, and the blind woman always rejoiced, when she heard his step. So her grandfather said, "The child must go to her sleep," and that was enough. He called through the open door a good night, took the forthcoming Heidi by the hand, and together they climbed the mountain under the sparkling, starry heavens.

Chapter 17
A Recompense

Peter came up with his goats the next morning, as usual, and with him the doctor. This good gentleman had done his best to engage the goatherd in conversation, but had scarcely been able to extract an intelligible monosyllable in answer to his questions. Peter was not easily trapped into communicativeness. So the silent company clambered up the steep hillside to the Alm hut, where Heidi stood awaiting them with her goats, all three as bright and happy as the early sunbeams.

"Are you coming with us?" said Peter, who repeated this question every morning, either in the form of an invitation or a challenge.

"Of course I am, if the doctor is going," answered Heidi.

Peter eyed the person named a little askance.

After the Alm uncle had greeted his guest with affectionate warmth, he hung the lunch bag over Peter's shoulders. The lad found it heavier than usual, by the addition of a large piece of delicate dried meat. Should the good doctor be pleased with the pasture, he might like to stay and eat luncheon with the children. Peter stood grinning from ear to ear, for he suspected some unusual luxury.

They began the ascent. The goats surrounded Heidi, each one wishing for the place beside her, and each pushing and crowding his neighbor a little. So for a while she was carried along with them, and did not resist. At last she stood still, saying, in a warning voice, "Now you must all run on properly, and not keep coming back to push and crowd me. I must walk a little with the doctor." Then tapping Snowball, who was always nearest her, gently on the shoulder, bidding her be especially good today, she worked her way out of the flock, ran back to her friend, took his hand, and held it tightly in hers.

There was not much trouble in finding subjects of conversation with this little companion, who began at once about the goats and their droll activities, about the flowers and the rocks, the birds and the snow-field, so that the time flew by, and they were at the summit without knowing it. Meanwhile Peter had cast many a threatening glance sidewise at the doctor, which might have caused the gentleman some uneasiness, but which fortunately he did not notice.

As soon as they reached their usual resting-place Heidi took the doctor to her favorite seat where the view was finest. Seating themselves on the sunny grass they looked about them. The heights above and the green valley were swimming in the golden autumn sunshine. From some lower Alp the faint tinkling cowbells came sweetly and softly like a song of peace and all the air was filled with pleasant sounds.

On the great snow-field above golden sunbeams glowed and shimmered here and there, while gray old Falkniss raised his rocky towers in majestic silence, standing strongly contrasted against the blue of heaven. The morning wind blew softly and caressingly, tenderly stirring the last blue harebells, which had outlived their companions of the great army of summer flowers, and now stood languidly waving their drooping heads in the warm sunlight. Overhead the great eagle circled in graceful, sweeping flight. Today he did not scream, but with widespread wings floated silently through the air in ecstasy of motion.

Heidi looked everywhere, at everything, all was so full of beauty. With sparkling eyes she glanced at her old friend, to be sure that he, too, saw as she did. As his eyes encountered Heidi's, dancing with joy and happiness, he said, "Yes, dear child, it may all be lovely, but how can one who carries a sad heart in his bosom feel the charm properly, or rejoice?"

"Oh," cried the child, with untouched gladness, "no one here carries a sad heart in his bosom; only in Frankfort are there such!"

The doctor smiled a little, but fleetingly. Then he said, "If some one came from Frankfort bringing all his sadness with him, what could be done to help him here? Do you know, Heidi?"

"If such a one does not know how to help himself, then he must tell all to the good God," said she confidently.

"That is a good thought, my child, but if he knows that his sorrow comes from God, what then can help him in his misery?"

Heidi had to think for a time about this new problem, though she was perfectly convinced that God could provide a balm for all sorrow. She sought for an answer from her own experience.

"One must wait," she said after a while, "and

must always think that soon the good God will bring something to make one happier; that something will come out of the trouble, but one must keep perfectly quiet, and not run away. After a while it will be quite plain how God had all the time something good in his thoughts, though we did not know it."

"Always keep that beautiful belief, Heidi," said the doctor. For a while he sat, gazing now at the rocky pinnacles, now into the gleaming valley.

During all this time the goatherd had been fully occupied in giving vent to his vexation. It was so long since Heidi had been to the pasture with him, and to see her now, sitting there with that old gentleman, and with never a word for him, was more than Peter could endure. It made him very angry. Placing himself in a hollow behind the unsuspicious doctor, where there was no danger of being seen, he doubled up first one fist and swung it in the air, and then two fists, and repeated the pantomime, and the longer they sat there the more vigorous and frightful became his action, and the higher he swung his fists in the air behind their backs.

But the sun had now reached the place in the heavens that indicated the time for their midday meal. Perceiving this, the lad shouted suddenly as loud as he could, "It's time to eat!"

Heidi rose at once, and wished to bring the bag to the place where they were sitting, so that her friend might eat without disturbing himself, but he declared that he was not hungry, and would only drink a glass of milk, and then climb higher up the mountain. Then Heidi discovered that she, too, was not hungry, and would only drink some milk, and furthermore would bring the doctor to the great moss-grown stone where Thistlebird had almost fallen over once, and where the sweetest and most nourishing herbs grew. So she ran over to Peter to explain to him that he was to get a glass of milk for the doctor first, and then one for her, from Schwänli. The lad gazed at Heidi in astonishment for a moment, and then said, "Who will have what is in the basket?"

"You may have it," she said, "but first fetch the milk, and quickly."

Never yet had Peter accomplished any action so promptly as he did this. The contents of the satchel seemed always before his eyes, and he longed to get at it. As soon as his companions had begun to drink their milk he opened the lunch bag and peeped in, when he saw the wonderful piece of meat he trembled for joy, and peeped again to make quite sure. Slowly he put his hand into the bag, then quickly withdrew it, as if really afraid to take what was there. It had suddenly come into Peter's head how he had been standing behind the gentleman who had given him all this superb feast, and had threatened him with his fists; and sorrow for this conduct prevented him from eating his dinner with satisfaction.

After a moment or two he sprang up, and running to the hollow, again stretched out his hands in the air, and made signs of smoothing out all the motions he had before made of hatred and anger. He continued this strange action until he felt satisfied that he had obliterated all indications of unkindness, and could return to eat his longed-for dinner with a good conscience.

Heidi and her companion went wandering meanwhile over the pasture, and enjoying themselves exceedingly. But at last the doctor found that it was time for him to return, while it occurred to him that the little girl might well like to play about awhile with the goats. Heidi had no thought of such a thing. Could she let the doctor go all the way down the Alp alone? She had still a great deal to tell him, to point out the spots where in summer there were myriads of lovely flowers. She must tell him all their names, for her grandfather had taught them all to her.

At last, however, the doctor took leave of his little companion, sending her back while he himself went down the mountain. But as he turned back now and then, he saw the child, still standing where he had left her, and waving her hand, just as his own little daughter had stood watching him every day when he left the house.

The whole month was a series of beautiful, clear, sunny days. Each morning the doctor climbed up the Alm, and went off for a ramble. Generally he went with the uncle high up amongst the rocks, where stood the old weather-beaten pines that overtopped the crags, and where nested the great birds of prey, which, startled, would fly screaming over their heads.

In the companionship of the Alm uncle the doctor found the greatest pleasure, and was more and more surprised at his conversation, and at the knowledge he showed of all the mountain herbs, their healing qualities, and where they grew, as well as of the curly mosses that nestled amongst the gnarled roots of the old pine trees, and the almost invisible flowers hidden in the Alpine soil. His knowledge was great, too, of the habits of the animals thereabout, and he told many a humorous story of the tricks and gambols of these dwellers in caves and rocks, and of the inhabitants of the high tree tops. The time passed so quickly, that day after day the evening surprised them before they were aware of its approach and the doctor constantly said, in taking leave at sundown, "I never pass the day in your company without learning something new and valuable."

But on many days, and those the finest, the doctor chose to go with his little friend. They sat together on the lovely spur of the Alp where they had sat that first morning, and the child repeated her hymns and songs, and told her old friend all her bits of knowledge and all her thoughts. Peter sat behind them in his old place in the hollow. He did not, however, double his fists. He was quite tame.

And so the lovely month of September drew to an end. One morning the doctor came up with a clouded countenance. He must go back to Frankfort, he said, and the thought made him sad, for he loved the Alm and its friendly faces, and was sorry to leave them. The Alm uncle was sorry too, for he had become much interested in the good doctor, and as for Heidi, she did not know how to think of being deprived of the companionship of her dear old friend, and looked at him long and beseechingly.

"Come down the mountain a little way with me, Heidi," said the doctor, when he had bade adieu to the uncle. Heidi put her hand in that of her friend, and they went, but the child could not grasp the idea that he was really leaving them.

"Now you must go back to your grandfather, my child," and the doctor passed his hand several times tenderly over her curly hair, "and I must go. Oh, Heidi! How I wish I could take you back with me, and keep you always!"

At these words all Frankfort rose before the child's eyes, the many, many houses, the stone streets, Miss Rottenmeier and Tinette; and she said rather doubtfully, "I should like far better to have you come to us."

"Yes, that certainly would be better. So farewell,

Heidi," and the doctor held out his hand kindly to her. Looking into his face Heidi saw that his eyes were full of tears, but he said nothing more, and turned away quickly to go down the mountain.

Heidi stood still. Those loving eyes, and the tears therein, touched her tender heart. Suddenly she burst forth weeping, and ran after her departing friend, calling with all her might, "Doctor! Doctor!"

The doctor turned just as Heidi reached his side. Tears were streaming down her cheeks, and she sobbed out, "I will go with you to Frankfort, and stay as long as you want me; but first let me go to tell my grandfather."

The doctor soothed gently the excited child. "No, my dear Heidi," he said tenderly, "not just now. You must stay awhile longer under the pines, or you would soon be ill again. But come, I will make a request of you. If I am ever sick and alone, will you come to me then, and stay with me? May I feel sure that I shall have some one who will care for me, and love me?"

"Yes, I will surely come, on the very day, for I love you almost as much as I do my grandfather," said the still sobbing child.

Pressing her hand fondly, the doctor turned away, while Heidi stood and waved him farewell as long as she could see him.

Chapter 18
Winter in Dörfli

The snow lay piled up about the Alm hut, so that
it looked as if the windows touched the ground;
below them nothing of the building was visible,
and the house door had quite disappeared. If the
Alm uncle had been living there, he would have
had to do as Peter did, for it snowed hard almost
every night. Peter jumped out of the bedroom
window into the snow, where he was obliged to
fight his way along through the drifts with might
and main, using his hands and feet, and often his
head. His mother handed him the broom from the
window, and he brushed and shoved with that
until he reached the house door. He had to clear
away the heavy snow piled up against it, or it
would fall in and half-fill the kitchen should any
one try to enter. Moreover, if the snow were
allowed to freeze hard, then no one could get in or
out, and the inmates would be imprisoned. When
once it froze hard, however, Peter had an easy and

pleasant time of it. If he had to go down to Dörfli, he would creep out of the window and let himself down on the crust. Then his mother would give him his little sledge through the same opening, and he would seat himself on it and go off when and where he chose, for all ways led downward. The entire Alm was an unbroken coast.

But the uncle was not on the Alm this winter. He had kept his promise. As soon as the first snow began to fall, he closed the hut and the stalls, and went with Heidi and the goats down to Dörfli. Near the church and the parsonage stood an old, ruined building, which plainly had once been a spacious mansion. Many of the rooms were in pretty good condition still, though some of the walls had fallen wholly, some in part. The former owner was a brave soldier, who had served in the Spanish wars, had performed many deeds of valor and accumulated great wealth. He came back to his native village of Dörfli, built this big, handsome house, and tried to live there, but the attempt did not last long. Little Dörfli was too peaceful and dull after the stirring life he had led in the great world. He went away and never returned. Many years after, when it was quite certain that he was dead, a distant relation took possession of the house, but not before it had fallen too completely into ruin to be worth repairing. Only quite poor families, therefore, lived in it, who paid little for the privilege, and when a wall fell in or out, here or there, left it as it had fallen.

But this was many years ago. When the Alm uncle came first to Dörfli, he had occupied the decayed old house with his son Tobias. Since that time it had stood empty, for unless one knew how to prop up the falling walls, and mend the windows, and stop the holes and rents as they occurred, it was not really habitable. In Dörfli especially the winter was long and cold, the wind blew howling through the rooms from every side, the lights were extinguished, and the dwellers in the old house shivered and shook with cold and discomfort. No danger of that for the uncle, however; he knew how to make himself comfortable. He took the old house again as soon as he had decided to go down to the village, and through the autumn months went constantly to put it in order, and make it weatherproof. In the middle of October he moved down there with Heidi.

If one approached the house from the rear one entered an open space, where the wall had fallen in on one side utterly, while half of the other was left standing. A bow-window, whose glass had long since disappeared, was still to be seen, mantled with thick ivy to the roof, whose fine arches showed that here had been a chapel. Between this and the great hall adjoining, the door was quite broken away; but remains of a handsome stone pavement were visible, between which the grass grew high and rank. Here, too, the walls had fallen in part, as well as a portion of the roof, the remainder of which, save for a few thick columns, seemed about to fall upon the head of whoever might be beneath it. Here the uncle had made a partition of boards, and covered the floor with straw, for a lodging for his goats.

Then there were numerous passages, where sometimes the sky above was visible, and sometimes the green fields without, and the road. Beyond all this, there was a room with a strong oaken door hanging firmly on its hinges, a fine large room, in good condition, its dark panellings of oak quite unbroken. In a corner stood a huge stove, reaching almost to the ceiling, on whose white tiles, blue pictures were painted. There were old towers, surrounded by high trees, under which stood a hunter with his dogs; and there was a quiet lake under wide shadowing oaks, where a fisherman stretched his rod far over the water. Round the whole stove there was a seat built, so that one could sit at ease to examine the pictures.

This pleased Heidi exceedingly. As soon as she entered this room with her grandfather, she ran toward the stove, and seated herself to study the pictures. As she slid along the bench, she at last came quite behind the stove, and a new object of interest met her eyes. Between the stove and the wall was a quite wide space, and there was a rack that looked as if meant for drying apples. No apples were there, however, but Heidi's bed, exactly as it was on the Alm, a high pile of hay with the sheet tucked in all round, and the sack for coverlid. Heidi shouted aloud, "O Grandfather, this must be my bedroom! How beautiful! But where is yours? Where will you sleep?"

"Your bed must be near the stove, where you will not feel the cold. You may come to see mine."

The child danced through the long room behind her grandfather, who opened a door at the other end, and showed a small room where his bed was placed. Another door led out from this room. With curiosity, Heidi opened the door and stood still in surprise. Before her was a large kitchen, so large that she did not know what to think of it.

The grandfather had had a deal of work to make this room habitable, and there still remained much to be done. There were holes and big cracks on every side, where the wind came in, and yet so many had been already stopped with boards and planks, that the room looked as if little cupboards had been fastened to the walls everywhere. The big old door had been made fast with nails and wires, and could now be shut securely, which was a good thing, for beyond were only fallen walls, between which grew thick shrubs and brush, where armies of lizards and insects of all sorts harbored.

Heidi was delighted with their new dwelling, and when Peter came to see her the next day, to inquire how they were getting on, she had searched and peeped into all the corners and out-of-the-way places so thoroughly that she was perfectly at home, and could show him all about the premises.

The child slept famously in her corner behind the stove, but every morning, on awakening, she thought herself on the Alm, and felt she must rush to the hut door to see if the pines were not singing, while the deep snow was piled thereon, and weighed down the branches. She had to look about her for a long time to find out where she was, and had always a choking and stifled feeling when she realized that she was not at her home on the Alp. But when she presently heard her grandfather's voice talking to the goats, and heard them bleating heartily as if they said, "Come out, Heidi, make haste and come out," then she knew where she was, and sprang up and dressed as quickly as possible, to run into the spacious court where the stalls were. On the fourth day, however, she announced that she must go to see the grandmother, who ought not to be left alone so long.

To this her grandfather did not agree. "Neither today nor tomorrow," said he. "The Alm lies deep in snow, and it is still snowing there. If sturdy Peter can scarcely work his way through, a little one like my Heidi would be snowed up on the spot, quite hidden, and never more to be found.

Wait awhile till it freezes, then you can walk up on the crust."

It troubled Heidi a good deal that she could not go at once. Yet the days were so filled with all sorts of work now, that unawares one was gone and another came. Every morning and every afternoon she went to school, and learned eagerly all that was to be learned there. Peter, she scarcely saw in the school, however, for he was rarely there. The teacher, a mild sort of man, only said now and then, "It seems to me that Peter is missing again today. He can't afford to lose his schooling, but there is a good deal of snow up his way, and he probably cannot get through." Toward evening, when school was over, Peter came through well enough, and paid his visit to Heidi very regularly.

After a few days the sun shone again, and cast his beams over the fields of snow, sinking soon behind the mountain, however, as if it did not delight him to see the earth without its grass and leaves and flowers. The moon, however, rose large and clear, and shone the whole night through, and in the morning the whole Alp, from top to bottom, sparkled and glistened like crystal.

When Peter opened his window that same morning to get into the snow as usual, it did not feel at all as he expected. Instead of sinking in and floundering about, as he had done before, plump he came on to the hard crust. Away he flew, like a sled without a master, and only after much effort regained his feet, and began stamping violently to assure himself that the crust was really strong. He tried to drive his heels in, but only splintered off a tiny bit of the icy surface. The whole Alm was frozen as hard as a rock. Peter knew well that only under such circumstances Heidi could come up to the cottage, and he was content. Quickly he gulped down his milk when he had entered the cottage again, stuffed his bread into his pocket, and said hurriedly, "Now I must go to school."

"Yes, go and study hard," said his mother encouragingly.

Out of the window crept Peter again, for the door was fast. He drew his little sledge after him, and down he shot like a rocket over the crust. He flew along so fast that when he came to Dörfli, where the descent continues down to Mayenfeld, he still went on, for it seemed to him that he must exert great force over himself and his sledge if he wanted to stop in his course. But on he went until he came quite down to the plain, where the sledge stopped of itself.

He got off and looked about him. He had been carried even beyond Mayenfeld. Now it occurred to him that school must have begun some time ago, and that it would be over before he could get up there, as it would take him a full hour to climb the hill again. So he took his time to return, and so it was that he reached Dörfli just as Heidi had got home from school, and was sitting down to dinner with her grandfather. Peter went in, and having a big thought to express, which lay very near the surface, he got rid of it as soon as he entered.

"We've got it," he said, standing in the doorway.

"What? What? General, that sounds very warlike," said the uncle.

"The crust," replied the lad.

"Oh! oh! Now I can go up to the grandmother," said Heidi joyfully, for she had understood Peter's meaning at once. "But why did you not come to school, Peter? You could have come down well enough on your sled," she added reproachfully, for it seemed wrong to her that he should have stayed away when there was no need.

"Came down too far on the sled. 'Twas too late," returned Peter.

"That is called deserting," said the uncle, "and when men do that they must be taken by the ear, do you understand?"

Peter covered his ears with his hands in a great fright. For if there was anybody in the world whom he feared especially, it was the Alm uncle.

"And you an officer into the bargain!" said the uncle further. "It is twice as bad for you to run away in this fashion. What would you think if your goats were to run away, one here and one there, and take it into their heads not to follow, or obey you any more? What would you do then?"

"Beat them," was the laconic reply.

"And if a boy did the same thing, like an unherded goat, and should get beaten a little, what would you say then?"

"Served him right," was the answer.

"So, now, you know what you deserve, goat-general. The next time you go sliding down below into the valley, instead of stopping at the school, just come in here, and I will give it to you."

Now, at last, Peter understood the drift of the conversation, and that the uncle meant him when he spoke of a lad who ran away like an unherded goat. He was quite struck by the comparison, and stood staring into the corner, as if he saw something lying there such as he would use, in like circumstances, for the goats.

But the uncle resumed quite pleasantly, "Come now, sit down to table with us, and Heidi shall then go up with you."

Peter was delighted at this most unexpected turn of affairs, and twisted his face into all sorts of grimaces to express his pleasure. He obeyed without hesitation, and seated himself next to Heidi, who, however, had soon finished her dinner. She was so glad to go at last to see the grandmother that she could not eat. She gave her potato and toasted cheese to Peter, who had already received a plateful from the uncle, and so had a formidable pile before him. His courage did not fail him, however, and he advanced valiantly to the attack.

Heidi ran to the press to fetch her new warm mantle, which Klara had sent her. Now she could make the journey, with the hood over her ears, and be perfectly warm. She seated herself again by the lad's side, saying, as soon as he had finished his last bit, "Oh! Come now, Peter!" and off they went.

All the way Heidi had a great deal to tell her companion about Schwänli and Bärli, and how they would not eat in their stalls on the first day, and made no sound, and how she had asked her grandfather the reason, and he had replied that they felt as she did when she went to Frankfort, for they had never come down from the Alm before in all their lives. And Heidi said, "Peter, you ought to know just once what that dreadful feeling is."

The two children had now almost reached the cottage, and Peter had not spoken a word; he was so absorbed in thought that he could not even listen as usual. Now he stood still and said a little crossly, "I would rather go to school than get from the uncle what he promised me," and Heidi, being of the same opinion, strengthened Peter in his resolution.

They found Peter's mother sitting alone with her mending. The grandmother had to be in bed all day. It was too cold for her, and she was otherwise far from well. This was new to Heidi, who had always found her old friend seated in the corner at her spinning wheel. She ran quickly to the bedroom, where the grandmother lay in her narrow bed, with its thin coverlet, wrapped closely in the gray shawl.

"God be thanked and praised," said the blind woman, as she heard Heidi's bounding step on the floor. Ever since Peter had told her of the old gentleman from Frankfort, who had been every day up to the Alm, and often to the pasture with Heidi, she had felt anxious lest he should be able to persuade the child to return with him, and even after he had left, she still feared that some messenger would come and deprive her of her treasure.

Heidi stood by the bedside now, asking anxiously, "Are you very ill, Grandmother?"

"No, no, child! The cold has got into my bones a little, that is all," and she stroked the child's cheek lovingly.

"Shall you be quite well then, when the weather is warm again?" said Heidi.

"Oh yes, sooner than that, I hope. Please God that I get to my spinning before long. I meant to have tried today. Tomorrow I shall get at it," said the grandmother confidently, for she sensed that Heidi was frightened.

Her words had the desired effect. Heidi sat silent for a while, and then said, "Grandmother, in Frankfort they wear their shawls only to go walking. Did you think they wore them in bed?"

"Don't you see, Heidi, I wear the shawl in bed

that I may not be cold? I am so glad I have got it for the bedclothes are rather thin."

"But, Grandmother," said Heidi again, "at your head it goes down instead of going up. That is not the way a bed should be."

"I know that, child. I feel it very plainly myself," and the old woman fumbled at the thin little pillow, trying to get a better place for her head upon it. "You see this was never a thick pillow, and now I have lain on it for so many years, it has got all flattened out."

"Oh, if I had only asked Klara to give me my bed, to bring with me!" cried Heidi. "It had three big, thick pillows, one over the other, and I was always slipping down until I came to the flat part, and then had to pull myself up again where I ought to be. Can you sleep so, Grandmother?"

"Yes, indeed, it keeps one warm, and one can breathe far better when one's head is high," replied the grandmother, trying to raise herself into a better position. "But we won't talk about it any more. I have so much to be thankful for, that other old, sick people are without: the nice soft rolls every day, and this beautiful warm shawl, and your coming, as you do, to see me, Heidi. Are you going to read me something today?"

The little girl ran to get the book. She picked out one nice hymn after another, for she knew them all, and was glad to read them again. It seemed so long since she had done so.

The grandmother lay with folded hands, and her face, which had looked worn and troubled before, now assumed a peaceful expression, as if some great happiness had befallen her.

Presently Heidi stopped reading. "Are you better now Grandmother?" she said.

"I am well, Heidi. You make me well. Read it through, will you?"

The child read the hymn to the end, and as she came to the last verse:

"Even though my sight grows dim,
*   Brighter still my spirit burns;*
And I joyful turn to Him,
*   As the traveller homeward turns,"*

the grandmother repeated it once and again, while on her face there lay as it were a great, joyful expectation.

After a while the child said, "It is getting dark, Grandmother. I must go home. But I am so glad that you are better."

Holding the child's hand tightly in her own the grandmother said, "Yes, I am glad too, and even if I must keep on lying here, I am well. You cannot know—no one can—how terrible it is to be all alone for many, many days, to hear not a word spoken, and to see nothing, not a single ray of light. Then very heavy thoughts come to one. It seems as if it would never be light again, and as if one could not bear to live. Such words as you have just read to me, Heidi, bring light and happiness into one's heart again."

Then the grandmother let go the child's hand, and after she had said good night she ran out quickly, for indeed the night had already come. But outside the moon shone clear in heaven so that it was bright as day. Peter placed himself on his sled, with Heidi behind him, and like two birds through the air, they glided down the Alm together.

But later, when Heidi lay on her bed of hay behind the stove, warm and comfortable, her thoughts returned again to the poor old blind grandmother, with her thin pillow, and her darkness within and without. She wondered how long it might be before she could go again to read to her, and kindle the light that alone could help her to bear her loneliness. Long she pondered, seeking for something that would be of use to her old friend. At last it came to her. She knew now what to do, and could hardly wait for the morrow to begin to put her new plan into execution.

So wrapped in thought had Heidi been, that she had not yet said the prayer which she never forgot before going to sleep. She prayed now for her grandfather and for the grandmother, and slept thereafter profoundly till break of day.

Chapter 19
The Winter Still Continues

The following day Peter came down punctually to school, bringing his dinner in his satchel, as was the custom. When the children who lived in Dörfli went home at noon, those who came from a distance seated themselves on the table, and placing their feet against a bench, spread out their dinner on their knees. Thus till one o'clock could they enjoy themselves, and then school began again. Peter for once had got through an entire day in the schoolroom, and when it was over he went to see Heidi at her grandfather's.

As he entered the big room, Heidi, who had just preceded him, darted over to him, saying, "I know something, Peter."

"Well?" returned the lad.

"You must learn to read."

"Have learned."

"Yes, yes, but I do not mean like that. I mean, so that you can read any time, anywhere."

"Can't."

"No one will believe that of you any longer—
not I certainly," said Heidi eagerly. "The
grandmamma in Frankfort knew that it was not
true, and she told me not to believe it."

This piece of news surprised Peter very much.

"I will teach you to read. I know quite well
how," continued Heidi. "You must learn, and
then read a hymn or two to the grandmother every
day."

"That's nothing," grumbled Peter.

This obstinate resistance against something
that was good and right, and that Heidi had so
much at heart, excited the child indignation. With
flashing eyes she placed herself before the boy, and
said threateningly, "Then I will tell you what will
happen to you if you do not learn. Your mother
has already said that you must go to Frankfort to
learn all sorts of things, and I know where the boys
go to school there. Klara pointed out the big
schoolhouse to me when we were out driving. But
in Frankfort they do not stop going to school
when they grow up, but keep on even after they are
big men. I saw that myself. And you need not
think there is only one teacher there as we have
here, and such a good one, too. No, whole rows of
masters go together into the schoolhouse, and they
are all in black as if they were going to church, and
have black hats on their heads so high!" Heidi
indicated with her hand the height of the hats
from the floor, while cold shudders ran down her

254

listener's back.

"Then you will have to go in amongst all those gentlemen," continued Heidi with ardor, "and when your turn comes and you cannot read, nor even spell the words without mistakes, then you will see how the gentlemen will laugh, and make fun of you. It will be worse than Tinette, and you ought to know what it is when she makes fun of you."

"Then I will learn," said the boy, half angry, half complaining.

"Now that is right," said Heidi, softened at once. "We will begin right away," and she busily got together the necessary things, and drew Peter towards the table.

Among the many things that her dear Klara had sent her from Frankfort, in the big parcel, one which had pleased Heidi very much at the time, was a little book of the alphabet with verses. Heidi had thought of this book when she was making the plan for teaching Peter the previous evening. The two children now sat down together, their heads bent over the little book, and the lesson began. Peter had to spell out the first verse again and again, for Heidi was determined to have the lesson thoroughly learned. At last she said, "You cannot do it yet, but I will read it over to you one time after another, and when you know what it means then you can spell it out better." So she read:

"If your A B C is not learned today,
Go to be punished tomorrow, I say."

"I won't go," said Peter crossly.

"Where?" asked Heidi.

"To be punished."

"Then try to learn your A B C today."

So Peter set himself to the task, repeating the letters perseveringly, until Heidi said, "Now you know those three," and as she saw how much the couplet had helped her scholar, she wanted to go on and prepare the way a little for the next lesson. So she read several more verses, very slowly and distinctly.

"D E F G must follow straight,
Or sad misfortune will you await.

"Forgotten is your H I J K,
Very unlucky is that day.

"Who stammers over L and M,
Receives a punishment with shame.

"No wit goes fast, as it should do,
You learn right quickly N O P Q.

"But should you stop at R S T,
Something will hurt you terribly."

Here Heidi stopped, for Peter was as still as a mouse, and she had to look to see what he was about. All these threatenings and mysterious warnings had frightened him so terribly that he did not dare to stir, and sat staring at the little girl full of alarm. His looks stirred her tender heart and she said reassuringly, "You need not be so frightened, Peter. If you will come to me every evening, not as you go to school, but regularly, I will teach you, and if you learn as fast as you have today, at last you will know all the letters, and the other things will not happen. But remember, you must not let the snow keep you away."

Peter promised, for he was quite tame and docile after the fright he had received. He followed his little teacher's directions faithfully, and studied his letters every evening till he had them all by heart, and the verses too. The grandfather often sat in the room, smoking his pipe and listening to the exercises, and often the corners of his mouth twitched with suppressed laughter—it was so droll. Peter was generally rewarded with an invitation to supper after his tremendous exertions. This always consoled him, and removed any danger of his suffering from the fright caused by the verses, and their threatened punishments.

The winter days passed one after another, bringing the lad with them, who made fair progress with his alphabet. At last they reached the letter V, and Heidi read the couplet:

"Whoever mistakes the U for V
Must go where he dislikes to be,"

when Peter growled out, "See if I do!" But for all that he studied hard, just as if he feared some one coming up to take him by the collar from behind, to carry him where he disliked to be. The next evening came:

"If W is not learned at all,
Beware the rod upon the wall."

"There isn't any," said the lad scornfully, looking up at the wall.

"Then you do not know what my grandfather has in his chest. If that thick stick as big as my arm should be taken out, I think we should say, 'Beware the rod.'"

Peter did know that hazel stick, and bent over his W till he had mastered it.

"If you forget your X today,
Nothing to eat will come your way."

Looking searchingly toward the press, where the bread and cheese were kept, our scholar said crossly, "I never said I was going to forget my X."

"Well, if you won't forget it, we can learn another letter today, and that is the last but one."

Peter did not agree to this, but Heidi read the couplet:

"If from your Y you run away,
You will be laughed at all the day;"

and before Peter's eyes all the gentlemen in Frankfort rose up, with their tall, black hats on their heads, and laughter and scorn on their faces. He learned Y so thoroughly that he knew how it looked with his eyes shut.

But the next day found him in rather a high and mighty mood, for there was only one more letter to be learned. So when his patient teacher read:

*"Who stops and ponders over Z
unto the Hottentots must be led,"*

he called out scornfully, "Oh yes, but nobody knows where to find them."

"Truly, Peter, my grandfather knows all about them. I will run over to the parsonage and ask him," and Heidi jumped up and ran to the door.

"Wait!" cried Peter, who felt as if the Alm uncle and the pastor at his back would be upon him in a trice, and pack him off to the Hottentots, for he really had forgotten what to call Z.

The earnestness in his tone made Heidi pause. "What is the matter with you?" she asked, astonished.

"Nothing! Come back! I will learn it," he stammered out. But Heidi had begun to feel interested about these Hottentots herself, and wished to know where they did live, and she was going over to find out. But her pupil called after her so despairingly that she yielded, exacting extra work from him in return. Not only Z was mastered, but Heidi forced her pupil into words of one syllable, and Peter got a start this evening he had never had before.

The snow had become soft again, and thereafter more fell and yet more, so that for fully three weeks Heidi did not get up to see the grandmother. All the harder she worked with Peter, in order that he might be able to read the hymns. At last one evening the lad entered his mother's sitting room, and announced in his usual abrupt fashion, "I know how."

"What do you know, Peterkin?"

"How to read."

"Is it possible, my son? Mother, did you hear that?" cried Brigitte, full of admiration.

Of course the grandmother was much interested, and full of wonderment as to how this had come about.

"I must read you a hymn. Heidi told me to," went on Peter.

Brigitte quickly brought the book, and Peter began to read aloud. After every verse his mother said, "Who would believe it!" The blind woman also followed the verses intently, but she made no comment.

The day after, it happened that Peter's class at school had a reading exercise. When our young friend's turn came, the teacher asked, "Shall we skip you, Peter, as usual, or will you try, I will not say to read, but to stammer out a line or two?"

Peter began, and read two or three lines without a single mistake.

The teacher laid down his book and stared at the boy as if he had never heard reading before. "Peter," he said at last, "a miracle must have taken place. As long as with unbroken patience I worked daily over your reading, you never even learned your letters. After I gave up trying to teach you as a waste of time, here you are reading perfectly well. Whence comes in our age such a miracle, Peter?"

"From Heidi," answered the lad.

The teacher looked at Heidi, who was sitting quietly in her place, and had not in any way the appearance of a miracle-worker.

"I have noticed, indeed, a change in you, Peter," continued the master. "Formerly you were often a whole week without coming down to school at all. Now you never stay away, but come regularly. To what am I to attribute this change?"

"To the uncle," was the reply.

With increasing astonishment the teacher looked from Peter to Heidi, and from the little girl back to Peter again. Then he said cautiously, "You may read again." Peter did so, and satisfactorily. It was indeed true. He had learned to read.

As soon as he had dismissed the school the master hastened to the parsonage, to relate what had taken place that day, and to bear testimony to the good influence exerted by Heidi and her grandfather over those about them.

Every evening at home Peter read aloud a single hymn. Thus far he obeyed Heidi, but he never volunteered a second, nor did his grandmother ever ask for a repetition. Brigitte's delight, however, was undiminished, and often when the reader had long been fast asleep, she would say proudly, "We cannot be thankful enough, Mother, that Peterkin has learned to read. We may expect wonderful things from him now."

"Yes," said her mother, one night, "yes, it is well for Peter that he has at last learned something. But I hope the good God will soon let the spring come, so that I may have Heidi again. Something is left out so often when Peterkin reads to me. I have to think about it, and then I lose the place, and they don't do me the good that they do when Heidi reads them."

For the truth was that Peter, in order to make the reading as easy for himself as possible, left out all the long words or those that looked difficult. "There are enough left," he said to himself; "the grandmother will never miss them." So, naturally, the sense of the verses suffered in Peter's manner of reading them.

Chapter 20
Distant Friends Bestir Themselves

It was the month of May. The mountain brooks, swollen by the melting snow of spring, leaped down from every height to the valley. Bright and warm lay the sunshine on the Alp, which grew greener day by day. The last lingering snowdrift sunk away, and from out the fresh new grass the little early flowers peeped joyously, opening hourly to the sun's quickening rays. The merry spring breezes rustled through the branches of the old pines, shaking out the last year's rusty needles, to make room for the brighter green of their new array. High above all, the great eagle spread wide his majestic wings against the blue, cloud-flecked sky, and golden sunflames sought out and dried each lingering trace of winter's frost, and spread a warm mantle abroad over the wide Alm.

Heidi was again on the Alp. She ran hither and thither, and did not know which spot was the most beautiful. Now she listened to the wind, as with deep, mysterious murmurings it came toward her from yonder rocky crag, growing ever nearer, ever stronger, till it seemed to bury itself deep in the pine trees, shaking them and rustling them with a shout so joyous, that she joined in with all her force, and was borne this way and that as if she herself were a spring leaf.

Then away to the other side of the hut she flew, flinging herself down on the sun-bathed grass to peer in among the short blades, spying out the timid flower buds, and counting how many were already opened at the call of spring. The mazy dances of the flies and midges, rejoicing in the spring breeze, delighted the child, and she drew in deep inspirations of the scented air as it rose from the fresh, moist earth, and thought the Alp was never yet so beautiful as now. Every tiny living creature, she felt, must have its sense of perfect happiness as well as she, for they seemed humming and singing one to another, "On the Alp! On the Alp! On the Alp!" in continual chorus.

From the little workshop in the shed behind the hut came mingling with the rest the busy sound of hammer and of saw, a strain of homely music very dear to Heidi, for did it not belong to the old, happy life upon the Alm, yes, from the very beginning? Into the shop she ran with nimble feet, for she must know what her grandfather was working at so busily. Outside the door stood a new chair, all spick and span, and another, almost completed, was still under the uncle's skilful hands.

"I know what that means," cried Heidi joyfully; "we shall need these when they come from Frankfort. This one is for the grandmamma, and that for Klara. I suppose there will have to be another," the child went on falteringly, "or do you think, Grandfather, that Miss Rottenmeier will not come?"

"That I cannot possibly tell, my child, but it will be safer to have a chair ready, so that we can ask her to take a seat, if she is here."

Heidi stood looking for a long time at the armless, stiff wooden chairs, and making silent mental reservations of how Miss Rottenmeier would look if seated upon one. Presently she said slowly, shaking her head, "Grandfather, I do not believe she will sit on that."

"Then we will invite her to be seated on the beautiful turf-covered sofa," replied her grandfather composedly.

While the child was puzzling over this answer, the shrill whistle and shout that she knew well came suddenly to her ear. She ran out, and was at once surrounded by the bleating flock, which showed plainly that it shared her pleasure at being back upon the Alm again. Peter drove them all back, one to the right and one to the left, for he had something to give to Heidi. As he drew near, he handed her a letter. "There!" he said, leaving to Heidi any further explanation of the matter.

"Did you find this letter for me up in the pasture, Peter?"

"No," was the answer.

"Where, then, did you get it?"

"From the lunch bag."

The statement was a true one. On the previous evening the postman had given the letter to Peter to take up to the Alm, and Peter had placed it in his empty satchel. The next morning the lad put his bread and cheese into the satchel as usual, and went up the Alp with his goats. Of course he had seen the uncle and Heidi on his way up, but not until he had eaten his dinner, and was shaking out the last crumbs, did the letter again see the light. Heidi read the address carefully, then she ran back to her grandfather in the shop, and in high glee held out the letter to him. "From Frankfort, from Klara!" she cried. "May I read it to you right away, Grandfather?"

The uncle was ready, and so was Peter. The latter disposed himself to listen, uninvited, by placing himself firmly with his back against the doorpost, for thus he could best follow the reading.

Dear Heidi,

We have already packed up everything for the journey, and in two or three days we hope to start.

Papa is going away too, but not with us. He must go directly to Paris. Every day Dr. Classen comes, calling out almost before he enters the room, "You must go! You must go! Off to the Alp!" He cannot wait patiently until we are ready. I wish you could know how much he enjoyed his visit to the Alp. All through the winter he has been to see us almost every day. He would sit down by my side, day after day, and tell me about every day that he passed with you and your grandfather, and about the mountains and the flowers, the quiet that reigned up there so high above all the villages and roads, and the fresh, pure air. And he always said, "Yes, up there anybody would get well again!"

He himself is different, too, from what he was for a long time. He seems quite young and cheerful again. Oh, how happy I am, too, at the thought of seeing all the things he tells about, and of being with you on the Alp, and of making the acquaintance of Peter and his goats! But first I must be under treatment for six weeks in Ragatzbad. The doctor has ordered that, and then we shall take rooms in Dörfli, so that in fine weather I can be carried up the Alp to stay all day with you. My grandmamma will go with me, and stay all the time. She, too, is very glad to be able to see you again.

But just think, Miss Rottenmeier will not go. My grandmamma used to say to her almost every day, "How is it about the Swiss trip, my good Rottenmeier? Do not hesitate to say so, if you wish to go with us." But she always thanked my grandmamma in her most terribly polite fashion, and said that she would not be so bold. But I knew what she was thinking about. Sebastian had given a most frightful account of the Alp when he came back from taking you home, how terrible rocks overhung the path, and that everywhere there was danger of falling into chasms or over precipices, while the road went up so steep that it seemed as if one would certainly tumble over backwards; that goats, perhaps, but certainly not human beings, could ever climb up there without risking their lives. Miss Rottenmeier shuddered at this description, and has not seemed to care much since about the Swiss journey.

Tinette, too, has taken fright, and will not go with me. So we shall go all alone, grandmamma and I, though Sebastian will go with us as far as Ragatz, and then return.

I can scarcely wait until the time comes to see you.

Farewell, dear Heidi. Grandmamma sends you a thousand good wishes. Your true friend,

Klara

As soon as Heidi had finished reading, Peter darted away from the doorpost, swinging his rod right and left, and making it whistle angrily in the air. Away down the mountain scampered the goats, and the herd behind them, slashing still at his invisible enemy. This enemy was the expected company from Frankfort, against whom the lad was very bitter.

Heidi, on the other hand, was so full of delighted anticipation, that she planned a visit next day to the grandmother, to tell her all about the letter, who was coming from Frankfort, and especially who was not. It must all be of the greatest importance, Heidi believed, to the grandmother, who indeed, through her deep affection for Heidi, lived with the child everything that belonged to her life. So she started on the afternoon of the following day, for now she was able to make her visits alone. It was pleasant running down the sunny Alm, with a frolicsome May wind chasing behind her with many a helping gust.

The grandmother no longer kept to her bed, but was sitting again in her corner at her spinning. A strange expression, however, lay on her face this afternoon, as if she had heavy thoughts for companions. She had not slept all night, because of the anxiety which had come to her the evening before, when Peter came home in his anger. The old woman had half understood, from his broken sentences, that a crowd of people were coming from Frankfort to the Alm. What would happen then he did not know, and she was left to think that out for herself.

But now Heidi came bounding in, and set herself with such energy to her story that for a while she was more absorbed than ever in the prospect before her. But suddenly she interrupted herself, saying anxiously, "What is the matter, Grandmother? Are you not pleased with all this, too?"

"Yes, yes, child, I am pleased for your sake, that you have something to make you so happy," replied the grandmother, trying to look more cheerful as she spoke.

"But I can see quite well, Grandmother, that you are worried about something. Do you really think that Miss Rottenmeier may come after all?" asked Heidi, herself with some anxiety.

"No, no. It is nothing, nothing at all," said the old woman soothingly. "Give me your hand a little while, Heidi, so that I can feel that you are really here. It would surely be for your good, though how I should live through it I don't see."

"I will have nothing for my good that you cannot live through, Grandmother," said the little girl, so decidedly that a new fear arose in the grandmother's mind.

She had conceived the idea that the people from Frankfort were coming to take Heidi back with them, and now that the child was strong again, she knew that it would be good for her to go. This was the cause of the grandmother's great anxiety. But now she perceived that she ought not to let this be observed by Heidi, lest the affectionate child might for her sake refuse to go away. She cast about for an escape from this dilemma, but only for a moment, for there was but one.

"Heidi," she said, "I know of something that always does me good, and makes me contented again. Read me the hymn that begins, 'God will provide.'"

Heidi began as soon as she could get down the

old hymn book, and read in a clear tone:

"God will provide
On every side
    That which is best;
Should waves o'er roll
Thy shrinking soul,
    Trust Him, and rest!"

"Yes, yes, that is exactly what I wanted," said the grandmother with a lighter heart, and the troubled expression passed from her face.

Heidi looked at her thoughtfully, and then said, "'God will provide.' We know what that means, don't we, Grandmother?"

"Yes, yes," nodded the grandmother, "and as we know that He will provide everything just as it should be, we must trust to Him. Read it once more, Heidi, so that we can have it in mind, and not forget it again." The child read the words once more, and yet once more, to the blind grandmother.

It was evening when Heidi climbed the mountain. The bright stars came out gradually, one after another, twinkling and sparkling, as if they were sending their light down for her especial pleasure, and as she gazed at them looking down upon her from the blue heaven, she repeated aloud the grandmother's hymn, "God will provide." And all the stars seemed to nod assent, smiling down at her, and glowing with the glow in her own heart. Thus she reached the hut, where she found her grandfather too gazing upward at the sky, for it was a long time since the starry heaven had shone so brightly.

Not only the night, but the days too of this month of May were very clear and bright, and the uncle often noticed that the morning sun rose with the same splendor in the cloudless sky as that with which it had set, so that he said repeatedly, "This is a most remarkable month for sun. The pasturage will be very nourishing. Look out, general, that your jumpers and leapers are not too bold with all their good food."

And Peter swung his rod round and round after his manner, as if to say, "Never fear! I'll look out for them."

And thus the green month of May passed into the warmer June, with its long, long days so full of light, when all the flowers on the Alp bloomed forth, and everything glowed with many colors, and sweetest perfumes were spread abroad. Toward the end of June, Heidi went forth one day from the hut, where she had just finished her tasks of the morning. She wished to see whether the whole great bush of star-thistles was indeed open, for the flowers were so exquisitely beautiful with the sun shining through their transparent petals. But as she turned to run back to the hut, she suddenly gave such a cry at the top of her voice that the uncle rushed out of his shop at the unusual sound.

"Grandfather! Grandfather!" cried the child as if beside herself. "Come here—come here! See! See!"

The grandfather's glance followed the excited child's outstretched arm. Certainly it was an extraordinary sight that met his eyes—an unusual procession to come wending up their quiet Alm side. Two men led the way with an open litter, in which sat a young girl enveloped in many wraps. A horse followed with a stately lady on his back, a lady who looked about her in a lively manner, and chatted briskly with the young guide walking at her side. The bath-chair, well known to Heidi, came next, pushed by another lad, and then a porter with such a quantity of rugs, furs, and shawls that his basket was piled far above his head.

"They are here! They are here!" cried Heidi, jumping up and down for joy, and there they were indeed. They came nearer and nearer. At last they were at the grass plot in front of the hut. The bearers set Klara's litter on the ground, and the children kissed and hugged to their hearts' content. The grandmamma descended from her horse. Heidi ran to her with a tender greeting, and the lady turned to the Alm uncle, who drew near to bid her welcome. There was no stiffness in their meeting. They knew each other already as if they were old friends.

After the first words of greeting were over, the

grandmamma exclaimed with lively interest, "My dear Uncle, what a glorious place you have up here! Who could have believed it? A king might well envy it to you. And how blooming my Heidi looks, like a monthly rose!" She drew the child to her, stroking her sun-browned cheeks. "What is that for out-and-out magnificence! What do you say, Klara, my child? What do you say to it?"

Klara was looking about her in ecstasy. Anything like it she had never known or imagined. "Oh, how beautiful it is! Oh, how beautiful it is!" she cried. "I did not suppose it would be like this. Oh, Grandmamma, if I could only stay here always!"

The Alm uncle had rolled the bath-chair toward her, and spread the shawls and soft rugs over it. "It is better for the child to lie in her own chair than in the litter," he said, and without more ado lifted her gently from the straw litter and placed her comfortably in the bath-chair, covering her with rugs and tucking them in about her feet as neatly and handily as if his lifelong business had been the care of those disabled in limb. The grandmamma looked on in astonishment.

"My dear Uncle," she broke out, "if I knew where you learned the care of sick people, I would send all the nurses to learn their business at the same place."

The uncle smiled a little. "It comes more from practice than from study," he said sadly, in spite of the smile. Before his eyes, out of the long-vanished past, rose the figure of a man extended in a chair like Klara's, whose limbs were so stiffened and crippled that he could not move a joint. It was his captain, whom he had found on the battlefield after a fierce fight in Sicily, and whom he had rescued and cared for and tended until death ended his terrible sufferings. The uncle felt that the lame Klara was his special charge, and that he had almost a right to tend and watch her, and minister to her comfort as he well knew how.

The sky lay blue and cloudless over the hut, and over the pine trees, and far away over the high cliffs that rose in shimmering gray against it. Klara could not look about her enough. She was full of ecstasy over everything that she saw.

"Oh, if I could only run about as you do, Heidi, round the hut and under the pines!" she cried longingly. "If I could only go to look at everything that I have heard so much about, and never seen!"

Now Heidi made a great and successful effort. The chair rolled quite easily over the short, smooth grass, and under the pines. Here they stopped. Never had Klara seen such giant trees as these, whose long, broad branches grew down quite to the ground, each descending branch greater and thicker. The grandmamma, too, who had followed the children, stood filled with admiration. She did not know which was most beautiful, the full, murmuring crown, high up against the blue sky, or the straight, firm, column-like stems, with their powerful branches that told of the many years they had stood, looking down into the valley, where men came and went and where all was change, while they remained steadfast.

Heidi next rolled the chair to the stalls, in which certainly there was not much to be seen, for the animals were away. Klara called back, "Oh, Grandmamma, I long to see Schwänli and Bärli, and all the other goats, and Peter! I shall never see them if we have to go down as early as you said we must. It is too bad."

"Dear child, enjoy now the pleasure you are having, and don't think of what may escape you," said the grandmamma, following the chair that Heidi was pushing farther and farther.

"Oh! The flowers!" cried out Klara again. "Whole bushes of such pretty red blossoms, and all the nodding bluebells! Oh, if I could get out and pick them!"

Heidi darted to the flowers and brought back a great bunch of them. "But that is nothing, " she said, as she laid the flowers on Klara's lap. "If you go up with us once to the pasture, there you will see something! It is all covered with them. Red star-thistle, and bluebells, and thousands of bright yellow flowers, that make the place shine as if it was pure gold. My grandfather says that those are called sun's eyes; and then there are the brown ones, with little round heads, that smell so good. If you once sit down you never are willing to get up again, it is so beautiful!''

Heidi's dark eyes shone with longing to see again what she was describing, while Klara's soft blue ones seemed kindled thereby, and beamed in full reflection. ''Do you believe that I could get there, Grandmamma?'' she said. ''Can I ever get up so high? Oh, if I could only walk, Heidi, and so climb the Alp with you. All over it. Everywhere!''

''I will push you farther,'' Heidi thus comforted her, and in her zeal gave the chair such a shove that away it rolled, and might have gone on down the mountain had not the uncle caught it with his ready hand.

While the little party was standing under the pines the host had not been idle, but had brought out table and chairs for the dinner, set the pot upon the fire, and got everything in the process of cooking. Soon it was served and the company gathered to the repast.

The dining room with its azure ceiling, and the view down into the wide-stretching valley were much to the grandmamma's taste. A soft, cooling breeze fanned their cheeks as they took their frugal meal, and made sweet music for them in the trees.

''I never yet enjoyed anything so much as this. It is a truly glorious scene,'' declared the grandmamma. ''But what is this?'' she continued.

"Klara, are you really eating a second bit of cheese?"

In truth the second piece of golden cheese lay upon Klara's plate, and she bit into it and the thick slice of bread with real signs of appetite. "It tastes better than everything put together in Ragatz," she affirmed.

"That is right," cried the Alm uncle, well satisfied. "This is the effect of our mountain air. It always helps out where the kitchen is slender."

The gay little dinner went on most happily. The two elders understood each other perfectly, and their talk became more and more lively. But after a while the grandmamma glanced toward the west, and said, "We must soon be getting ready to go down, Klara. The sun is sinking, and the people will be here with the horse and litter."

At these words Klara's happy face became clouded. "Only one hour more, dear Grandmamma, one hour or two! We have not been into the hut at all, nor seen Heidi's bed. Oh, if only the day was ten hours longer!"

"Which is not quite possible, you know," said the grandmamma, but she really wished to see the hut herself. So they rose from table, and the Alm uncle rolled the chair with firm hand toward the door. It was far too wide for the narrow opening, but the uncle did not long bethink himself. He lifted Klara out and carried her into the hut straightway in his strong arms.

Once within, the grandmamma ran about peeping into every corner, making merry in her lively way over the housekeeping, which she was obliged to say was very neat and well-ordered. "Your bed must be up here, Heidi?" she asked and with nimble feet climbed the little ladder to the hayloft. "How sweet it smells up here! It must be a very healthful bedroom!" She went to the opening to look through, while the uncle came up with Klara on his arm, and Heidi trotted along behind.

Then they all stood admiringly about Heidi's nicely-made bed, and the grandmamma pensively inhaled deep breaths of the sweet-scented air. Klara was quite carried away by the charms of Heidi's bedroom.

"How nice it is for you here, Heidi!" she exclaimed. "From your bed you can look right into the sky, with the hay smelling so sweet all about, and the sound of the wind in the pines. I never heard of so jolly and perfect a bedroom."

The uncle looked significantly at the grandmamma.

"It seems to me," he said, "if the grandmamma is not opposed to it and will trust me, that the little girl might be left here for a while, and that she would gain strength. So many shawls and rugs of all sorts came with her that we can arrange a quite comfortable bed, and the grandmamma need have no anxiety as to the care that will be taken of her. I promise that."

The two children screamed for joy like two suddenly-freed birds, while the grandmamma's face was radiant with satisfaction.

"My dear Uncle, you are a charming man," she said with animation. "What do you suppose I was thinking of? I have been saying to myself all this time, would it not be a good thing for Klara to remain up here for a while? Would it not strengthen her? But then the care for the host, and the nursing and tending! And here you propose it, as if it were nothing at all! I must thank you, my dear uncle. I must thank you from my heart!" And the grandmamma shook her host's hand once and again and yet again, and the uncle shook hers in return, his face beaming.

The uncle went to work at once. He carried Klara back to her chair before the hut, followed by Heidi, who could not jump up high enough, she was so happy. Then he took all the shawls and rugs on his arm, saying, while he could not help laughing, "It is very fortunate that the lady grandmamma fitted herself out as if she were going on a winter campaign. We can put them all to good use."

"My dear uncle," replied the visitor gaily, "prudence is a fine virtue, and wards off many a calamity. If a body gets back from a journey over your Alp without having encountered storms and wind and rainspouts, he may be grateful, and so will we be, and my coverings are good for something. About that we are united."

While this little conversation was going on, they had both climbed up to the hayloft, and begun to spread the wraps over the bed, one after the other. There were so many that it looked at last like a little fortress.

"Now let me see a stalk of hay stick through, if it can," said the grandmamma, as she passed her hand over the bed on every side; but the soft wall was so impenetrable that truly not one came through.

She went down now to the children, who were sitting with beaming countenances, making plans of what they would do from morning to evening all the time they were to be together. But how long would that be? This was the question that was instantly laid before the grandmamma. She said that the grandfather knew best about that. They must ask him. As he presently appeared, they did ask him, and he replied that four weeks would be enough to enable them to judge if the air of the Alp performed its duty in strengthening Klara or not. Now the children rejoiced with a will, for the prospect of remaining together so long surpassed all their expectations.

At last the litter-bearer and the horse with its leader were visible, as they came toiling up the winding mountain path. The former was allowed to turn back immediately.

While the grandmamma was preparing to

mount her horse, Klara said gravely, "O Grandmamma, this is not at all a parting, even though you are going away. You will come every now and then to visit us on the Alp, to see what we are about, and that will be so jolly, won't it, Heidi?"

Heidi, who today had fallen from one pleasure into another, could signify her assent only by renewed jumping up and down.

The uncle descended the mountain with his guest, although she begged him not to take so much trouble, he insisted upon holding her bridle rein, declaring that he should give her his company as far as Dörfli, for the Alp was steep and the journey not without danger.

Now that she was alone, the grandmamma resolved not to remain in Dörfli, but to return to Ragatzbad, and thence to undertake from time to time her Alpine journeys.

Before the uncle returned, Peter came down with his goats. As soon as these descried Heidi, they ran toward her as usual. In a moment Klara in her chair, as well as Heidi, was surrounded by the flock, which crowded and pushed and peeped, one goat over the other. They were quickly named by Heidi, and one and all presented to Klara.

So it came about that the latter quickly learned to know the pretty Snowball, the lovely Thistle-bird, the grandfather's well-kept goats, and even the big Turk. Peter, meanwhile, stood apart, casting strangely threatening glances toward the happy girl.

When the children at last looked kindly toward him, calling out, "Good evening, Peter," he made no answer, but slashed at the air with his rod as if he would cut it all in bits. Then off he ran, and his followers at his heels.

But of all the beautiful things that Klara had that day seen on the Alp, there came now the best.

As she lay in the big, soft bed in the hayloft, to which Heidi had also clambered, and looked through the round opening up into the starry heavens, she cried out, delighted beyond measure, "Oh, Heidi, look. It is exactly as if we were driving in a high open carriage right through the sky!"

"Yes, and do you know why the stars are so happy, and twinkle their eyes so?" asked Heidi.

"No, I do not know why. What do you mean, Heidi?"

"Because they see, up there in heaven, how the good God provides everything good for his children, so that they need have no anxiety, and may be quite sure that everything that happens will be for the best. That makes them happy. See how they twinkle—they want us to be happy too. But you know, Klara, we must not forget to pray to the good God, and beg Him to remember us, when He provides for His children, so that we can be quite sure and need not fear anything."

Now the children sat up in bed, and said each her evening prayer. Heidi immediately put one round arm under her head, and in a trice was asleep. Klara, however, lay awake for along time, for such a bright, star-lined sleeping room she had never before seen in her life.

In fact she had scarcely seen the stars at all, for she never went out of the house in the evening, and the thick curtains within were always closed long before the stars came out. So now when she shut her eyes she had to open them again at once to see if really those two wonderfully bright ones were still sparkling and twinkling as Heidi said they did. And they were always there, but Klara could not look enough at their gleaming light, until her eyes closed of their own accord, and in her dreams even she saw yet the two great shimmering stars.

Chapter 21
More About the Life on the Alp

The sun had just climbed over the cliffs, and cast his first golden beams downward toward the valley. The uncle stood quiet, reverently looking about him as he did every morning, and saw how the silvery mist lying over hill and vale gradually melted away, and the world emerged from the shadows of darkness as the new day awoke.

Brighter and brighter became the thin clouds of morn, until the sun arose, and poured out his golden beams over rock and wood and height. At last the uncle went into the hut, and quietly mounted the little ladder. Klara had just opened her eyes, and was gazing, completely bewildered, at the bright sunbeams that streamed through the round opening, and danced and flickered on her bed. She did not know what she saw, nor where she was. But soon her eyes fell on the sleeping Heidi by her side, and the friendly voice of the grandfather met her ear, saying, "Have you slept well? Do you feel rested?"

Klara assured him that she was not at all tired, and that, once asleep, she had not awakened through the night. This was very satisfactory to the uncle, and he began at once and helped Klara to dress, as cleverly and handily as if it were his calling to be a nurse, and to take care of sick children.

Heidi also opened her eyes, and saw with astonishment what her grandfather was about, and watched him till he carried Klara, completely dressed, in his arms down the ladder. She could not wait a moment longer. She rose, dressed herself with lightning speed, and ran down the ladder and outside, to see what next her grandfather would be doing.

The evening before he had pondered, when the children had gone to bed, as to how he could get the bath-chair under shelter. It could not be pushed in through the hut door; that was too small. At last an idea came to him. He took off two of the big shutters from the shed, which made an opening big enough to allow of the chair being pushed through into the workshop; then he replaced the shutters, without making them fast. Heidi came down just as her grandfather, having placed Klara in her chair, had rolled her into the sunshine in the middle of the grass plot. There he left her, and went toward the goat stalls. Heidi ran to her friend's side.

The fresh breeze of morning fanned the children's faces, and the spicy perfume of the pines was carried toward them on every breath of air. Klara was leaning back in her chair, drawing in deep draughts of the delicious fragrance, and feeling better than ever before in her life. In fact, she had never yet breathed the pure morning air, surrounded by everything fresh and beautiful in nature, as she now did. Then, too, the sweet clear sunshine lay on her hands, and on the grass at her feet, with no overpowering heat, but with a warmth that was delightful. That life on the Alp could be like this, Klara had never been able to imagine.

"Oh, Heidi, if I could only live here always, always!" she said at last, turning about in her chair from side to side, and drinking in the air and the sunshine.

"Now, you see, don't you, that it is exactly as I told you it was," replied Heidi, delighted. "The most beautiful spot in the whole world is at my grandfather's on the Alm!"

At this moment the grandfather himself came out of the stalls toward the children, bringing two mugs full of foaming, snow-white milk, one of which he gave to Klara, and the other to Heidi. "This will do my little friend a deal of good," he said, nodding to Klara. "It is from Schwänli, and is strength-giving. To your good health! Drink now!"

Klara had never tasted goat's milk, and she felt impelled to smell it a little before drinking. But when she saw that Heidi drank hers eagerly, without once stopping, it tasted so very good to her, Klara decided to try, and found it as sweet and spicy as if there were sugar and nutmeg in it. She emptied her mug with enjoyment.

"Tomorrow we will take two," said the uncle, who had looked on with satisfaction as Klara followed his granddaughter's good example.

Peter came at his usual hour with the flock, and while Heidi was giving and receiving her usual morning greetings, and caressing, and getting pushed about, the uncle drew Peter aside, out of hearing of the bleating of the goats, which made a deal of noise whenever they had Heidi to themselves, and bade him give attention to his words.

"From today forth you are to give Schwänli her own way. She knows where to find the most nourishing herbs, therefore, if she wishes to climb, you are to follow her. It will do the others no harm, and if she chooses to go higher than you usually go, do not hold her back, do you understand? Even if you do have to clamber a little, it is no matter. You are to go where she wishes, for in this she is wiser than you are, and she must have the best, so that she may give some famous milk. Why are you gaping so over there, as if you would like to swallow some one? Nobody will interfere with you. Now off with you, and remember!"

Peter was accustomed to obey the uncle's orders promptly. He took up his line of march at once, but it looked as if he feared an ambush somewhere, for he continually turned his head and rolled his eyes about. The goats had managed to push Heidi a little way up the hill with them. That was what Peter wanted. "You must come too," he said, pressing in among the goats. "You must come too, if some one is going to follow up Schwänli."

"No, I cannot," cried Heidi. "I cannot go with you for a long, long time, as long as Klara is with us. But some time we are both going up. My grandfather has promised that we shall."

With these words Heidi freed herself completely

from the goats, and ran back to her friend. Peter stood, making passes with his fists toward the bath-chair and its occupant, until the frightened goats fled away past him. After them he went without stopping, until he was out of sight, for he feared that the uncle might have seen him, and he did not care to know what sort of impression his first action had made on the uncle.

Klara and Heidi had thought of so much to do today that they hardly knew where to begin. Heidi proposed, first of all, to write to the grandmamma the daily letter which she had promised her. The grandmamma had not been quite sure whether it would agree with Klara on the mountain, and whether it would really benefit her health, so she had engaged the children to write to her each day, and to tell her everything that happened. Thus she would know immediately if she was needed up there, and could stay quietly at Ragatz in the meantime.

"Must we go into the hut to write?" asked Klara, who was perfectly willing to send news to her grandmamma, but was so comfortable in the open air that she did not wish to move.

Heidi knew how to manage that. She ran into the hut and brought out all her school materials for writing, together with the little three-legged stool. She put her reading book and portfolio on Klara's knees, so that she could write on them, and seated herself on the stool with the bench for a table, and thus they both began to write to the grandmamma.

But after every sentence that Klara wrote, she would lay down her pencil and look about. It was too beautiful. The wind was no longer so cool; it only softly fanned her face, and whispered lightly to the pines. In the pure air the little merry midges danced and hummed, and a great stillness lay on all the wide fields. Calmly quiet, the great mountain peaks gazed down into the vale, which was everywhere at peace. Only, at intervals, the joyous sound of a yodelling herdboy's song came through the air, and was echoed back from the crags.

The morning went past, the children scarcely knew how, and the grandfather came with the steaming dishes and brought dinner out to them, for he said that Klara must stay out-of-doors as long as a ray of sunshine remained. After dinner Heidi rolled the bath-chair under the pines, for the children had arranged to pass the afternoon there in the cool shade, and to tell each other everything that had happened since Heidi left Frankfort. Under the trees they sat, and the faster they talked the louder the little birds sang above in the branches, for the chatter of the children pleased them, and they wished to join in. Thus the day passed, and now it was evening, and the goats came rattling down the mountain path, the driver behind, with a scowling brow and sullen mien.

"Good night, Peter!" said Heidi, as she saw that he did not mean to stop.

"Good night, Peter!" called out Klara kindly.

He gave no answer, but drove his goats along, snarling at them as they went.

When Klara saw the grandfather driving the pretty Schwänli to the stall to milk her, she was seized with such a longing for the spicy milk that she could hardly wait until it was brought to her. She was astonished at it herself.

"This is really strange, Heidi," she said, "for as long as I can remember anything, I have eaten only because I was obliged to. Everything that I got to eat tasted of cod-liver oil, and I have thought a thousand times, 'If only I didn't have to eat!' And now I can hardly wait until the grandfather comes with the milk!"

"Yes, I understand it very well," said Heidi, for she remembered the days in Frankfort, when everything seemed to stick in her throat, and she could not swallow a morsel. Klara did not fairly understand it yet. She had never before passed an entire day in the open air, and such a life-giving air, moreover, as this mountain region could boast.

When the Alm uncle appeared with his mug she took it gratefully, and finished it even more quickly than Heidi did hers. "May I have a little more?" she asked, handing her mug back to the grandfather. When he brought back the mugs to the children, there was upon each a high cover.

In the afternoon the Alm uncle had taken a walk over the green Maiensäss, to a mountain cottage where they made the sweetest, yellowest butter, and had brought back a nice round ball of it. He had cut two good thick slices of bread, and spread them well with butter. These were for the children's supper. They both bit into these slices so heartily that the grandfather stopped to watch how far it would go, for he was well pleased with their appetites.

When Klara went to bed that night she did not spend much time watching the twinkling stars, but followed Heidi's example and closed her eyes at once, and there came to her a sound, healthy sleep, such as she had never known before.

In this delightful manner the next day passed, and the next, and then there came a great surprise for the children. Two strong porters came up the mountain, each carrying on his basket a high bed, ready made from the factory, with a white coverlet, clean and brand-new. The men brought also a letter from the grandmamma. She wrote that these beds were for Heidi and Klara, that Heidi was to take hers with her in the winter to Dörfli, for in the future she must sleep in a proper bed. The other one could stay on the Alm for Klara when she came again. Then the good lady praised the little girls for their long letters, and encouraged them to write every day, so that she should continue to know all that they did, and how Klara's health improved.

The grandfather went upstairs, removed the covering from Heidi's hay bed, and spread the hay about in the loft. Then he came down, and with the help of the men carried the beds up to the loft. He pushed them close together, so that the two pillows were opposite the round hole, for he knew how much pleasure the children had in the morning and evening view which this afforded them.

The delight in her new life increased with Klara from day to day, and she could not tell her grandmamma enough of the uncle's goodness and care for her, and how lively and amusing Heidi was, far more so than in Frankfort, and how every morning when she awoke her first thought was, "Thank heaven, I am still on the Alp!"

So the grandmamma rejoiced much that things were going on so well, and decided to postpone her visit to the Alm a while longer, for in truth the steep mountain ride was rather a trial to her. The grandfather certainly took an extraordinary interest in his little charge, for no day passed that he did not think out something that he knew would strengthen her. He made every afternoon long excursions amongst the rocks, going higher and higher, and brought back each time a bundle of sweet-scented herbs, so that the perfume of the thyme and wild pink filled the air, and at night all the goats ran smelling toward the stalls, where the sweet bundle lay. But the uncle took the precaution to shut the door, for he had not climbed up over the high rocks for these rare herbs in order that the flock generally should have a meal, without the trouble of getting it for themselves. The forage was all intended for Schwänli, so that she might give strengthening milk, and it was easy to see that this unusual care agreed with her, for she tossed her head higher every day, and rolled her eyes right proudly.

It was now the third week that Klara had passed on the Alp. For several mornings, when the uncle brought her down to place her in her chair, he had said, "Won't this little daughter try once to stand up for just a moment?" Klara did try, to please him, but she always said immediately, "Oh, it hurts me so!" and clung to him for support. But every day he coaxed her to try a little longer.

For years there had not been such a lovely summer on the Alm. Every day the sun moved through cloudless heavens, and every little flower opened its petals as wide as possible, and glowed and sent its perfume up toward him. Every evening he threw his purple and rosy light over the rocky pinnacles and on the snow-field opposite, and then plunged into a flaming sea of gold. Heidi told her friend over and over about all this, for only above in the pasture was it rightly to be seen. She told her with especial enthusiasm how up there, over the great slopes, troops of shining golden heather-roses bloomed, and so many bluebells that it seemed as if the grass had grown blue, and near them whole bushes of brown flowers that smelled so sweet that it seemed as if one could never get away when once one had sat down to enjoy them.

On one special occasion, sitting under the pines, Heidi had been prattling about the flowers, and the sunset, and the shining rocks, and it caused such a longing in her own breast to see them that she suddenly jumped up and ran to her grandfather in the shop, who was sitting at his workbench. "Oh, Grandfather," she cried out before she reached him, "cannot we go tomorrow to the pasture? It is so beautiful up there now!"

"Yes, we will," said he assentingly, "but then the little daughter must do me a favor. She must try standing up alone for me this evening."

Heidi came back to Klara exulting over this good news, and the latter promised at once to try to stand on her feet as often as the uncle wished, for she was overjoyed at the thought of this trip to the beautiful goat pasture. Heidi was so excited that she screamed out to Peter, as soon as she saw him coming down, "Peter! Peter! Tomorrow we are going with you, and shall stay all day."

For reply, Peter growled like an irritated bear, and struck angrily at the innocent Thistlebird who was trotting by his side. Fortunately she knew what was coming in time, and jumped away.

Tonight the little girls climbed into the beautiful high beds, with their heads so full of plans for the pleasure of the coming day, that they promised each other to lie awake all night to talk about it till it was time to get up. They had scarcely laid their heads on their pillows, however, when their chatter ceased suddenly. Klara saw a big, big field before her in a dream, that was heavenly blue, so thickly did the bluebells cover it; and Heidi seemed to hear the eagle calling from on high, "Come! Come! Come!"

Chapter 22
Something Happens That No One Expected

Very early the next morning the uncle stood for a while before his hut, and looked about to see what the day would be. A reddish golden glow lay on the highest peaks; a fresh wind began to move the branches of the pines; the sun was about to rise. He watched how upon the high mountain tops the green ridges began to turn golden, and how the shadows in the valley gradually grew less deep, until the rosy light poured down upon them, and height and depth were flooded with gold. The sun had risen.

Now the uncle brought the bath-chair out of the shop, placed it before the hut ready for the journey, then went up to the loft to wake the little girls.

Just at this moment Peter came climbing up. His goats no longer ran confidently, as was their habit, by his side, round and about him up the mountain, for Peter now continually thrashed right and left with his rod like a crazy creature, and where he hit, it hurt. The lad had reached the highest pitch of bitterness and anger. For weeks he had not once had Heidi to himself as he used to have her. When he came up in the morning, no matter how early, the stranger child was always there in her chair, and Heidi had no eyes but for her. When he came down in the evening, there stood the chair under the pine trees, and Heidi had no word for him. She had never once been to the pasture with him through all the long summer, and now, today she was coming, but the chair and the strange girl were coming too, and what good would that do him?

Peter knew how it would be, and this was what had brought his inward fury to the highest pitch. His eyes fell on the chair, which was standing so proudly on its rollers, and seemed to stare at him like an enemy, an enemy that had already done him so much harm, and today would do still more.

Peter looked about. Everything was quiet, nobody in sight. Like a wild creature he threw himself upon the chair, seized hold of it, and gave it a mighty shove toward the steepest part of the decline. Away flew the chair, and instantly disappeared.

Peter rushed up the Alm as if he had suddenly become winged, not stopping once until he reached a big blackberry bush, behind which he concealed himself. He had no desire for the uncle to catch sight of him. He was anxious to see what would become of the chair, nevertheless, and this bush was placed most conveniently on the edge of a spur. Here, half hidden, he could look down the Alm, and if the uncle appeared, could conceal himself in a trice.

What a wonderful thing met his view! Far below him his enemy was plunging down, as if driven by an ever-increasing power. Now it turned over and over, then made a big leap, then threw itself down again on the earth, and rushed to its ruin. Bits of it flew in every direction; feet, arms, cushions, everything was thrown into the air.

Peter felt such an unbounded joy at the sight, that he jumped up with both feet together. He laughed aloud; he stamped for joy; he leaped about in a circle; he ran to the same place again and looked down, broke out into laughter again, and again leaped about. He was really quite beside himself with delight at the overthrow of his enemy, for he saw all sorts of pleasure that would follow for him. Now surely the stranger would be obliged to go away, because she would have no means of moving about. Heidi would again be alone, and would come with him to the pasture, and be at his call mornings and evenings, and everything would be back in the old order. But Peter did not bethink himself of what it is to do a bad deed, and of what follows.

Just then Heidi came running out of the house toward the workshop. Behind her was the grandfather with Klara in his arms. The workshop door stood wide open; the two shutters were standing against the side of the building; all within was bright as day. Heidi looked here and there, ran round the corner and came back again, her face betokening the greatest astonishment. At the moment her grandfather joined her. "What does this mean? Have you rolled the chair away, Heidi?" asked he.

"I am looking for it, Grandfather, and you told me that it stood near the workshop door," said the little girl, casting her eyes about everywhere.

The wind had in the meanwhile grown stronger; it clattered at the workshop door, and threw it slamming against the wall. "Grandfather, the wind has done it," said Heidi, and her eyes grew big at the discovery. "Oh, dear! If it has rolled down to Dörfli, we cannot get it back until it is too late for us to go."

"If it has rolled down, it won't come back at all, for it has been broken into a hundred bits," said the grandfather, coming round the corner to look down the mountain. "But 'tis strange that it should have gone down," he added, as he looked back and remembered that the chair would have had to go round the corner of the hut before starting down the mountain.

"Oh, what a pity! Now we cannot go today, and perhaps never," lamented Klara. "Now I shall certainly have to go home, for I have no chair. Oh, what a pity! It is too bad!"

But Heidi looked up in perfect confidence at her grandfather, and said, "You can find some way for us to go up to the pasture, and to keep Klara here too, can't you, Grandfather?"

"We will go up to the pasture as we intended to," said the Alm uncle, "and see what will happen next."

He went into the hut, brought out a pile of shawls and put Klara on them upon the sunny grass. Then he went to fetch for the children their morning's milk, and to bring Schwänli and Bärli from their stalls.

"I wonder why the others have not come up yet," said the uncle to himself, for Peter's whistle had not yet been heard.

Then taking Klara on one arm and the wraps on the other, "There now, forward!" he said, going on in front. "The goats can come with us."

Heidi liked this. One arm round Schwänli's neck and the other round Bärli's, she strolled along behind her grandfather, and the goats were so happy to be climbing the mountain again with Heidi that they almost squeezed her together between them from pure tenderness.

Arrived at the pasture, the little party saw the goats eating on the slopes in little groups, and Peter lying at full length on the grass.

"Another time I will teach you to go by without stopping, lazybones! What do you mean?" said the Alm uncle.

Peter sprang to his feet at the sound of the Alm uncle's well-known voice. "Nobody was up," he answered.

"Did you see anything of the chair?" resumed the uncle.

"Which one?" returned Peter crossly.

The uncle made no reply. He spread out the shawls on the sunny slope, and set Klara down, asking her if she was comfortable.

"Just as comfortable as if I was in the chair," said she, thanking him, "and I am in the very nicest place. It is beautiful, perfectly beautiful, Heidi," cried she, looking all about.

The grandfather was preparing to go back. He bade them enjoy themselves together, and when it was time, Heidi was to fetch the dinner from the satchel that he had put yonder in the shade. Peter was to get their milk, but Heidi must make sure that it was brought from Schwänli. Toward evening the grandfather said he would return, but first of all he must go to see what had become of the chair.

The sky was deep blue. No cloud was to be seen in any direction. The great snow-field opposite glistened as if with thousands of gold and silver stars. The gray pillars of rock stood high and firm, as from ancient time, in their place,and looked sternly down into the valley. The big eagle balanced himself in the azure, and over the heights the mountain wind blew cool upon the sunny Alp.

The children were unspeakably happy. Now and then a goat came and lay down a little while by their side. The tender Snowball came most often, and laid her head against Heidi, and would scarcely have gone away, had not one or another of the herd driven her. Thus Klara learned to know them apart, so that she was no longer likely to mistake one for another; for each one had an entirely different face, and its own manner. They were now so well acquainted with Klara that they would rub their heads against her shoulder, which was their surest sign of confidence.

Thus the hours passed by. Then it came into Heidi's head that she would just go over to the place where all the flowers were, to see if they were open, and as lovely as the year before. If they waited until the grandfather came up in the evening, she was afraid that they would be closed. The desire grew so strong in Heidi that she could no longer resist it.

A little doubtfully she asked, "Will you be angry, Klara, if I run off for a while and leave you alone? I should like so much to see how the flowers look. But wait a moment!" An idea had occurred to Heidi; she sprang aside, and tore off a pair of fine branches from the green bushes. Then she took Snowball by the neck and led her to Klara's side.

"There, you will not be alone now," said Heidi, and gave Snowball a little push. The pretty creature understood, and lay down. Then Heidi threw the branches into Klara's lap, and the latter said that she did not mind being left alone with the goats. It was something that had never happened to her before.

So Heidi ran off, and Klara began to feed Snowball, giving her leaf by leaf to eat from her branch, and the goat became quite tame, and drew the leaves slowly one by one from her hand. It was easy to see that she was happy there, for she did not make any motion to go away, though she was constantly stirred up by the big Turk.

It seemed delightful to Klara to be sitting here alone, with this gentle goat that looked up at her as if she wished for protection. A greater desire arose in the girl's heart than she had ever yet experienced, to be for once mistress of herself, and to be able to help others, and not always be waited on and tended. And many thoughts came into Klara's mind that she had never known before, and an unknown longing to live always in the beautiful sunshine, and to do something that would give pleasure to others as Snowball was now giving her pleasure. A wonderful happiness filled her heart, as if everything that she knew and could do were different from what it had ever been before and more beautiful. She felt so brave and so well that she had to catch the little goat about the neck, and cry out, "Oh Snowball, how beautiful it is up here! If I could only stay here always with you!"

In the meanwhile Heidi had reached the flower plot. She gave a cry of joy. The whole place was covered as with glistening gold. Here were the shining buttercups; thick clumps of bluebells rocked to and fro, and a strong spicy odor was wafted over the sunny hillside, as if precious balsams were being spread abroad. The sweetest perfume came, however, from the little brown flowers Heidi so loved, which showed their round heads here and there between the upraised chalices of gold. Heidi stood still and gazed, and drew in the sweet air in long inspirations. Suddenly she turned, and out of breath from excitement reached at length the place where Klara sat.

"Oh, you must certainly come," she cried out. "They are so beautiful, and everything is so beautiful, and they will close in the evening. Don't you think that perhaps I can carry you?"

Klara stared at the excited Heidi with astonishment, but she shook her head.

"No, no. What are you thinking of, Heidi? You are much smaller than I am. Oh, how I wish I could walk!"

Heidi looked searchingly around; a new idea had come to her. Over yonder, where Peter had been lying on the ground, he was sitting now and staring at the children. He had been sitting there for hours staring at them, as if he could not rightly understand what he was looking at. He had destroyed the chair that everything might come to a standstill, and the stranger no more be able to stir; and a short time afterward there she came, and was sitting on the ground by Heidi's side. It could not be, and yet it was; he could see that whenever he wished.

Now Heidi called out to him, saying, "Come down here, Peter!" and her voice sounded very decided.

"Won't come," he said in reply.

"Yes, you must. Come, I cannot do it alone; you must help me. Come quick!" urged Heidi.

"Won't come," cried he again.

At this Heidi ran down the mountain a little way toward the lad. She stood there with flaming eyes, and cried out, "Peter, if you do not come this instant I will do something to you that you will not like. You may believe it!"

These words were a sharp thrust for Peter, and he was seized with dire anxiety. He had done something wrong, which he thought nobody knew of. He had been delighted with his deed up to this moment, but now Heidi was talking as if she knew all about it, and was going to tell her grandfather, and Peter was dreadfully afraid of that person. If he should learn what had become of the chair! Peter was becoming more and more uneasy. He rose, and went toward Heidi.

"I am coming, but then you must not do it," he said, so tamed with fear that Heidi took pity on him.

"No, no; now I will not," she replied. "Come with me. It isn't anything to be afraid of, what I want you to do."

When they reached Klara, Heidi directed that Peter should take her firmly by one arm, while she herself held her by the other, and that thus they should lift her up. This succeeded pretty well, but now came the most difficult part. Klara could not stand alone. How was it possible to hold her up and bring her forward at the same time? Heidi was too small to support her with her arm.

"You must take me round the neck, quite fast, so, and then you must take Peter's arm and cling fast to that. Then we can carry you."

Now Peter had never given any one his arm before. Klara took hold of it well enough, but

Peter held it stiffly, hanging down by his side.

"That is not the way to do, Peter," said Heidi very decidedly. "You must make a ring with your arm, and then Klara can put hers through it. She must hang on to it fast, and you must on no account give way, then we shall get on nicely."

They did not get forward very rapidly, however. Klara was not very light, and the pair were not well matched; on one side it went up and on the other down, which caused a decided uncertainty in the support.

Occasionally Klara tried to move a little upon her own feet, but drew them quickly up again.

"Just put your foot straight down once," urged Heidi. "Afterward it won't hurt you so much."

"Do you think so?" asked Klara doubtfully. She obeyed, however, and ventured one firm step on the ground, and then another, crying out a little at each. Then she raised her foot again, and set it down more gently. "Oh, that did not hurt me nearly so much," said she, delighted.

"Do it again," said Heidi earnestly.

Klara did it again and still again, and presently she cried out, "I can, Heidi! I can! Look! Look! I can take steps one after the other."

Heidi literally screamed for joy.

"Oh, oh! Can you really take steps? Can you walk? Can you really walk? Oh, if my grandfather could only see you! Now you can walk, Klara! Now you can walk!" she exclaimed again and again in her delight.

Klara held tight to her two supporters, but at every step she became somewhat firmer; they all three felt sure of that. Heidi was beside herself for joy.

"Now we can go together every day to the pasture, and all about the Alp, wherever we wish," she said. "And you can walk all your life, as well as I can, and need not be pushed about in your chair, and will be well. Oh, this is the very greatest pleasure that we could have!"

Klara agreed with all her heart. Certainly there could be no greater happiness in the world than to feel strong, and able to go about like other people, and not lie suffering all day long in a sickchair.

It was not very far over to the flower field. They could already see the glistening of the buttercups in the sun. Now they had reached the clumps of bluebells, between which the sunny grass looked so inviting.

"Mightn't we sit down here?" asked Klara.

That was just what Heidi liked, and down in the midst of the flowers the children seated themselves. For the first time in her life Klara was seated on the dry, warm grass. All about her were the swaying bluebells, the shining buttercups, the red centaury, the spicy prune flowers. Everything was beautiful, so beautiful!

The children sat still for a long time, rejoicing in the new happiness that had come to them, which with the sunshine, and the perfumes of the flowers, seemed to fill their hearts almost to overflowing. Peter, too, lay still and motionless in the bed of flowers. He had fallen fast asleep.

Softly, gently, came the breeze to them, sheltered as they were by the huge rocks, and paused, sighing, through the shrubs. Now and then Heidi rose and ran about on either side, for everywhere it seemed more beautiful, the flowers thicker, the sweet scents more delicate, as the wind wafted them hither and thither. She could not be content without trying each favorite resting place.

Thus the hours passed by, and the sun had long passed the meridian, when a little troop of goats came very solemnly toward the flowered-covered slope where the children were. This was not a usual feeding place; they were never driven to this spot, for they did not like to graze in the flowers. They looked like an embassy, with Thistlebird at the head. Undoubtedly the goats had gone forth to find their companions, who had left them alone so long; for goats keep very good account of time. When Thistlebird discovered the three missing ones in the middle of the flowery slope, she gave utterance to a loud bleat, in which the others joined in chorus, and the whole flock came trotting toward them.

This awakened Peter. He sat up and rubbed his eyes very hard for a moment, for he had dreamed that he saw the bath-chair standing before the hut door, all unharmed with its red covering, and in waking had thought the buttercups were the yellow nails of the unfortunate chair. Now his anxiety came back to him. Although Heidi had promised not to do anything to him, yet the fear of discovery had grown very lively within him. He felt quite tame, and willing to do as he was bid, and to obey in everything exactly as Heidi should direct.

When they got back to the pasture again, Heidi hastened to get the lunch bag and to keep her promise faithfully, for it was in reference to the midday meal that she had threatened Peter with punishment. She had noticed in the morning how many good things her grandfather had placed in the bag, and she had rejoiced beforehand at the thought of how Peter would like getting his share of them. When, therefore, he was so obstinate and disobliging about helping Klara, she gave him to understand, or meant to do so, that she would not give him anything to eat, though Peter had interpreted her words very differently. Now the little girls took piece after piece from the bag, and made three piles of them, which were so high that she said to herself with satisfaction, "He shall have everything that we do not need."

Taking each portion to its owner, she seated herself by Klara's side, and the children enjoyed their dinner thoroughly after their unwonted exertions. And it happened just as Heidi had foreseen; when Klara and herself had eaten all they possibly could, there still remained so much untasted that Peter received a share quite as large as the third he had had in the beginning. He ate quietly everything that came to him, even to the last crumb, but not with his usual appetite. For something seemed to lie heavy at his stomach that choked him, and made his food stick in his throat.

The children had taken their dinner so late, that soon after they had finished eating the grandfather was seen coming up to fetch them. Heidi flew to meet him. She wished to be the first to tell him what had happened, but she was so much excited over her news that she could hardly find words with which to utter it. He soon made out, however, what she wished to say, and an expression of real delight came over his face. He hastened his steps, and as he came up to Klara he said to her, smiling pleasantly, "So now we have tried, and we have won!"

He raised Klara from the ground, passed his left arm around her waist and held his right as a firm support for her hand, and she marched along with this steady support at her back much more surely, and with less fear than before. Heidi ran about them shouting for joy, and the uncle looked as if some great good fortune had befallen him. He soon took Klara in his arms, however, saying, "We must not overdo it. It is quite time to get home." And he set himself at once to the work, for he knew that Klara had made such unusual exertions that she needed rest immediately.

When Peter came down to Dörfli with the flock that evening, a large knot of the villagers were gathered together, and crowding each other a little here and there, the better to see what was lying on the ground. Peter wished to see too. He elbowed and pushed right and left till he got through the crowd.

Now he saw it.

On the grass lay the central piece of the bath-chair, with a part of the back hanging to it. The red covering and the shining brass nails proved what a handsome chair it must have been when perfect.

"I was here when it came to be carried up the Alm," said the baker, who stood near Peter. "It was worth five hundred francs at least, I will wager. I should like to know how it happened."

"The wind might have driven it down. The uncle himself said so," said Barbel, who stood by, admiring the red covering.

"It is pretty lucky that nobody else did it," said the baker again; "he would catch it, I'm thinking. When the gentleman in Frankfort finds it out he will have the thing looked up. I am glad, for my part, that I have not been up on the Alm these two years past. Suspicion may fall on anybody who has been up there lately."

Many different opinions were uttered, but Peter

had heard quite enough. He crept furtively out of the crowd, and ran with all his speed up the Alm, as if some one were after him to catch him. The baker's words had frightened him terribly. He knew now that at any moment a policeman might come from Frankfort to investigate the affair, and it would come out that he was guilty, and they would take him and send him to the house of correction. Peter saw this in prospect, and his hair stood on end for fear.

Disturbed beyond measure he reached his home. He would give no answer to anything; he would not eat his potatoes, he crept to his bed as fast as he could, and lay there groaning.

"Peterkin must have been eating sorrel again. He has a stomach ache. Hear how he groans," said his mother Brigitte.

"You must give him more bread. Give him a piece of my roll tomorrow morning," said the grandmother pityingly.

When the children looked from their beds out into the starlight that same evening, Heidi said, "Haven't you realized all day, Klara, what a good thing it is that the good God does not grant our prayers, no matter how earnestly we pray to Him, if He has something better in store for us?"

"Why do you say that now, Heidi?" asked Klara.

"Don't you know how I prayed in Frankfort that I might go home right away? And when the good God did not let me go I thought it was because He had not listened to my prayer. But you see, if I had gone away then, you would never have come here, and you would not have been cured on the Alp."

Klara became very thoughtful. "But, Heidi," she said, after a pause, "if that is true, we ought never to ask for anything, because the good God must always know of something better for us than we can know about."

"Yes, yes, Klara, this is the way it is," said Heidi eagerly. "We must pray to God every day, and tell Him everything, everything; so that He can know that we do not forget Him, and then He will not forget us. Your grandmamma told me so. But we ought never to think that God has forgotten us because He does not grant our prayers, and so stop praying, but rather pray in this way: 'Now I am sure, dear God, that there is something better in store for me, and so I will be happy, because you will provide.'"

"How did you think of all this, Heidi?" asked Klara.

"Your grandmamma told me first, and then it happened, and I knew it was true. But I meant to say, Klara"—and Heidi sat up in her bed—"today we ought to thank the dear God particularly for the great happiness He has sent us in letting you walk."

"Yes, you are right, Heidi; I am glad that you have reminded me. For sheer happiness I had quite forgotten."

So the children prayed, and thanked God in their own way that He had cured Klara who had been sick so long.

Next morning the grandfather proposed that the children should write to the grandmamma in Ragatz, and ask her to come up to the Alm, as there was something worth seeing there. But the children had made a different plan. They had proposed to give the grandmamma a very great surprise. Klara was to practice until she could take a little walk, supported by Heidi alone, but the grandmamma must not have the least suspicion of it. And they begged the uncle to tell them how long he thought it would take. When he said not more than a week, they proposed to write a letter inviting the grandmamma urgently to be at the end of a week on the Alp. But not a word of the surprise was to be breathed.

The days that followed were the most delightful of all that Klara had passed on the mountain. Every morning she woke with the happy sound ringing in her heart: "I am well, I am well! I need lie no longer in a chair. I can go about by myself like other people!"

The walking exercise followed, and she went better and better, and took a longer walk each day. The unwonted exercise brought such an appetite with it, that daily the slice of bread and butter had to be bigger, and the grandfather stood by and watched it disappear with immense satisfaction. And he always brought a big jug of the foaming milk out to the children now, and filled mug after mug for them. At last the week was over, and the day came that was to bring the grandmamma.

Chapter 23

A Parting, But Not Forever

The day before she was to start, the grandmamma had sent off a letter to the Alm, so that her arrival would not take them by surprise. Peter brought this letter as he came up toward the pasture. The Alm uncle had already come out before the hut with the children, and stood ready with Schwänli and Bärli by his side. The goats shook their pretty heads in the fresh morning breeze, while the children patted them, and wished them a happy journey to the pasture. The uncle looked with satisfaction, first at the fresh faces of the children, and then at his clean, well-bred goats. His face wore a very happy expression.

At this moment Peter made his appearance. When he saw the little group he drew near very slowly and held the letter out to the uncle. The moment it had left his hand he sprang back timidly and looked quickly behind him, as if something might be coming of which he was afraid, then with one leap he was off, and up the mountain.

"Grandfather," said Heidi, who was much surprised at this queer conduct on the part of the goatherd, "why does Peter behave exactly like the big Turk when he sees a rod behind him?"

"Perhaps Peter sees a rod behind him that he deserves," replied her grandfather.

The lad ran up the nearest slopes at one pull. As soon as he was out of sight of the hut it was different, then he stopped and turned his head in a scared fashion in every direction. Suddenly he gave a jump and looked behind him, as frightened as if some one had seized him by the nape of his neck. From behind every bush, out of every thicket, he thought the police from Frankfort might be ready to spring upon him. The longer this anxious dread lasted the more unhappy Peter was, and he had at last not one quiet moment.

Heidi soon went into the hut to put everything in order, for she wished the grandmamma to find it looking very neat when she came. Klara found so much amusement in watching these proceedings on the part of Heidi, that she always came in to look on while her friend worked. They were both so well employed that the early morning hours slipped away, and it was almost time for the visitor to arrive before they knew how late it was. Then they came out and seated themselves to await the great event.

The grandfather joined them. He had taken a walk that morning, and brought home a big bunch of dark-blue gentians, which looked so beautiful in the bright sunlight that the children exclaimed at the sight. He carried them into the hut. Every now and then Heidi sprang up from the bench, in hope to descry some sign of the grandmamma's procession.

There it was at last, just as Heidi had expected it would be! First came the guide, then the grandmamma on her white horse, then the porter with his basket piled with wraps, for the lady never would go up the mountains without plenty of means of keeping dry and warm. They came nearer and nearer. Now they had reached the summit, and the grandmamma from her horse caught sight of the children.

"What do I see. Klara, my child? What is this? You are not sitting in your chair!" the grandmamma cried, quite startled, and hastened to dismount. But even before she reached the children she clasped her hands together and said, "Is it you, Klara, or is it not? Your cheeks are red, and round as apples. Child, I should not know you!"

The good lady darted toward her grandchild, but in a trice Heidi had slipped from the bench, Klara had risen quickly, supporting herself on her little friend's shoulder, and the two girls were calmly taking a little walk. The grandmamma stood perfectly still, at first from fright. She thought that Heidi was undertaking some unheard-of thing.

But what was it that she saw? Upright and steady Klara was walking by Heidi's side. The children came back after a few minutes, both with rosy cheeks, both with beaming faces. Now the grandmamma threw herself upon them. Laughing and crying at once, she clasped Klara in her arms, then Heidi, and then again embraced her granddaughter, finding no words to express her joy.

Presently she spied the uncle, who was standing by the bench looking at the group with a contented smile. The grandmamma took Klara by the arm, and with increasing surprise and delight that it was indeed so, that the child was indeed walking by her side, moved with her toward the bench. Then she stopped, and seized the uncle by both hands.

"My dear good Uncle! How can we ever thank you? This is your work! It is your care and nursing—"

"And our good Lord's sunshine and mountain air," added the uncle, smiling.

"Yes, and Schwänli's good sweet milk too," added Klara. "You must see how I drink the goat's milk, Grandmamma, and how good it is!"

"I can see that by your cheeks, Klara. No, I really do not know you; you have grown round and plump, as I never dreamed you could be. Is it really my Klara? We will not lose one moment, but telegraph to my son in Paris. He must come to see you immediately. I will not tell him why. It will be the greatest happiness of his whole life. How shall we arrange this, my dear Uncle? You have sent the men down again, I suppose?"

"Yes, they have gone, but if you are in such haste, we can send the goatherd down. He will have time enough."

The grandmamma wished to send a dispatch at once to her son. He ought not to be deprived of his happiness a single hour. So the uncle went a little to one side, and gave such a searching whistle through his fingers that the echo came back from the rocks far above them. Before long Peter came running down. He was as white as chalk, for he thought that the uncle was whistling him down to be punished.

Only a bit of paper was given to him, however, which the grandmamma had in the meantime written, and he received the order to take this paper to the post office in Dörfli. The uncle said he would attend to the payment later, for it was not safe to give Peter too much to do at once. Thus Peter set out quite relieved, his paper in his hand, for the uncle had not whistled him to his deserts, and no policeman was to be seen.

The party now seated themselves comfortably at the table, and everything that had passed was rehearsed to the grandmamma from the beginning. It took a long time to finish the story, for they were constantly interrupted by questions, and expressions of thankful surprise.

"And my weak, pale, lame little grandchild is transformed into this blooming, round-faced maiden! It is a fairy tale, I do believe," cried the grandmamma, and delighted the children by showing how completely their plan of surprise had succeeded.

Mr. Sesemann, in his turn, had planned a surprise. He had set out one fine sunny morning from Paris, and travelled on to Basle without stopping, and on again the following day as quickly as possible. He had been seized with an irresistible desire to see his daughter, from whom he had been separated all summer. He had arrived in Ragatz just as his mother had left for the Alm; had followed in a carriage to Mayenfeld, and on to Dörfli, for he thought the walk up the Alm would be enough for him to undertake.

He was quite right, moreover, the steep climb was very fatiguing to him. He saw no cottage anywhere; and he knew, too, that halfway up he should have found the dwelling of goat-Peter, for he had heard the description of the mountain path often enough. There were little footpaths visible everywhere, crossing and recrossing each other.

Mr. Sesemann began to be afraid that he was mistaken, and that the mountain cottage lay on another part of the Alp. He looked about, hoping to see some human being. It was perfectly quiet. Nowhere a sound to be heard; not a living creature to be seen; only a mountain breeze fanned the air, while insects hummed, and a bird sang in the clear sky. Mr. Sesemann stood still, and let the Alpine wind cool his heated brow.

Somebody came running down the mountain. It was Peter, with his dispatch in his hand. He ran as the crow flies, not following the path on which Mr. Sesemann was standing. As soon as the runner was near enough, Mr. Sesemann beckoned to him. Hesitatingly and timidly Peter advanced, sidewise, not in a straight line, and as if he could not put one foot before the other properly, but must drag one behind him.

"Well, my lad, this way!" said Mr. Sesemann encouragingly. "Just tell me if by this path I shall come to the cottage where an old man lives with a child call Heidi, and where the people from Frankfort are staying?"

A smothered cry of fear was the only answer, and Peter dashed away with such tremendous force that he went heels over head down the steep slope, and rolled in involuntary somersaults farther and farther, just as the bath-chair had done, only fortunately Peter did not come all to pieces like the chair. Meanwhile the dispatch received terrible treatment, and flew away, torn into bits.

"A singularly bashful mountaineer," said Mr. Sesemann to himself, for he supposed this conduct to have been caused by the unexpected appearance of a stranger before the simple Alpine boy. After he had watched Peter's powerful movement down the hillside for a little, he went on his way.

Peter could not stop himself, no matter how he struggled. He rolled on and on, and now and then over and over. But this was not the worst for him at this moment. The worst was the knowledge that the policeman had arrived from Frankfort, for Peter did not doubt that the stranger who had asked the way to the Alm uncle's hut was he. At last he tumbled into a bush, about halfway down the last slope toward Dörfli, and there he stuck fast. He lay still for a moment to collect himself, and think what to do next.

"This is first rate. Here comes another!" said a voice close to Peter. "And who will get a shove tomorrow, I wonder, and come tumbling down like a half-made potato sack?"

It was the baker who was joking in this manner. He had come up the hill a little way to refresh himself after his hot day's work, and had quietly watched Peter as he rolled, not unlike the bath-chair, down the steep mountain side.

The lad hastened to regain his feet. A new fear had seized him. Now the baker knew, too, that the chair had been shoved down. Without a single glance backward, Peter turned again up the mountain. If he could have had his way he would have liked to creep into his bed, for he felt safest there. But his goats were up above, and the uncle had strictly charged him to come back quickly, because they ought not to be left very long alone. Peter groaned aloud and limped on. It must be. He must go up again. But he could not run. The anxiety and the manifold bruises that he had just received distressed him too much. So on he went, limping and groaning all the way up the Alp.

Mr. Sesemann reached the first cottage soon after he had seen Peter, and when he thus knew that he was on the right path he went on more courageously. At last he saw his goal before him. There stood the Alm hut, and there the dark tree tops of the old pines waved to and fro.

Mr. Sesemann went gaily along the last ascent, picturing to himself his daughter's pleased surprise. He was quickly discovered and recognized by the party before the hut, where a surprise was ready for the father of which he had no idea. As he came up the last steps of the hill, two figures came toward him: a large girl with fair hair and a rosy face, supporting herself upon the smaller Heidi, out of whose dark eyes streamed glances of happiness.

Mr. Sesemann started. He stood still, and stared at the approaching children. Suddenly great tears rolled down his cheeks. What remembrances were rising in his heart! It was the image of Klara's mother that rose before him; so had she looked—such golden locks, such rosy cheeks. Mr. Sesemann did not know if he was awake or asleep.

"Papa, do you not know me again? Am I really so much altered?" And with the words Klara was clasped in her father's arms.

"Yes, you are altered! Is it possible? Is it reality?" The father drew a step or two backward to see if the picture would not vanish from before his eyes. Then again he folded her in his arms, and then held her off from him, to gaze on her rosy cheeks and to see how firmly she held herself.

By this time the grandmamma had come up, for she could not wait another moment, she was so desirous of seeing her son's happy face.

"What do you say, my son? The surprise you have given us is good; but ours for you is far better, is it not?" and she kissed her son affectionately. "But now you must come up to the hut to make the acquaintance of the uncle, who is our great benefactor."

"Certainly, and I ought to say a word to our little friend here," said Mr. Sesemann, as he shook Heidi's hand. "How is it? Fresh and healthy once more on the Alp? But it is useless to ask—no Alpine rose could look more blooming. This is a pleasure to me, child, a real pleasure."

Heidi looked affectionately up into Mr. Sesemann's face. How good he had always been to her! And that now, here on the Alp, such a great happiness should have befallen him made Heidi's heart beat rapidly for joy.

Mrs. Sesemann carried her son off now to see the Alm uncle. The two men stood holding each other's hands, and Mr. Sesemann expressed his gratitude and astonishment at what seemed to him almost a miracle. The grandmamma turned away, for she had said all this a few moments before, and she wished to have another look at the old pines. Here, under the shade of the trees, where the broad branches left a free place, stood a great cluster of most wonderful dark-blue gentians, as fresh as if they grew there naturally. She clasped her hands with pleasure and astonishment.

"How splendid! How lovely! What a sight! Come here, Heidi, my dear child. Did you arrange this for me? It is perfectly wonderful!"

The children were by her side in a moment. "No, no, I did not do it," said Heidi; "but I know who did."

"That is just the way it looks up in the pasture, and more beautiful yet," said Klara. "But guess, Grandmamma, who brought you these flowers early in the morning from the pasture!" And Klara smiled so merrily that the grandmamma began to think the child had been up there herself before her arrival. But that indeed was a thing impossible.

A slight noise was just then heard under the

pines. It was made by Peter, who had just got back. When he saw from afar who was there with the Alm uncle, he had made a wide circuit, and was creeping secretly along under the trees. The grandmamma recognized him, and a new idea took possession of her. Peter must have brought these beautiful flowers down for her, and now was hiding himself for bashfulness. No, that could not be permitted, he must have a little recompense.

"Come, my lad, come here. Quick! Don't be afraid!" said the grandmamma, and peered, as she spoke, through the trees at Peter.

The lad stood still, stiff with fear. Escape was no longer possible to him. He had but one idea left. "It is out!" His hair stood on end, and pale and trembling he crept out from behind the pines.

"Come, my boy. Don't stay there," said the grandmamma, meaning to encourage him. "Now tell me, did you do it?"

As Peter did not raise his eyes, he did not see where the lady was pointing. He did not see that the uncle was standing not far off at the corner of the hut, piercing him with his clear gray eyes, and that the most dreadful of all people in the world, the policeman from Frankfort, was standing by his side. Trembling and quivering in every limb. Peter gave forth a loud cry; it was "Yes!"

"Now, now," said the grandmamma, "what does all this fright mean?"

"Because—because—it is all broken to pieces,

and can never be mended," stammered the lad, and his knees shook so that he could no longer stand.

The grandmamma went toward the corner of the hut. "My dear uncle," said she compassionately, "is that boy really cracked?"

"No, not in the least," said the uncle reassuringly. "The boy is only the wind that chased the bath-chair down the mountain, and now he is expecting his well-earned punishment."

The grandmamma could hardly believe this, for she did not find Peter at all mischievous in appearance; and then, he had no reason for destroying this very useful bath-chair. The uncle, indeed, had only a suspicion to sustain his assertion, a suspicion that he had conceived after the deed. The scowling looks that Peter had cast at Klara from the very beginning, and all the signs of dislike he had manifested toward the visitors to the Alps had not escaped the uncle. He had put this and that together, and was quite convinced that he understood the whole story which he now confided to the grandmamma.

When he had finished, the lady declared with great energy, "No, my dear Uncle, no, no! The poor boy has been quite enough punished. One must be merciful. Here come strange people from Frankfort and carry off his Heidi from him for whole weeks at a time, his only happiness, and truly a great happiness, and he sits up there alone day after day and looks on. No, no, one must be forgiving. Anger has overpowered him, and driven him to a revenge which was rather a stupid one, I must acknowledge, but anger makes us all stupid."

With this the grandmamma went over to the poor fellow, who was still trembling and shaking violently. She sat down on the bench under the pines, and said kindly, "Now come here, my lad. I have something to say to you. Stop shivering and shaking, and listen. You must obey me. You pushed the bath-chair down the mountain, to break it in pieces. It was very wrong, and you knew it, and that you deserved to be punished you knew also, and so you tried very hard to prevent anybody from finding out what you had done.

"But now you see, whoever has done a wrong deed and thinks that no one knows it, deceives himself. The good God sees and hears everything, and as soon as He sees that anybody has done wrong, and wishes to hide it, He awakens quickly in that person the little watchman that He has placed in everybody at his birth, and that is allowed to sleep until that person has done something wrong. The little watchman has a little sting in his hand, and with that he keeps pricking the wrongdoer, until he has not one moment's peace. And then he worries the tormented person with his voice, for he calls out continually, 'Now they are coming to punish you! Now it is all found out!' So he is always anxious and frightened, and has no comfort, not one bit. Have you not felt something like this, Peter, just now?"

Peter nodded quite abashed, but consentingly, for the description was exact.

"And yet, in one way, you were wrong in your calculation," said the grandmamma further. "Just see how that wrong thing that you did has turned out to be the best, the very best, for the person toward whom you felt so unkindly. Because Klara had no chair in which she could be carried up the mountain to see the lovely flowers, she made great exertions to get to them; and so she learned to walk, and walks better and better every day. If she stays here, at last she will be able to go to the pasture whenever she chooses, much oftener than if she had to be rolled up in her chair. So you see, Peter, the good God can turn anything that is meant to be wicked into something good for the person who was to be hurt. And only the evildoer has the sorrow and harm. Have you understood all that I have said, Peter? Well, then, think on it, and every time you have an inclination to do something wrong, think of the little watchman inside of you with his sting and disagreeable voice. Will you promise me that?"

"Yes, I will," replied Peter, still more depressed, for he did not know in the least what the end of this was to be. There was the policeman, standing all this time beside the uncle.

"Well, that is good. Now the thing is settled,"

returned the grandmamma. "But I mean to give you something in remembrance of the people from Frankfort, something that you will like to have. So now tell me, have you ever wished for anything very much? What is it? What would you like best to have?"

At this Peter raised his head, and stared at the grandmamma with big, round eyes. He had been expecting something horrible to happen to him, and now he was to get something that he wanted very much! He scarcely knew what to think.

"Yes, yes, I am in earnest," said the grandmamma. "You shall have something that you will like very much, to remind you of us, and to show you that we do not remember what you have done to harm us. Do you understand, my boy?"

At this Peter's prospect began to clear up a little, and he understood that he had no punishment to fear, and that the good woman before whom he stood would save him from the power of the police. He felt a sense of relief as if a mountain were lifted that had been weighing him down to the ground. He had also learned that it is wiser to acknowledge at once what one has done that is wrong, than to wait until it is found out, so he said, "And I lost the paper too."

The grandmamma had to ponder a little over this abrupt announcement, but she soon discovered the connection, and said kindly, "Yes, yes, that is very good of you to tell it. Always confess anything you have done that is wrong, and then it can be repaired. Now tell me what you wish for."

Peter realized now that he had leave to wish for anything in the world, and he felt almost dizzy. The whole fair at Mayenfeld swam before his eyes, with all the beautiful things that he had stood for hours looking at and never even hoped to possess, for Peter's fortune was never so great but that everything there cost at least its double. There were the handsome red whistles, which he could use for his goats so nicely; there were the tempting knives with round handles, toad-stickers they were called, with which one could do a lively business in the hazel copses.

The boy stood deep in thought, trying to decide which of these two was the more desirable, and he found it impossible to choose. Presently a luminous idea came to him, by which means he could wait until the next fair, and have time to think it well over.

"A penny," he said, quite decided.

The grandmamma laughed.

"That is not extravagant. Come here!" She drew out her purse and took from it two florins, upon which she placed four pennies. "We will make a little calculation," she said. "Here we have as many pennies as there are weeks in the year. You can take a penny every Sunday, and so have one every week all the year round."

"All the rest of my life?" asked the boy

innocently.

At this grandmamma began to laugh so immoderately that the uncle and Mr. Sesemann broke off their conversation to hear what it was about.

The grandmamma kept on laughing.

"You shall have it, my lad. There shall be a clause in my will to that effect—do you hear, my son? A penny a week to the goat-Peter as long as he shall live."

Mr. Sesemann nodded approvingly, and joined in the laugh.

Peter gazed at the money in his hand, to see if it were really true, then he said, "Thank God!" and ran off in a most unusual fashion. But this time he kept his feet, for he was not driven by fear but by joy, a joy such as Peter had never known. All fear and anxiety were gone, and he was to have a penny every week for the rest of his life!

Later in the day, when the party had finished their merry dinner before the hut, and sat there talking over all sorts of things, Klara took her father, whose face beamed more and more with joy each time he looked at her, by the hand, and said, with a sprightliness that no one had ever observed in the delicate and languid child, "Oh, Papa, if you only could know what the grandfather has done for me! So much every day that it would be impossible to tell it all, but I shall never forget it in all my life. And I shall always be thinking how I can do something for him, or send him a present, that will give him half the happiness that he has given me."

"This is also my greatest wish, my dear child," said her father. "I am at this moment thinking of it, of how we can in some small measure repay what we owe to his kindness."

With the words Mr. Sesemann rose and went toward the uncle, who was sitting beside the grandmamma and talking with her very animatedly, but who rose as his guest came toward him.

"My dear friend," said Mr. Sesemann, taking the old man's hand very affectionately, "let me say a word to you! You can easily understand that for many years I have not known real happiness. What were all my money and possessions worth to me when I glanced at my child, and felt that I could never make her sound or well, no matter how much I might accumulate? Next to our good Heavenly Father, I feel that you have healed her for me, and have given me, as well as the child, a new life. Now tell me how I can show you my gratitude. Recompense you I cannot, but what I possess I place at your disposal. Speak, my friend, is there anything I can do?"

The Alm uncle had listened in silence, while surveying the happy parent with a benevolent smile.

"Mr. Sesemann will well believe that I have my

share in the pleasure of this cure, which has been worked on my beloved Alm. My trouble is more than repaid," said he, in his decided manner. "I thank Mr. Sesemann for his kind offer, but I need nothing whatever. As long as I may live, I have enough for myself and for my grandchild. I have one wish, however, and could that be fulfilled I should for this life feel no further concern."

"Name it, name it, my dear friend," begged Mr. Sesemann.

"I am old," continued the uncle, "and cannot live very much longer. When I go, I cannot leave the child anything, and she has no other relatives; no one person who would take charge of her and care for her. If Mr. Sesemann will give me the assurance that Heidi need never go out into the world to seek her bread among strangers, he will have richly repaid me for what I have done for his daughter."

"But, my dear friend," said Mr. Sesemann, "there can never be any question of that at all. The child belongs to us. Ask my mother, ask my daughter, if they would ever dream of allowing Heidi to go to anybody else as long as they were living. But if it would be of the least comfort to you, here is my hand upon it. I promise you that this child shall never in her life go out to earn her bread amongst strangers. I will provide against that, now and after my death. I will see too that this child of yours is not made to live amongst strangers, no matter how favorable the circumstances might be. We have experienced that. But she has made friends for herself. I know such a one. He is in Frankfort, closing up his affairs, to be able to go where he will and give himself some rest. That is my friend Dr. Classen, who means to return here in the autumn, and to establish himself, taking council with you, in this neighborhood, for he has never felt so well elsewhere, he says. So you see the child Heidi will have henceforth two protectors near her. May you both live long and happily together!"

"God grant this may be so," said the grandmamma, and she shook the uncle's hand for a long time with great cordiality. Then putting her arm round Heidi's neck, for the child stood near her, she said very tenderly, "And you, my dear child, you must also ask for something. Tell me now, have you no wish that you would gladly have fulfilled?"

"Yes, indeed I have," answered Heidi, and looked at the grandmamma with much satisfaction.

"Well, tell me at once, my child."

"I should like to have my bed from Frankfort with the high pillows and the thick coverlet, because the blind grandmother has to lie with her head down and can scarcely breathe, and then she will be warm enough under the coverlet, and not have to wear the shawl in bed because she is so cold.''

Heidi had said this without stopping to breathe, she was in such haste to express this darling wish of hers.

"Oh, my dear Heidi, what are you saying?" cried the grandmother, much moved. "It is a good thing that you reminded me of this, for in great happiness it is so easy to forget one's duties. When God sends us everything that is good, we ought to think of those who are deprived of so much! We will telegraph to Frankfort at once. This very day Rottenmeier shall pack the bed, and it will get here in two days. God willing, the grandmother shall sleep well in it!''

Heidi danced round and round the grandmamma, as the easiest way to express her delight. But suddenly she stood still, and said, "Now I must go down to tell the grandmother all about it. She will be anxious because I have not been to see her for so long.''

"No, no, Heidi, what are you thinking of?" said her grandfather reprovingly. "When one has visitors it is not proper to run away and leave them.''

But the grandmamma supported Heidi.

"The child is right, my dear Uncle," said she. "The poor grandmother has for a long time been deprived of enough on our account. We will all go together to see her, and I will take my horse from her cottage. Then we will go down to Dörfli and will telegraph at once to Frankfort. What do you think of it, my son?''

But Mr. Sesemann had not yet had time to talk over his trip. He therefore begged his mother to be quiet a little while, and not to start off so hastily, as he wished to say a few more words to the uncle.

Mr. Sesemann had proposed to travel a little with his mother through Switzerland, and to see if Klara were strong enough to make a short distance with them. Now, it was all so different. He could have the most delightfully interesting trip with his daughter, and he would make use of these beautiful late summer days for that purpose. He therefore proposed to pass the night in Dörfli, and the next day to take Klara away from the Alm, in order to journey with her to meet her grandmamma in Ragatzbad, and from there farther.

The uncle took his foster daughter on his arm, and followed with firm steps the grandmamma and Heidi. Last of all came Mr. Sesemann, and in this manner they went down the mountain.

Heidi went dancing and jumping along by the grandmamma's side, and the latter wished to know all about the poor blind woman, how she lived, and how everything went on in her house, especially in winter.

The grandmamma listened with the liveliest interest to Heidi's account, until they reached the hut. Brigitte was just then busy hanging Peter's second shirt in the sun to dry, so that when he had worn the other long enough he could change. She caught sight of the company and ran into the cottage.

"Now they are all going away, mother," she said. "There is a whole procession of them, and the uncle is carrying the sick child."

"Oh, must it really be?" sighed the grandmother. "Are they going to take Heidi with them? Did you see that? Oh, how I wish I could take her hand once more! If I could only hear her speak again!"

At this moment the door flew open, and Heidi came leaping in, up to the corner where the old woman sat, and hugged her tightly. "Grandmother! Grandmother! My bed is coming from Frankfort, and all the three pillows, and the thick coverlet. They will be here in two days—the grandmamma says so."

Heidi was not able to bring out her words fast enough, in her impatience to see the great delight of the grandmother, who smiled, but looked rather sad.

"Oh, what a good woman she is! I ought to be glad that she is taking you away with her, Heidi, but I shall not live long after it."

"What? What? Who told the good old grandmother such a thing as that?" It was the friendly voice of Mrs. Sesemann, and her hand grasped that of the blind woman, which she pressed warmly. "No, no, there is no talk of any such thing. Heidi is going to stay with the grandmother, and always make her happy. We wished to see the child again, but we came to her. We shall come up to the Alm every year, for we have good reason to thank God for the goodness He has shown to us up here, where He has performed a miracle on our dear child!"

With this the light of true happiness came over the face of the grandmother, and with speechless joy she pressed the hand of the kind Mrs. Sesemann, while two big tears rolled slowly down her face. Heidi recognized the look of happiness, however, and was contented.

There were hot tears shed the next morning when it was time for Klara to take leave. The girl was very loath to part from her friends, and from the beautiful Alm where she had felt well, as she had never felt before. But Heidi comforted her, saying, "It will be summer again before we think of it, and then you will come again, and it will be more beautiful than ever. Then we can begin at once to walk about, and go up every day with the goats to the pasture, and see the flowers, and everything will be delightful from the be-ginning."

Klara wiped the tears from her eyes, for Heidi's words had comforted her a little.

"Give my good-bye to Peter," she said, "and to all the goats. I wish I could give Schwänli something. She has helped so much in making me well."

"You can do that easily enough," said Heidi. "Send her a little salt. You know how she likes to lick it from my grandfather's hand in the evening."

This counsel pleased Klara. "Oh, I will send a hundred pounds from Frankfort," she cried, "as a remembrance of me."

Mr. Sesemann here beckoned to the children, for he must be going. Mrs. Sesemann's white horse had been sent up for Klara. She could ride down now. She no longer needed a litter.

Heidi stationed herself on the most prominent part of the slope, and waved her hand to Klara until there was no longer a sign of horse or rider to be seen.

The bed from Frankfort has arrived, and the grandmother sleeps so soundly every night that she will certainly get new strength from it. The good grandmamma has also not forgotten the hard winter on the Alp. She has sent a big package to the goat-Peter's cottage, and in it were all sorts of warm things, so that the grandmother could wrap herself up very snugly, and not shiver from the cold in her corner.

In Dörfli a great building is going up. By the advice of the uncle, the doctor has purchased the old building that he and Heidi live in, which was formerly a fine house, as one might see from the room where the stove with the beautiful tiles stood. This part the doctor is to have arranged for his lodging. The other part will be put in condition for the uncle and Heidi, for the doctor recognizes in his old friend an independent man, who must have his own dwelling-place. Quite at the back Schwänli and Bärli will have comfortable winter lodgings.

"My dear friend," said the doctor recently to his companion, as they stood together on the walls, "you must look at the thing from my point of view. I share all your pleasure in the child as if I were her next nearest relative. I must also share all duties. In this way I shall have a kind of right to our Heidi, and can hope that she will care for me in my old age, and stay with me and nurse me. That is my dearest wish. She shall be recognized as my heiress, and when we leave her behind, you and I, we need not be anxious about her comfort."

In the meantime Heidi and Peter sat together at the grandmother's side. The former had so much to tell and the latter so much to hear that they pressed closer and closer against the happy blind woman, who listened intently to the little girl's account of the exciting events of the past summer, when Heidi's visitors prevented her from going to the cottage.

And of the three who sat thus together, each looked happier than the other, because of being all once more together, and because of all the delightful things that had taken place.

At last the grandmother said: "Heidi, read me a hymn of praise! It seems to me that I ought to do nothing but praise and glorify our Lord God, for all that He has in His mercy granted us, His poor children."

About the author:

Johanna Spyri

Born in the small Swiss town of Hirzel in 1827, Johanna Spyri is famous for her delightful children's stories.

After her marriage in 1852, she moved with her husband to the city of Zurich, where she began to yearn for the simple country life that she had known as a child. Her memories of the Swiss mountains, her love of nature, and her glowing imagination are evident in the story of the beloved little girl, HEIDI.